# FOUR KINDS OF RAIN

*Robert Ward* (signature)

# FOUR KINDS OF RAIN

## ROBERT WARD

ST. MARTIN'S MINOTAUR
NEW YORK

This is a work of fiction. All the characters, organizations, and events portrayed in this novel are either products of the author's imagination or are used fictitiously.

www.stmartins.com

Book design by Jonathan Bennett

Library of Congress Cataloging-in-Publication Data

Ward, Robert, 1943–
    Four kinds of rain / Robert Ward.—1st ed.
        p. cm.
    ISBN-13: 978-0-312-35780-1
    ISBN-10: 0-312-35780-X
    1. Psychologists—Fiction. 2. Baltimore (Md.)—Fiction. 3. Art thefts—Fiction. I. Title.

PS3573.A735F68 2006
813'.54—dc22

                                                    2006045472

First Edition: October 2006

10  9  8  7  6  5  4  3  2  1

FOR JEFFREY AND GAYLE LEWIS

# ACKNOWLEDGMENTS

Thanks to John Lansing; Sascha Blair; Gwenda Blair; John Manciewicz; Dan Pyne; the late Bill Sackheim; Jo Anne Sackheim; the wonderful artist Susan Hall; Baltimore Police Detective Matt Bauler; my best pals in Baltimore, Jed and Julia Dietz; Mary Jo Gordon; Detective Nick Giangrosso; Dr. Larry Horowitz; Chuck Lorre; Lee Lankford; Dr. Bob Huizenga; Mike and Toni Andreen; Bob Asahina and his wife, Linda Ashour; Pat McGuire; Nina Marino; Rick Kaplan; David Milch; Lukas Ortiz; Gary Phillips; Michael Schur; Susan Steiner; Wendy Martin; Dr. Jeff Schwartz; Lenny Levitski; Brent Staples; Jeff Weber; and Robert Wallace. Special thanks to my wife, Celeste Wesson, who read every draft; my son, Robbie, who I kicked around the ending with time and time again; Dr. Brent Walta; R. D. Laing; Sol Yurick, who introduced me to radical psychotherapy many years ago; and the great Michael Connelly, who read the book and got it to my brilliant and charming agent, Philip Spitzer. Phil, in turn, sent the book to the right man, Michael Homler, at St. Martin's, who is not only a terrific editor but now a good friend. Love to all of you.

# PART I
## RAIN and SNOW

# CHAPTER ONE

Even after three vodkas and an Ambien, it had taken Bob Wells two hours to fall asleep. Now he lay in his bed dreaming that he was running through a maze of dark city streets, while sharp little stilettos of ice stuck in his chest. Somewhere ahead of him in the gathering dark, a voice screamed, "Terrorists. Terrorists . . . they're coming! The terrorists!" He knew that panicky voice so well, knew it nearly as well as he knew his own. He turned a dream corner and saw the screamer lying there, near a battered old phone booth, his sore-covered head hanging in the gutter.

Bob Wells woke up with a start. There it was again. The panic dream of ice rain. A lethal injection that fell from the night sky, accompanied by a high-pitched scream, the same scream he could hear for real now, somewhere out there on the wet city streets.

He got out of bed, went to his bedroom window, and with some effort pushed it open. The cold wind and sleet blew in from the harbor. Bob stuck his head out into the night and looked down the far end of Aliceanna Street. The homeless guy was there, just as he'd been the night before, the guy everybody called 911, lying in the gutter, right next to the battered and windowless telephone booth. Loaded on rotgut and crack, he held his wine bottle in the air and screamed: "Here they come! The terrorists! They're in the air! They're here! Terrorists! Terrorists!"

Bob listened to 911 rave, his hysterical voice cutting through his rapidly beating heart. Finally, he shut the window, sighed, took off his sweat-soaked pajama top, quickly threw on his old wool crewneck sweater, and reached for his black Levi's.

Bob buttoned his old navy pea jacket against the sleet as he headed down the slippery street. He was ten feet away when the terrified, wide-eyed, filthy man looked up at him.

"I know you," he said. "The fucking terrorist."

"Nah, Nine," Bob said. "No terrorists, man. It's just me. Bob."

The drunken, panicked wreck looked at him through rheumy eyes.

"Dr. Bobby?" he said. "Dr. Bobby, that you?"

"Yeah," Bob said. "That's me. What's up, Nine?"

"They're coming," 911 whispered. "They're coming. I heard it from my people."

"Right," Bob said. "So, if they *are* coming, maybe the smart thing to do would be to get off the street?"

911 bit his scabby lower lip and looked at Bob in a cagey way.

"So you might think," he said. "But then again, maybe that's exactly what they want me to do. After I get to the shelter, boom, the death strike hits there."

"I don't think so," Bob said, moving even closer. "You know why?"

"Why?"

" 'Cause I talked to your people just a few minutes ago and they told me that tonight is just a street action. Anybody in the shelter is safe, Nine. Okay?"

911 looked frantically around like a frightened gerbil.

"Also it's cold and wet out here," Bob said, looking up at the sky. "You could get real sick and then you'd be playing right into their hands."

From beneath the street grime, 911 assumed a thoughtful stare. "You're right," he said. "They would just love that, bro."

"Of course they would," Bob said. "Hey, the thing is, I gotta go to St. Mary's shelter right down on Broadway, so maybe you'd like to keep me company, huh?"

"Like riding shotgun on the stagecoach to Dodge," 911 said.

"Just like that," Bob said.

"Maybe we should go now, before they come," 911 said. Like he'd just thought of it. Like *he* was taking care of Bob.

"Let's do it," Bob said.

As 911 tried to unfold his bones from the street, Bob gently took his arm, a mistake he wouldn't have made earlier in the night, when he was less wasted.

911 pulled away quickly and kicked Bob squarely in the balls. Stunned, Bob went down on his knees, groaning and holding his crotch, as the homeless man scuttled away.

"Oh no, man. You can't fool me," 911 screamed. "You almost had me, dude, but I saw through you! You fucking terrorist son of a bitch!"

Bob fell over on his side as the pain shot through his stomach and lodged somewhere near his Adam's apple. He lay there and it occurred to him, for maybe the hundredth time that day, that he seriously needed out of this shit. Up, up, and away, like forever, for good. No more, baby. No more friend of the friendless. No more poor folks. No more 911s.

As the burning pain subsided, Bob Wells entertained a small, almost funny thought. If any of his neighbors looked out their windows just now, they'd see *him* there and think, Look at the poor, homeless son of a bitch out in *this* shit. Pathetic.

And they'd be right, Bob thought, dead right. Because this was it. This was his life. The grand and once near-glorious Bob Wells was lying in the street after being kicked in the balls by a madman. Not only that, but the madman was one of his own patients, a wretch he'd helped get off the streets time and time again.

Cold winter sleet raining down on his face, Bob began to laugh. It was perfect really, just fucking perfect. Slowly and with great delicacy, Bob picked himself up and limped up the dark wet street toward home.

# CHAPTER TWO

During this period, the last "normal" phase of his career, Bob's life had taken on a ghoulish regularity. When he was done with the last patient of the day in his dying psychology practice, he'd come up from his knotty pine basement office, make sure his little row house was locked (he'd been robbed five times in the last two years), and trudge on down the street to American Joe's bar. Here he would meet his old pal, the semiretired labor reporter Dave McClane for happy hour and the two old cronies would belt back their well drinks. Dave drank something foul called Misty Isle scotch and Bob Popov vodka, which tasted, he suspected, not unlike Sterno. Despite their vows to "tone the drinking down," and get into a "health bag for the new year," more often than not one drink would turn into two and two into four. By six o' clock, they would both be whacked and as the darkness settled like blue ink over downtown Baltimore, the boozy glow of the afternoon would shade into a sour feeling of discontent. The approaching night held little excitement for two middle-aged, divorced men and that lack of promise often lurched Bob Wells into a tailspin of melancholy.

"Twenty-two years of marriage to Meredith and it's all she wrote," he said to Dave, as he rocked back on his heels, standing at the bar. "I spend all my time assessing other people, watching them, learning about them so they can deal with their hang-ups and yet I never saw it coming."

Big Dave McClane shook his head and grabbed a handful of Spanish peanuts from the plastic dish that Gus Smetana, the bartender and proprietor, had just set in front of them.

"But that's the way, huh, Bobby?" Dave said. "Isn't the husband always the last one to know?"

"I guess so," Bob said, slightly irritated that Dave answered his own lame self-pity with an even lamer cliché.

"Of course, Darlene left me, too," Dave said, snapping up another handful of the foul peanuts. "But that was a long time ago. And it wasn't for somebody else."

"Thanks for reminding me, bud," Bob said bitterly.

Dave looked a little hurt.

"Come on, Bobby," he said. "You know I didn't mean it that way. Personally, I can't understand why she would ever leave you for Rudy fucking Runyon. The guy's a total asshole."

"Yeah, but a *rich* asshole," Bob said. "Saw the happy couple just the other day."

"Where?" Dave said, running his big hand through his graying and disheveled hair.

"Over at Hopkins Hospital," Bob said. "They had a seminar on bipolar disorder. Just as I'm about to go inside, I see this huge black limo drive up. Man, it's about a hundred feet long. The driver parks and opens the back door and out pops Dr. Rudy and the lovely Meredith."

"Brought the limo, huh? Heard his publisher pays for it," Dave said.

" 'Ask Dr. Rudy,' " Bob said, in a voice that mimicked the announcer's on Rudy's nationally syndicated radio show.

"'Whether it's love or loss, Dr. Rudy has the answers,'" Dave said. "Gotta hand it to him, though, the guy's done all right for himself."

Smetana came over and showed off his gleaming new dentures. "Hey, lads," he said. "Hate to break up this high-toned conversation, but it's last call for happy hour."

"And what a happy hour it's been," Dave said. "You want a last drink, Bobby?"

"Why the hell not?" Bob said, smiling with what he hoped would look like his devil-may-care grin.

"The thing is," Dave said, "you gotta be a personality. You could write a book, Bobby, all you been through. The activist shrink, man."

Bob laughed, as he picked up his vodka and ice.

"Yeah, that would sell maybe ten copies."

"Whatever," Dave said. "You're still a hero to me, Bob-a-ril," Dave said, putting his big arm around Bob's shoulders. "All you done for people down here. You stuck with your youthful dreams, baby, helping the people who needed it most, and that means a hell of a lot. You never sold out, and not too many guys can say that."

"Yeah, well, maybe I should have," Bob said. "'Cause this poverty shit is getting old, right?"

"Ah, you don't mean it, Bob. It's not in you. You're a working-class hero."

Dave opened his arms and gave Bob a drunken hug. Bob felt himself blush. Jesus, Dave could get sentimental when he was loaded. But what the hell, now that all his other friends had run for the burbs, and Meredith had cashed in with Rudy, what it came down to was Dave McClane was his best friend. He managed to give Dave an embarrassed little hug back.

"Well, I gotta get back, Dave-o," Bob said.

"Sure you don't want to take a run down to the Lodge?" Dave said. "Heard there's going to be a little birthday party tonight for Lou Anne."

"Ah, the fair Lou Anne Johnson," Bob said. "You make your move on that girl yet?"

Now it was Dave's turn to blush. He'd had a crush on the buxom waitress at the local artists' bar, the Lodge, for over three months, but was too shy to tell her.

"Not yet," Dave said. "You think she's a little young for me?"

"Young?" Bob said. "She's almost forty. Damn cute, too. You ought to tell her you're crazy about her before some other guy gets there."

"Well, maybe I will," Dave said. "What about you, Bob? When are you gonna find a new woman?"

"Never," Bob said, moving to the door. "I'm all done with that."

In his mind's eye he suddenly had an image of Dave and Meredith, Rudy and himself . . . all of them young, marching in the streets to fight city hall from building the beltway through Fells Point. Young, angry, dangerous . . . friends and lovers. He shook his head and the image floated away. There was a time when he liked to recall his romantic radical youth, but now it was too painful to remember.

"I'll see you at the Lodge Thursday night, bud," Bob said, as he got to the door and looked out into the icy street.

"Long live the Rockaholics," Dave said.

That was the name of Bob's oldies band. The Lodge was their one steady gig and Dave was their number one fan. But then he had always been Bob's number one fan, ever since they were kids and Dave had been a roadie for Bob's old band, the Nightcats.

"Take care, bro," Bob said.

"You too, bro," Dave said.

Bob stumbled, half-crocked, out into the freezing night. He felt warmth and a brotherly tug toward Dave, but he felt something else, too. Something like contempt. After all, any man who could be *his* fan ... well, that made him lower than Bob himself on the food chain. And since Bob felt like a failure and a sack of shit, what then did that make Dave?

As he walked past the narrow row houses toward his own place on Aliceanna Street, Bob was suddenly overwhelmed with a feeling of dread. This was it, truly all there was. After all the sound and fury of his activist youth, fighting city hall, giving his life—his *whole* fucking life—for some ideal of equality, some dim utopian fantasy, this was what it had come down to. A few patients, barely enough money to scrape by, and crummy well drinks with Dave. Meanwhile, all his other old pals, the once-radical shrink gang, lived in the burbs and watched their kids grow, go to college, and prosper. Jesus, some of his old college friends were already grandparents. And most of them were multimillionaires.

Christ, Bob thought, he'd been as brilliant as any of them. But somehow, for all his youthful brains and passion, he'd missed the boat. Not that he was all *that* old; he was still in his early fifties. Which meant he was just old enough to know that he had used up his store of luck, or to put it like the old Marxist he once was, his capital was spent, the workers of the world had never revolted, and, face it, his life as a useful member of society, even as marginal as it had been for the past ten years, was now kaput, finished, ancient history.

In the past month, Bob's last grant from Johns Hopkins Hospital had dried up. Named after his old mentor and radical psych teacher, the Roger E. Director Grant had been renewable yearly, and when things were tight it had always pulled him through. But this year the board had denied Bob's request and when he'd petitioned them they'd written him a fucking e-mail, saying that "the grant was for groundbreaking new work in the field of psychology," and that "a person as well-established" as Bob couldn't be "eligible for it in the new millennium."

Bob didn't have to be a CIA decode specialist to know what that really meant: "You're an old washed-up hack and if you're not rich and famous by now, it's not our job to fund your worthless fucking practice."

God help him . . . he didn't know what he was going to do next. If only he'd sold out years ago, taken a job as a corporate shrink . . . back when he had heat on his career. The thought of being broke, going into his dotage eating at Denny's, getting the early bird special with the old-age pensioners. Wearing a spit-mottled cardigan sweater, wandering around the pier at Fells Point, staring through the restaurant windows at happy, successful people who were eating oysters and crab cakes.

Oh Jesus, such thoughts made him panic. It was like someone had sent electricity through his body. Juiced him up . . . with a zap of fear.

It hadn't always been this way, of course.

No, it hadn't been so bad when Meredith was still around. But living alone, there were some nights he thought about, *really* thought about, downing a whole bottle of Ambien and checking out for good. Leave the Gandhi bit for some young sucker with a need to save this sad, violent world.

Bob walked on, feeling a pain in his right knee, an old lacrosse injury from his days at Hopkins. Lacrosse. Running all day in scrimmages and then *after* a killer practice doing another two miles on the track. Was it possible that he had ever been that young? Or was that merely a dream?

A dream like his marriage . . .

In spite of what he'd said to Dave, about how he'd been blind-sided by Meredith's defection, the truth was he'd seen it coming. It was as much his own fault as Rudy's (the son of a bitch). If he hadn't gotten into the goddamned poker games with Ray Wade, fat Lenny Bloom the social worker, and their buddies. If he hadn't lost his life savings in his early middle-aged "swinging guy" period. It had all seemed so innocent when they started. Just a few old friends getting together once a week for a low-stakes game. But disastrously for Bob, his little hobby soon blossomed into a full-bore gambling addiction. The excitement of the games gave him a rush, like the wild old days, fighting the cops. And for a while, maybe six months, he'd been on a tear, coming home with his old corduroys stuffed with bills. He'd become so cocky that he'd talked Ray Wade into getting him into "bigger games," a favor slick Ray was only too happy to grant. After all, Bob was a cardsharp's dream. He was a bold and reckless player. No matter what lousy cards he held in his hand, he always managed to convince himself that the next one he drew would be the one that filled an inside straight. When these moments of "inspiration" came, it was almost as though he heard a voice from, well, not God exactly, Bob didn't believe in God, but from a higher power of *some* kind. (Was it the same higher power that had convinced him he had to live a noncompromising life as an urban saint? Probably.) Thus "inspired," Bob would suddenly throw caution and common sense to the wind. He raised the stakes and stayed in, until the bloody end. It was a huge rush to play cards that way, brave, dangerous. Poker made him feel alive, gutsy, and, most of all, young.

It also made him broke.

By the end of one solid year of wild drinking and poker playing, Bob and Meredith's life savings had dwindled down to sub-nothing. All their retirement plans, which had once included

Ambrose Bierce–like dreams of moving to Mexico and buying a cottage in San Miguel de Allende, or homesteading in economical and left-friendly Costa Rica, were now washed up.

Poverty at this precarious age was a bitter pill to swallow. Meredith wept at night, tossed and turned in bed. She railed and screamed at him until she was all screamed out. Then one day three years ago she'd *moved* out. Out and in with Bob's old friend and current nemesis, the pop shrink star Dr. Rudy Runyon.

Now she lived in luxury in Rudy's 1920s mansion in Roland Park, played tennis every day at the Roland Park Country Club, and confined her trips downtown to occasional stop-ins at the shelter on South Broadway, where Bob worked a couple days a week, and where Rudy made yearly public appearances to keep up his image as the champion of the homeless.

Bob let himself into his little row house, took off his coat, and flopped on the faded yellow couch. He reached for the vodka bottle on the sideboard and poured himself a stiff drink.

God, the agony of it, getting old with the same depressing patients.

He took a sip and reminded himself not to go down that dark path. Don't hate your patients. No, no, that was no good at all. After all, he did *try* to help them, didn't he? He worked his butt off trying to get the manicurist Ethel Roop to keep her ballooning weight down. But every time they seemed to be making some headway, she'd relapse. The last time had been just a few days after Christmas. She'd gone on an eggnog-and-cinnamon roll binge and gained fifteen more pounds. Christ, she'd be better off taking some kind of new designer diet pill than talking to him. A pill he couldn't prescribe because he wasn't a psychiatrist. And what about Perry Swann, the masturbating bus driver? Hadn't he worked forever to get him to see that his problems were related to his unfinished business with his mother, who'd sexually molested him when he was three years old? But what good had this startling insight done? Two weeks ago Perry had jerked off in front of a woman just outside the Greyhound bus terminal and been busted for public lewdness. Which meant suspension from his job, a trial, and probably a cancellation of his health insurance, and *that* meant bye-bye Bobby Wells. Another patient down the tubes and how the hell would he find a new one to replace him?

Of course, there were his elderly patients at Church Home Hospital and St. Mary's shelter, but those were welfare recipients for which he received a small stipend from the Department of Welfare.

No, what he needed were some more paying patients.

Christ, face it, the only interesting (and solvent) patient he had nowadays was the haunted and paranoid art dealer, Emile Bardan, who usually sat through the fifty-minute hour terrified by fears that Bob hadn't been able to help him with at all. And what if Emile decided Bob was useless? What then?

Bob couldn't bear thinking about it.

He'd done it, all right. Royally fucked up his life.

What he needed, he thought, as he headed upstairs to his Ambien and blessed oblivion, was a miracle. That was it. Some way to see things anew. Life looked at through a new pair of glasses, a vision that would spring him into action.

But what in God's name that vision might be, the good shrink Bob Wells didn't have a clue.

# CHAPTER THREE

On the surface, at least, Emile Bardan seemed a brilliant and successful guy. He owned a lot of real estate, ran a new art gallery that dealt in antiquities a few blocks away on South Broadway, and lived in a smartly refurbished end-of-the-row nineteenth-century redbrick row house in nearby Canton. He was thin and handsome, in his thirties, obviously well-educated, and Bob gathered from his offhand comments that he did quite well with the ladies.

But for all of that, Bardan was a terrified man. He was obsessed by the recurrent feeling that his enemy and rival, a Brit named Colin Edwards, was going to steal one of his prized acquisitions, the mask of Utu. Indeed, the fear so overwhelmed him that Emile was no longer sure if he was in his right mind.

"Perhaps," he told Bob, "I'm just paranoid, but maybe . . . maybe it's really going to happen. That's what's driving me nuts. I just don't know."

As a hungover Bob made breakfast the next morning, he remembered what Emile had told him about the mask.

"It's a mask of the Sumerian sun god," Emile explained, sitting cross-legged and nervously wringing a monogrammed linen handkerchief in his hands.

He picked up a large art book he'd brought with him and brought it over to Bob, who looked down at a color photo of the mask.

Bob knew very little about art, but one glance at the strange and terrifying green mask made him shudder. Utu's eyes were almond shaped, the mouth was oversized, with nightmarishly thick red lips, and his ears were pointed. Golden streaks slashed the sun god's green cheeks, and his forehead was adorned with three huge red rubies. Utu was hardly sunny; rather, he radiated a fierce malevolence.

"He's very . . . intimidating," Bob said.

"Yes, he is," Emile said. "The Sumerians didn't have cozy gods. And if you think the picture is hellish, well, you should see the real thing sometime. It's very powerful. It had to be because our boy here was not only the sun, the giver of life, but you can see from his fierceness, he was something else, too . . ."

"He looks angry," Bob said, realizing at once that it was a lame and obvious statement.

"That's right," Bardan said. "Old Utu was also the avenger of the dead. The god of justice and vengeance."

"Right," Bob said. "Well, I can definitely see why you value the piece."

Bob handed the book back to Emile Bardan and sat back down in his seat.

"Where the hell was I?" Emile said, looking down at the floor.

"You were talking about Colin Edwards," Bob said.

"Yes," Emile Bardan said. His voice was pitched higher when he spoke about Edwards, and he gritted his teeth.

"We've known each other all our adult lives. I met him in Cambridge years ago, when we were both students. We ended up in the business and we often bid against each other at auctions. I usually won, and Colin has hated me ever since. He's a rich, smooth bastard and something else, too: a thief. He's been involved in any number of art thefts, but he's very slick. Never been caught."

Bob felt hopeful for the first time. This was the most Emile had ever told him. Now the trick was to keep him talking.

"I'm not sure I understand, how he's related to the mask?"

"He wanted it badly, but I outbid him for it and he's been toying with me ever since."

"Toying?" Bob said. "How do you mean?"

Emile flashed his big brown eyes.

"You'll think I'm paranoid."

"Try me."

Another long silence. Bob waited, trying hard not to let Emile feel his own desperation. Finally, the trim little man spoke.

"Okay. For example, he sends people around to my town house to watch me. And I get phone calls all the time. Even in the middle of the night. He doesn't say a word. Then hangs up. He's seriously fucking with me."

"The thing I don't understand is," Bob said, "if he wants to steal the mask, why would he put you on guard like that?"

"Because that's how he is," Bardan said, "It's personal with him. It's not enough for him to simply steal the mask and sell it. He's got to break me down in the process."

"Sounds sadistic."

"Totally," Emile said. "The most sadistic bastard you'd ever want to meet."

Suddenly, unexpectedly, Emile began to weep. Bob waited for him to use the Kleenex box, which was sitting on the little end table by his chair.

"Have you called the police, Emile?"

"Of course. But you know what they say. 'Sorry, we can't do a thing until a crime is actually committed.' Meanwhile, I can't sleep, can't think. Colin's watching me, waiting for me to slip up, and then he'll grab the mask."

"I take it you have it well guarded," Bob said. "Locked in a safe."

"Of course," Emile Bardan said. "But this war of nerves, it's really getting to me. I think what I really need is some sleeping pills. When I can't sleep I get nuts. And I'm afraid I'll make a mistake. Think you can write me a prescription?"

Bob bit his lower lip and felt a twinge of anxiety. Since he wasn't an MD he couldn't write prescriptions, but instead had to refer his patients to a psychiatrist who could give them the pills they invariably wanted. The problem was once they'd met a Dr. Feelgood, many of them jumped ship. Why spend their lives talking to Bob when the pills changed their mood in a matter of hours?

"I could refer you to someone," Bob said. "But let's try to work on this without medication. You don't want to add addiction to your other problems."

Emile Bardan only shrugged and picked at his pink socks.

"I know what you think," he said.

"What's that?" Bob said.

"You think I'm making the whole thing up."

"Not at all," Bob said. "But now that you mention it, are you sure he's really got people watching you?"

"Of course," Emile said. "They were on my roof the other night."

"Edwards and his men? You saw them?"

Emile shut his eyes and massaged his temples with his thumb and forefingers.

"Heard them," Bardan said. "I got my pistol and headed up the fire escape. By the time I got up there, the helicopter was already in the sky."

"And you're sure this . . . helicopter had taken off from your roof?"

Bardan's thin and elegant face squeezed into a frown.

"See? That's what I'm talking about. You don't believe me. I'm telling you, the guy is after me. He's driving me crazy."

Bardan's eyes were wide with terror and it took Bob a full fifteen minutes to calm him down. At the session's end, they'd agreed to meet twice a week for the next few months, during which Emile Bardan's stories had become even wilder. He was sure his phones were tapped, he was certain Edwards had hidden cameras in his living room and office. He lived in fear that one day when he went to check on the mask, it would be gone and there would be nothing he could do.

In the beginning Bob had believed him, but as the stories grew more elaborate he began to wonder how much of it could possibly be true. Perhaps all of it was a mere projection, some kind of neurotic persecution fantasy that caused Emile to fixate and obsess on Colin Edwards.

Bob wasn't sure where the truth actually lay, but his instinct told him that there was something else going on in Bardan's heart, some terrible secret that perhaps made him feel that he *deserved* to have the mask stolen from him. Sometimes, when Bardan talked about Edwards stealing it, there was almost relief in his voice, as though he wished Edwards *would* steal it so the whole torturous ordeal could finally be over with.

Emile Bardan seemed to be suffering from some terrible guilt, a guilt that could only be expiated by losing the mask. But whenever Bob tried to broach the subject, Emile would get uncommunicative, cross and recross his thin legs, and stare moodily down at Bob's frayed Indian rug.

They had reached an impasse, not unusual in therapy, of course, but before Bob could work through it, Emile announced he had to go to London for a time to check on some possible acquisitions for his gallery.

Bob asked him what he would do about the mask when he was gone. Emile frowned and said he'd hired two guards.

"Expensive guards," he said, as he left the room that day. "The kind that will shoot to kill, if necessary."

"Let's hope it never comes to that," Bob said, using his best optimistic voice.

"I'll see you when I get back," Emile said.

As Emile left that day, Bob smiled and wished him a good trip, but the truth was he hated to wait for two whole weeks. Given the tenuous nature of their relationship, two weeks could set them back two months, maybe longer. God, what rotten luck. He finally gets an interesting paying patient and the guy leaves. Maybe forever.

Meanwhile, what was he supposed to do about his overdue credit card bills, his late mortgage payment? Bill collectors were starting to hassle him. At first they were polite, but after a few calls they had threatened to come pay him a visit. He had to think, come up with something. What he needed, he found himself saying as he climbed into bed at night, was inspiration. In the old days, in his youth, inspiration could come from anywhere. He'd be walking down the street and he'd see two people talking, maybe they'd just be waiting for a bus, but the way they were huddled together would make him think of one of his patients, and he'd suddenly *know* what that patient's problems were all about. Because his antennae were out, because he was fully alive.

That was what it was all about, he thought. Becoming alive again.

# CHAPTER FOUR

Dressed in his old Hopkins sweatshirt and his father's watch cap, Bob ran through Patterson Park. Sometimes, he thought, as he moved his legs in long, loping strides, sometimes when he was a kid, running would give him ideas, too.

Now he jogged by the dilapidated Chinese pagoda, which had been there ever since he was a child. He remembered when the People's Republic of China had sent it to Baltimore. There had been a ribbon cutting, pictures in the paper and on television. But now the pagoda was rotting, and on late-night jogs he'd once seen a dozen rats running out of it. Kids used it for sex, and junkies to shoot drugs.

Like everything else in his life, Bob thought, the pagoda was past its prime.

Bob ran harder and watched the steam come from his mouth. He could still run. He wasn't a hopeless case, yet. He just needed to work harder. Find a reason to keep moving. Hey, he'd be okay. Of course he would. It was just a matter of time, wasn't it? Something would happen. And boom, he'd be on top again.

Running, like this, with the endorphins flowing, he could nearly believe it.

But even the run had its perilous side.

At least once a week, an unmarked beige Crown Victoria would pull up beside him, somewhere near Linwood Avenue or at the east end of Baltimore Street.

Inside, Homicide Detective Bud Garrett would be sitting behind the wheel. Garrett's eyes sagged down to his lips, and he'd lost most of his once-thick brown hair. He sported a lame comb-over, three or four lost strands that looked like broken feelers on an insect. Beside him in the passenger seat was his fat, brutal partner, Ed Geiger. Geiger had a gut, and a big, untrimmed mustache. When Bob looked at him he always thought of Hitler.

The Crown Vic was there again today.

"Hey, hey, look at the jock," Geiger said.

"Yeah," Garrett said. "Dr. Bobby's gonna get himself on *Survivor.*"

They both brayed at that one. Bob said nothing but kept running as the police car kept pace. As he tried to cross the street at Linwood, the two detectives pulled in front of him, blocking his path.

"What the fuck?" Bob said.

"Oooh, you shouldn't curse," Garrett said, getting out of the car.

"What the hell do you guys want?" Bob said.

"You got any drugs on you?" Geiger said. "I think you better let us look and see."

"Yeah," Garrett said. "Assume the position, Bob."

"This is bullshit," Bob said. But he didn't resist. He wasn't in the mood for a beating today. He spread his legs and leaned on the roof of the car, as Geiger roughly patted him down.

"Nothing here today," Geiger said as he finished. "The hero is clean."

"Save anybody from mental illness today, Bob?" Garrett said.

"No," Bob said. "But I did teach a class in how to avoid police harassment."

"Whoaaaa," Geiger said. "Score one for Dr. Bobby."

Bob gave them a quick little smile like they weren't getting to him and, suddenly, had a mental image of himself punching Garrett's nose in a street demonstration thirty years ago. Yeah, those were the days . . . the whole hood out fighting city hall, and Garrett trying to shove Bob off the street with his baton. Bob had surprised him with a short left hook, right in the snout.

A glorious, terrific shot . . .

An impulsive shot that had earned him fame in the hood, and the enmity of the cops for the rest of his life.

"Hey, Dr. Bobby," Garrett said. "I see that old pal of yours, the Jew boy, Rudy? I hear he's got his own radio show."

Bob said nothing.

"Hey, that's not all he's got," Geiger said. "I hear he's got Bobby's ex-wife . . . the gorgeous Miss Meredith."

Bob glowered at them.

"Ohhh, I think he's getting mad," Garrett said.

"I'm getting scared," Geiger said.

"Fuck you both, officers."

"No, but Bobby," Garrett said, "how come you ain't got a show? I think you should have one. Could be called *The Saint*. You could dispense advice to the coloreds and the immigrants around here about how to achieve sainthood."

"First, you gotta lose all your money gambling," Geiger said. "That way you remain pure as the driven snow."

That one hit Bob hard. How the fuck did they know about that? Ah Christ, what was he thinking, around here, *everybody* knew everything.

"Then you gotta live in a shithole house, 'cause saints can't have nice pads," Garrett said.

"And no nookie," Geiger said. "You gotta get no nookie at all."

"You guys done with your comedy routine?" Bob said.

"Sure, Dr. Bobby," Geiger said. "For now. Have a nice jog."

They headed back to their car, laughing as they shut the doors. Bob turned away from the street and ran slowly across the frozen baseball diamond, into the park. As he ran he began to feel a pain in the pit of his stomach. In the old days, when he was a respected member of the community, the cops wouldn't have hassled him like that. Why? Because his old pals at Hopkins, and in the radical community, wouldn't let them get away with it.

But that was another world. Now they knew he was alone, weakened. They could do anything they wanted to him. And who was going to back him? No one. He was an animal cut out of the pack.

It was almost as if he were a criminal, he thought. Some street punk . . . but in a way it was worse because a criminal, like Ray Wade, for example, had his own crew, his own network. The cops didn't mess with Ray like they did him. Why? Because they had more respect for a criminal than they did an idealistic loser, like Bob. It was true. After all these years on the job, he had less power than a common street criminal. The idea was perverse, but instead of depressing him it made him laugh.

Maybe, he thought, he'd be better off if he actually *were* a criminal.

He laughed again and dismissed the idea. When you were desperate, hell, you were likely to think of some very weird shit.

# CHAPTER FIVE

Thursday night was the only time he still felt alive. That was the night Bob played with his band, the Rockaholics, at the funky artists' bar called the Lodge. Up on the small bandstand, Bob wailed away on lead guitar, doing the old blues and rockabilly tunes he'd loved since he was young. The group was made up of a middle-aged black drummer, Curtis Frayne, a fashionably bald, young bass player named Eddie Richardson, and a really good thirty-five-year-old Chinese organist/sculptor named Ling Ha. The Rockaholics played all the old tunes from the rockabilly catalog: "Be Bop a Lula," "Woman Love," "Blue Suede Shoes," and "Honey Don't." They usually attracted a decent crowd and while he was up there on the stage at the end of the bar, riffing on his old Les Paul, Bob was transformed. The aches in his knees disappeared. The pain in his neck, which seemed to get sharper every day, didn't bother him at all. These were the last good times, Bob thought, just about the only thing that pulled him from the depression and bitterness that strangled his mind.

But even this pleasure was imperiled. The problem with the Rockaholics was that nobody in the band really sang that well. A few years back, Bob had done a fair imitation of the old-time stars, Carl Perkins, Gene Vincent, and Eddie Cochran. But he couldn't hit the high notes anymore and nobody else in the band

was even half as good. Lately, there had been some complaints
from the hip younger artists, and bikers, who drank and danced at
the Lodge that the band's limited song list had become too predictable. There was even some talk of getting a new and younger
group, the Fliptones, as the house band. When Bob heard this
mutinous idea, he felt panic rise in his chest. Losing the gig was
unthinkable. Something had to be done about finding a real
singer. So for the next three weeks the band tried out prospective
leads. They were a motley crew, starting with a huge truck driver
named Jerry Jim Marx, whose act consisted of screaming streams
of obscenities into the mike ("Fuck me, eat me!!"). Next was a
skinny little punkette of a woman named Dukey Thorn who was
covered in tattoos. She looked cool, like many of the artists themselves, and for a minute Bob was hopeful. But then she sang.
Any relationship between Dukey's caterwauling voice and the
song's melody was purely coincidental. Finally, there was a big
black woman, a computer techie who worked at the ESPN Zone,
named Dee Dee Wallingham. She claimed to love "old-time"
rock, but sang every song like Celine Dion, her chubby fist tight-
ened over her heart. Her voice was a high-pitched wail, and she
managed to turn even "Knock on Wood" into a ballad.

Things looked desperate until one rainy night, just an hour before their gig was scheduled to start. Bob was hanging out at the
Lodge, doing the sound check with Curtis and the already half-
wasted Dave McClane.

"Hey," Dave said, pouring down his fifth glass of Evan
Williams bourbon. "Check it out. I'm the world's oldest roadie."

"And the world's best," Bob said.

Dave gave Bob his sweet, appreciative smile and Bob gave him
a thumbs-up. How old was Dave anyway? A couple of years older
than Bob and heading for the barn. Bob wondered if Dave had any
money. That was a subject that never came up and sometimes it

irritated him. Dave knew all about Bob's financial ruin but offered little information about his own situation. At one time,
maybe eight or nine years ago, Dave seemed to be doing pretty
well, even published a couple of magazine pieces in *GQ*, and
there was talk of a book contract for his "working-class" novel.
But somehow the book never got finished. And when Bob remembered the little he'd read of it, he figured that maybe it was
a good thing. The characters, one of whom was obviously based
on Bob, were all idealized caricatures of working stiffs. Noble
workers against evil bosses. The old social realism of the lamest
and most obvious kind. Yes, Bob decided as he checked his amp,
it *was* probably a good thing that Dave didn't publish it. The critics would have raked him over the coals. This way he could still
harbor the fantasy that he was too sensitive for the cruel world of
commercial book publishing.

"Hey Bobby," Dave said, talking into the mike, his glasses
glaring from the house lights on the stage. "This level good for
you?"

"Great, Dave. Now if you could only fucking sing."

Dave laughed and did a little Elvis imitation through the
mike.

*"Hey, hey, hey, I'm all shook up."*

He shook his belly, which was starting to hang over his thick
leather belt. Bob looked up and saw Lou Anne Johnson coming
out of the kitchen with a cup of chili in her hand. She looked up
at Dave, who smiled nervously at her and suddenly burst into his
own little rockabilly song.

*"Hey hey, there's a girl Lou Anne. She's so good looking she could kill
a man. Lou, Lou, Lou, Lou Anne, I need you, baby, doncha unnerstan'!"*

Lou Anne's mouth dropped open as Dave finished up with a
little pelvis swivel, and dropped creakily to one knee.

"Whoa, check him out," Curtis said, bringing a beer from the bar.

Bob laughed as Lou Anne put her chili down on a table, then ran up onstage and gave Dave a hug.

"My own local Elvis," she said.

"Damn," Dave said. "If I had known I was gonna get this kind of reaction I woulda started singing a year ago."

Bob laughed and waved at him. Oh man, he loved the old Lodge, had since the day he first started hanging out here. It was one of the true benefits of not moving out to the burbs. Out there, there weren't any hangouts. Everybody was home playing computer games. But here at the Lodge, in good old downtown Baltimore, you had characters. People like the Finnegan Brothers, two bikers who supplied the hood with grass, speed, and coke. (Not that Bob used the stuff himself anymore. He was terrified of a heart attack.) They were scary dudes, even just sitting around half-wasted like they were now. He looked at them sprawled in their back corner seats, dressed in their leathers. They were creepy, yeah, but he needed those kinds of creeps. Besides, they were loyal to the guys in the hood. Once when some dudes from Belair Road had come around the Lodge to mess people up, the Finnegan Brothers had beaten them senseless and driven them back to their own neighborhood. He felt a kind of bond with them, the kind that he would never have experienced out in posh Roland Park. And there were wild artists like Tommy Morello, the steel sculptor, who was showing in New York, as well as Baltimore. And Gabe DeStefano, the poet who only wrote poems about boats in Chesapeake Bay. Sure the poems were bad, but he loved the kid—and his crazy idea that Baltimore was sacred—just the same. The Lodge was his spiritual home, he thought, and if he couldn't play here anymore, man, he just didn't know. . . .

As Bob took a long sip of Jack Daniel's and tried to banish the evil thoughts from his mind, the front door opened and a very wet woman came hustling in out of the rain.

Bob looked up, and felt something happening in his chest. Jesus, she was something . . . she had thick blonde hair and the most beautiful, sensual lips. And her skin . . . he hadn't seen anything like it before. It was soft and white, and her nostrils flared a little, and her eyes . . . Christ, he'd never seen eyes like those. They were small, almond-shaped, and green. They seemed to hold a secret, or a promise.

She placed the steel tip of her open umbrella on the floor, shook it a little, looked around, and smiled nervously.

"Hi," she said shyly, looking at Bob, then quickly away. "My name's Jesse Reardon. I waitress down at Bertha's and I heard you all need a singer for your band."

Bob looked at Dave, who did a little Groucho Marx move with his eyebrows.

"I'm Bob Wells," Bob said. "Do you have any experience?"

"Sure," Jesse said, smiling at him. "I sang with a band for a little bit in West Virginia. Back in Beckley. Called the Heartaches?"

Bob loved her smoky voice, the way she seemed to be asking him if he'd ever heard of her old band. There was something just so damn lovable about her.

"Rock 'n' roll?" Bob said. He feared she was a country singer, which just wouldn't cut it with the hip artists at the Lodge.

"Sure," Jesse said. "Some blues, too. If you want I could, you know, sing something?"

Bob nodded, smiled hopefully at Curtis, who nodded.

"Where's Ling and Eddie?"

"Out in the kitchen," Curtis said. "Stealing food."

"Well, go get 'em," Bob said. "We want to give Miss Reardon here a chance to sing."

Bob turned to Dave, who looked at him with a childish excitement on his face. Jesus, she is so damn good looking, Bob thought. If she can only sing . . .

---

He helped her off with her soaking raincoat and folded it neatly over a chair. She wore a black sweater and blue jeans and a red ruby ring. Bob looked at her cheekbones, the curve of her lips, her small, perfect breasts. He felt his heart jump into his throat, and he silently told himself to cool down. From the kitchen the other band members filed out. Ling was eating an egg sandwich and drinking a beer. Eddie had a crab cake with saltines. Both of them checked her out, and Bob could feel the electricity in the room.

"What would you like to sing?" Bob said.

She looked around at the holiday lights that were still strung over the bar, smiled at him slyly, and said, "How about 'Blue Christmas'?"

"Yeah," Bob said. "That's a good one."

"You gonna sing it like Elvis?" Ling said.

"Un-uh," Jesse said, as she took the steps and grabbed the mike. "Charles Brown."

Bob looked at Ling and they both laughed. The lady knew Charles Brown. . . .

"All right," Eddie Richardson said, nodding to her. "Let's do it."

Bob waited for Curtis to hit the bass drum for the downbeat, then opened with a short, blistering blues hook. Next to him Jesse Reardon leaned into the microphone but hesitated as though she was too scared to sing. Then she looked at Bob, who nodded and smiled, as if he had total confidence in her. She shut her green eyes, opened her mouth, and began.

The effect was immediate and stunning. Jesse Reardon's voice was smoky, seemed to be crushed with heartache. Bob felt a jolt of electricity run up his back. He turned to look at Curtis, who had a smile big enough to light the entire club. Jesse sang on, doing the song a second time and Bob noticed Dave and Lou Anne rocking back and forth in perfect time at the front table, a huge smile on Dave's face.

At the song's guitar break, Bob ripped out a blistering solo . . . causing Jesse to smile at him, then look away. She grinded her hips in a subtle but sexy way and sang the last line again.

*I'll have a blue, blue, blue Christmas.*

The band worked up into a tight, screaming crescendo and Jesse gave a low, hot moan, "Oh yeeeah," as the tune ended. The bartender, Jimmy Jackowski, a big Pole who usually didn't much care for the band, looked up at the stage and said, "Fuckin' A, now that's music."

Jesse Reardon looked a little embarrassed.

"I was a little off in the timing because I haven't done this for a while. I could do another one, if you want?"

"No need," Bob said.

Jesse's face fell as she looked down at the floor.

"Oh well," she said. "Thanks for the chance."

Bob looked at the other band members, who all nodded their heads at once.

"You want the gig, you got it," he said.

"Oh my God," she said. "Really?"

"Really," Bob said. "We don't *have* to hear any more. That was totally cool. What do you say?"

"Yeah," she said. "I say oh yeah."

"Welcome to the Rockaholics," Ling said.

"Thanks," Jesse said. "I feel like I just won *American Idol.*"

There was a cheer from some leather-jacketed art students in the back of the bar, and suddenly Bob was hugging Jesse Reardon and feeling the warmth of her body, her lovely breasts crushing against his chest.

"Let's do another tune," Curtis said. "You know 'Tell Mama'?"

Jesse bit her bottom lip, smiled from the corner of her mouth, and said:

"Tell Mama *all about* it, baby!"

Everyone laughed and Bob screamed into the lead, as the band kicked in behind their new lead singer.

That night the new lineup, ragged and unrehearsed as it was, was a huge hit. And Bob Wells heard himself play better, tougher, tighter than he had in twenty years. The crowd went wild. Old and Young Finnegan grabbed Lizzie Littman, the porn film-maker, and danced on the bar. Tommy Morello picked up Lou Anne Johnson, twirled her around, and tossed her to Dave, who caught her and crashed to the floor. Gabe DeStefano was so thrilled he wrote five really bad poems about boats and the bay. Even old, drunken Wyatt Ratley, a burn victim from a fire at Larmel Steel, and one of Bob's patients, got up and did a kind of clog dance with two sexy Maryland Institute girls who'd stopped by. At the end of the night, the band was called back for four en-cores, and even after three whiskeys and five beers, Bob was barely tired at all. In fact, he hadn't felt this good since . . . well, since his old street-fighting days.

The only blight on the evening was that the music was so loud, and so good, that it attracted some street people who were hang-ing out outside the front door.

After trying and failing to come in the front door, 911 and two of his gutter pals got in through a back window, and started a fight right in the middle of "Money."

Dave McClane intercepted them as they tried to leap onto the dance floor, and Nine immediately kicked him in the balls. Dave fell back right into Lou Anne's waiting arms, howling in pain. Old and Young Finnegan quickly restored order, however, by throwing Nine and his smelly buddies bodily out into the street. Other than that, things rocked at the Lodge in a way they hadn't for a long time.

As they packed up their amps and guitars at 3:00 A.M., Bob thought about the old Dinah Washington song: "What a Difference a Day Makes." She had it dead right, he thought. His life looked considerably brighter the minute Jesse had walked through the door.

# CHAPTER SIX

During the next few weeks, Bob tried hard not to think of Jesse Reardon. He tried not to think of her lips, her breasts. He tried not to think of the way she swayed into the mike, or the smell of her perfume so close to him as he leaned into her, singing harmony on "Rainy Night in Georgia." He tried to forget her little half smile, and her laugh . . . so fully alive . . . so wonderful . . . God help him.

He tried to forget her because he was sure, absolutely sure, that she *must* be seeing a guy, though none ever showed up at any of the Lodge gigs. Then Dave told him that he'd heard that Jesse had been married to a redneck house painter named Dwight Reardon who'd gotten hooked on pills and booze and was living in the street.

Which meant she was free, but not for long. Every man at the Lodge was hitting on her. Christ, she'd caused a sensation. He had to do something, make a move. . . .

But he did nothing. Doubt had overtaken him. He was twelve years older than she was, and not in the greatest of shape. What shot did he have?

None.

Who was he kidding?

But still, the way she sang with him onstage, the way she leaned into him. Was it really all just part of the act?

Christ, he had told himself, told everybody, that he was through
with women. Been there. Done that.

But from the moment she had walked in out of the rain he was
a goner.

As the first days of spring bloomed across the city, Bob Wells al-
ternated between wild hope and total despair. On some nights,
after playing with Jesse at the Lodge, he knew, beyond the
shadow of a doubt, that she loved him. Wasn't it obvious in her
every stare, the way she worked with him onstage, pouting her
sensual lips at him, touching him as she danced by. And how
about afterward, at the late-night party with Dave McClane and
Lou Anne, and Ray Wade and his wild mom, Dorsey? All of them
drinking shots and laughing until two or three in the morning like
they were young again. It was obvious to everyone there that she
was crazy about him.

And yet, when he finally screwed up his courage and asked her
out to dinner, on a proper adult date, she made up some lame excuse about having a cold.

It drove him crazy. Bob couldn't eat, couldn't sleep, even with
Ambien.

He was so turned on by her, just saying her name over and over,
"Jesse, Jesse," made his heart beat faster. He was alive again, really alive, in a way he hadn't been for years.

Meanwhile, the chemistry between them wasn't lost on the
public, either. Their gigs had grown to three times a week, one at
the Lodge and two other nights at the Horsemen Lounge and the
Chesapeake Grill. Here they were, in middle age, and they were
a local sensation. Hanging out, having real fun, even making a little money . . . why, it would have all been perfect, except for
Bob's increasing romantic desperation.

His nerves were so ragged, he'd started matching drinks with Dave again, in the warm afternoons at American Joe's.

"Christ, David," he said as they downed their shots. "I'm crazy about her. What the hell am I going to do?"

Dave laughed and shook his head. "It's going to be all right, Bob. I think she just wants to be sure. She's letting you chase her until she catches you."

"But what's the point of that?" Bob said. "She already knows how I feel about her. Maybe I'm just wrong about the whole deal."

"No way," Dave said, grabbing a handful of peanuts. "I'm telling you, she's crazy about you. Lou Anne says so, too."

Bob managed a tortured smile. He was jealous of Dave's relationship with Lou Anne, which seemed perfect in every way. The lucky bastard.

"That's great about you two," Bob said, as his stomach twisted and turned. "It's really working?"

"Oh yeah," Dave said. "So far, I mean. We stay up late watching old movies, and she makes these great waffles. You have to bring Jesse over one morning and have breakfast with us. Maybe this weekend."

"That would be great," Bob said.

Except maybe he'd ask her and she wouldn't want to. The past two days she hadn't even returned his phone calls. It made him sick . . . dizzy . . . being in love . . . it was awful. And all the insight he brought to other people's love affairs did him absolutely no good at all.

"You know what, Bobby," Dave said, grabbing another handful of peanuts. "I'm thinking about asking Lou to move in with me."

"You're kidding?" Bob said. "Isn't it a little soon?"

"Maybe," Dave said. "But what the hell, when you know, you know, right?"

"I guess so," Bob said, feeling his stomach flip again.

He felt like he knew. He wanted her but she kept saying he'd get tired of her, that she needed time, time for what? To find some other guy?

"I mean, none of us are getting any younger," Dave said. "If not now, when?"

"Yeah, I guess you're right," Bob said. "It's just that I'd be careful. You don't want to make a wrong move."

Dave smiled and ran his hand through his hair.

"The only wrong move, as far as I'm concerned, is losing Lou Anne to some other guy because I didn't move fast enough. Some guy with a lot of money, like one of those D.C. lawyers who like to hang out at the Lodge when they come over to check on their rental properties. You know the guys . . . fucking speculators from over in D.C. I see them eyeing her. Guys with money, man, that's my enemy."

The words stuck in Bob's craw. Everything Dave said about Lou Anne was twice as true for Jesse. Rich lawyers from Fells Point were always falling into Bertha's Mussels. He'd been in there a couple of times and seen them talking to her.

"Jesse, you look great today."

"Jesse, what *is* that perfume? Doesn't she smell terrific?"

"Jesse, baby, those high heels are really sexy."

Christ, if he didn't make a move soon . . . he'd lose her. The thought made him sick to his stomach. He couldn't sleep, he couldn't stand it. He had to have her. What the hell was he going to do without her? That was the roughest part of all. Having deadened himself to the world for so long, now that he was feeling alive again, he couldn't imagine going back to the same old daily routine.

No, he couldn't, he really couldn't bear it.

What the hell was he going to do?

* * *

It was four in the morning and Bob walked around his house in a loop, by the bed, into the hall, down the end of the hall to the bathroom, around the bathroom, and back down the hall to his bedroom again. He made this loop seven times, then put on his sweater and leather jacket and walked down the steps and out the front door.

He stood outside her apartment, looking up at the dark second floor. She was up there sleeping, he was sure of it. This was madness, standing out here like an adolescent, but that was how he felt now, like a crazed kid who was just getting his first shot of hormones.

What should he do? Throw pebbles at the window? Start singing a love song? Christ, he had no idea how to act. He was like a zombie brought back to life but with no memory of what it was like to be human.

What would be a cool and subtle move?

He walked around in a circle trying to come up with it.

But it was no use. No good. He had not one idea.

Finally, afraid that he might chicken out entirely, he walked up the marble steps and saw her name on the buzzer: REARDON, J.

There was nothing else to do or say.

He started to push the button but the light came on in the hall.

Amazingly, she was standing there, dressed in a black nightgown that flowed dramatically to the floor.

She opened the door and smiled at him in a curious way.

"Bob, I happened to look out the window a minute ago and you were out here walking around in circles. Is something wrong?"

"Can I come in?"

"All right. But just for a while."

He looked down at the floor as he brushed past her. Slowly, he walked up the stairs to her apartment.

\* \* \*

Her place was funny, he thought. Though it was an apartment in the city, it might as well have been a rustic cabin in the West Virginia hills. There were pictures on the fireplace mantel of a glen somewhere in the mountains. There was an old rocker, obviously carved by some backwoods furniture maker. There was a couch with a handmade quilt thrown over it.

Bob felt swept away by the simple beauty of it all. He looked at her as she sat on the couch across from him. She was barefoot, and suddenly Bob had an intense desire to kiss her feet. The thought unnerved him even more.

"What's wrong, honey?" she said, in her smoky voice.

"What's wrong?" Bob said. "You barely talked to me tonight."

"I had to go home. I had to think," she said.

"And?" he said.

"Bobby, I do care for you . . . but I don't know . . . I don't know if I can go through it."

Bob moved to the edge of his seat. He felt as though he might fall off into space.

"Go through what?" he said.

"You'll hate me if I tell you," she said.

"Never," Bob said. "For God's sake, tell me what it is."

"If I was a little younger," she said. "It really wouldn't matter. But the way things are now . . . I'm almost forty, and I can't see myself . . ."

She faltered and a tear rolled down her cheek. Bob started to move toward her but she put up her hands, palms out, and shook her head.

"No, stay there," she said. "I can't trust myself to be honest if you hold me."

"All right," Bob said, feeling his arms trembling. "But tell me. Now."

"Okay," Jesse said. She wiped away her tears and began.

"I heard . . . I heard around town . . . God, this is so hard for me, I just hate confronting people . . ."

"It's all right," Bob said, falling back on his professional manner. "We have to be honest with each other."

"Okay, then," she said. "I heard from a lot of people that you . . . you lost all your money playing cards with Ray Wade and some other guys. That your practice had fallen off and that you're in a lot of trouble financially . . . and Bobby, I know you'll think I'm a gold digger, but I can't put myself through that kind of pressure again. 'Cause I know what it will do to you. And to me. Nothing good can come out of being poor."

Bob was stunned. He sat back in his chair in a self-consciously slow way so as not to fall backward. People had told her that he was a loser. He wanted to scream out, "Who? Who said it? I'll find the sons of bitches and kick their asses."

But what would that accomplish? He had to suspend his anger and dismay at the public humiliation he'd suffered (though it was hard . . . Christ, everyone knew . . . everyone knew he was broke, oh Jesus, the humiliation of it), and deal with the situation at hand.

He smiled, a big generous smile, and looked across the room.

"That's the problem with rumors," he said. "They're usually based on half truths. Here's the real story. Yes, when my wife left me I did go through a wild period where I lost quite a bit of money gambling. I think, honestly, that it was my own way of paying for my sins. I'd been careless with Meredith's love. I'd grown to take her for granted. I didn't listen when she told me that she was lonely, that she needed contact with me . . . and when she left me for Rudy Runyon I was devastated. I went through a period of real self-hatred. How could I have become such an uncaring and unfeeling person? I felt that I had to pay somehow for screwing up, so I played cards and I lost. Quite a bit of money, I admit. But nowhere near all of it. Fortunately, my mother and father left me a good-size inheritance. That part of my savings was never touched. So, you can tell your friends at the Lodge, or whoever they are, that they're dead wrong about my financial situation."

He looked at her directly and she winced at his words.

"You're mad at me," she said. "I knew you would be."

Bob got up from the chair and joined her on the couch. He took her hand and looked into her eyes. The same look he gave his troubled patients.

"I'm not at all upset that you questioned my financial situation. I don't think any woman should get involved with a guy who's broke. It's a recipe for disaster. What upsets me is you didn't come to me as soon as you heard all that bullshit."

She put her head on his chest and wept.

"I didn't feel . . . like I had the right. I was afraid you'd hate me and never see me again. I'm sorry I doubted you, Bobby. I mean it."

Bob put his right hand under her chin and gently lifted it toward his face.

"Jesse," he said. "You should know better. I love you."

"I love you, too," she said. "I do. But I can't stand being broke. I don't know what I'd do if I had to be poor again."

"You don't have a thing to worry about," Bob said. "Not one thing."

They kissed and Bob was flooded by a warm bath of emotion. God, he was in love, and he was loved back. Could there be anything better than this? No, of course not.

He slipped his hand under her nightgown, felt her warm, soft breast and was swept away by tenderness. Oh God, she was so beautiful, lovely, and now she was falling down on her knees in front of him.

And then he was holding her head in his hands as she unzipped his pants, and Bob felt as though he would never die. But even as he said her name again and again, he had a terrible foreboding. He had lied, and she had believed him, and even as he was swept away by the romance of it all, he knew that he had to make that lie come true. She was dead right. Nothing good could come for either of them if they were both poor.

# CHAPTER SEVEN

She loved him. It was amazing, as though it had been ordained, as though it were fate. He had almost lost himself in despair, ended up like so many other guys, hanging in the bars, talking about the lost days of youth, bitter and alone.

But she loved him and that changed everything.

Now, when he awoke in the morning, he looked out into his narrow, wire-fenced backyard and saw the first tendrils of spring blooming in the world. There was real greenery in his backyard. The idea made him laugh with joy. Hell, even the word "greenery" was fantastic. "Greenery," what a marvelous word, so simple and yet so descriptive. What wonderful, inventive human being had first come up with the word "greenery"? People were inventive, endlessly so. They could invent language. Art, music. And best of all, they could reinvent themselves.

On the suddenly Technicolor street, Bob noticed his neighbors. There was Maria Chacón, and her two beautiful babies. He found himself stopping and admiring the children. "Look at those two cool guys," he said. Maria reminded him gently that the kids were *niñas*, and Bob found this fantastic, as well.

All last year he'd assumed that Maria's kids were boys. Why? Because he had never bothered to ask her. Because in his depression he had assumed that he hated them all. Damn foreign assholes moving into the neighborhood, probably into some kind of drug-running bullshit. He'd told himself this negative crap all last year, every single time he saw them.

Or, to be more precise, every time he failed to see them. Because now it was obvious that he hadn't really seen them at all. Never seen the kids, or Maria, or her handsome young husband, Javier, who worked down at Harborplace and was so obviously devoted to his family.

Bob was stunned by his new vision, by how human, vulnerable, hopeful, and kind they were. Hey, he bet they'd like Jesse. Well, of course they'd like Jesse. Who wouldn't? Hell, they'd *love* Jesse. He told them to make sure they came down to the Lodge to hear the Rockaholics. He told them that his girlfriend was the lead singer and Maria was so happy for him. She said to him, "You know what, Bob, you look like you had a miracle," and Bob thought, Yeah, that's right. It really is that, a real honest-to-God miracle.

And when he dropped in down at Pop Ikehorn's corner store, he was stunned that the old guy smiled at him. Granted, it was a toothless, yellow gum smile, and the guy still looked like a two-hundred-year-old corpse, but how many times had old Pop *ever* smiled at anyone over the years? Like none, zero. The old guy with the curling yellow fingernails and the hair sprouting out of his ears, the old guy who sat hunched behind his cash register with his spit-mottled cardigan with one shiny silver button from the Sample Store, left over from say 1958, and he half dared you to say hello to him but even grumpy old Ikehorn couldn't hang in there with his loser's attitude against the new-and-improved Bob. No way, Jose. Now he smiled at Bob and even asked him to . . . *gasp* . . . reach into a bag of ancient pork rinds, which he had been eating since maybe 1945, and Bob, happy, goofy, mood-enhanced, did just that. He reached into the horrific bag and he grabbed hold of one, half convinced that at any second maggots were going to squirm onto his fingers, and he picked the weird, green, moldy thing out and took a big unhealthy bite out of it. It tasted like somebody's science project and he could barely manage to keep it down. But when he was done gagging, he smiled and said, "Mmmm-mmmm, tasty," and old Pop smiled and said, "That'll keep you young, young man," which may have been the first time he'd said anything but "Fucking niggers are taking over the city" since Bob had first met him fourteen years ago.

The love Bob and Jesse felt for each other only enhanced their communication onstage and soon the Rockaholics were jamming with a new level of passion, as the two of them played off each other.

In love himself, Dave managed to slip a short piece into the Scenes section of the *Baltimore Sun* with the title "Rockaholics Really Rock!" The piece was pure Dave, overgenerous in its assessment of the band's talents, though dead-on regarding Jesse. "The purest soul and blues singer this town has seen in twenty years!" Jesse was embarrassed and thrilled by the write-up and kissed Dave on the head, as the four of them ate Lou Anne's waffles after staying out all night. "Nobody is going to believe I'm *that* good, honey!" she said modestly. But she was dead wrong. Dave's over-the-top review brought in the fans, and soon the Rockaholics were playing at the Lodge two nights a week and people had to be turned away at the door. Onstage, the excitement of the crowd coursed through them and Bob and Jesse communicated in a near-subliminal way. Jesse had started to move around the stage now, rocking to the music, and sometimes they moved toward each other as if they were stalking each other. Bob would come toward her, desire on his face, as he blasted his way through "Hold On," and Jesse would back off, fear in her lovely face. Then Bob would lunge at her, and she'd sidestep him just in

time to avoid a collision. It was sexy and a little comical, and
something they didn't have to plan. It just happened one night
and they incorporated it into the act. It worked, drove the audience wild. The onstage chemistry between them was now so hot
that when Bob came near Jesse, riffing out, she'd touch his shoulder and then blow off her finger. The crowd loved that, as well.
They were the toast of downtown, interviewed on the radio and
on a local morning television show. There was even talk of a
record label getting together with them to do an independent CD.

"It's too great," Bob said, as they headed out with Lou Anne
and Dave to yet another party. "How old are we, twenty?"

"That's too old," Lou Anne said. "I'm eighteen, baby."

"Yeah, darlin'. Eighteen is just about right," Jesse said, hugging Lou Anne as if she were her best high school girlfriend.
Which is how they felt. The two of them had gone through so
many of the same things, bad men and low-paying jobs and tough
childhoods, that they were like twin sisters.

"I just love Lou Anne," Jesse said. "I can tell her anything."

"She's the greatest," Bob agreed. "The best."

What was a little odd, Bob thought, was how Lou Anne and
Jesse's relationship seemed to mirror that of Bob and Dave. Lou
Anne positively worshiped Jesse. She baked blueberry pies because Jesse said she liked them. She gave Jesse back rubs in the
little room off the stage where the band got ready for their perfor-
mances. When Jesse came offstage, sweat pouring off her, Lou
Anne stood by with a towel and rubbed her down.

Some nights Bob thought it was a little much, but then immediately chided himself for questioning it. Jesse was a star, so why
shouldn't Lou Anne, as her best friend, worship her, as well?

The four of them were great pals and Bob told himself to cool it
with all the lame questions. Enjoy. Accept. Be grateful for what's
been given.

* * *

Not only was Jesse a fantastic lover but also a great listener. She wanted to know all about his work and his wild past. After a two-hour lovemaking session, Bob lay in bed, his hand on her left breast, and said: "Come on, Jess, you don't want to hear about that ancient history, do you?" But Jesse had laughed and *insisted*. She wanted to know everything, how he'd gotten into psychology and what it was all about. So Bob started telling her the story of his life, how he'd fallen into it when he was attending Hopkins in the seventies and how he and a group of his radical friends had studied Jung, and his theory of the collective unconscious. At that point he had to stop the story to explain to her just what that was. "Remember," she said, "I'm jest this ignorant old country girl." Bob kissed her on the head and assured her that wasn't true at all. Naked, he held in his stomach as he reached up to the bookshelf and pulled down his musty old paperback copy of *Memories, Dreams, Reflections,* and just touching that book gave him a shock. He remembered Meredith and Rudy and himself all sitting there talking about archetypes and how the mandala was the symbol of wholeness in a divided world, and how they had felt they were on to something so deep, so wonderful, the secrets of the unconscious mind, and in their youthful arrogance so much more than that, the secrets of the *universe* even. He hopped back into bed and began to explain Jung to her, how he had started with Freud but then developed the collective unconscious theory, in which all mankind dreams and shares the same myths, even though they are expressed symbolically in different ways. She caught on right away, and was thrilled not only by what Bob was teaching her but by the fact that she could understand it.

"That's the thing," she said. "I never knew I was smart enough to go to school. I was told I was a dummy by my daddy so often that I just stayed away from books and ideas."

"That's a terrible thing that was done to you, Jess," Bob said. "In our country the poor are made to feel that they are stupid, so they'll stay right in their place."

She shook her head and tears came to her eyes.

"Oh Bobby," she said. "And to think now I have my own personal guru."

Bob shook his head, but she was all over him, kissing him with her lovely lips and asking him to tell her more. And so he did. He told her about how he and his friends wanted to use their therapy to wake up the world, because they all believed society was moving into a new kind of consciousness, and it was beyond anything the old straight political leaders could see or understand. They thought they could show people the way to a new spiritual growth, beyond material possessions. A world governed by a grace and harmony. And most of all kindness, compassion.

After going on for a while, Bob stopped and felt slightly embarrassed. Surely she must have heard enough by now. But she only snuggled up closer to him and said, "Bobby, I could listen to you talk for the next hundred years. Do you know what it's like to grow up in a place like Beckley where talk is considered unmanly, where the only strength is the strength of your arms and back? Where if you're a woman you would never even think to go to college?" She suddenly broke into tears at the thought of it and Bob patted them away, then heard himself telling more of his old stories, the ones he'd sworn he'd never tell again, not because they were dull but because they hurt so badly to recall. Because to tell her about those days of bright hope when he and Rudy and Meredith and the others lived together in a big-shingled house on St. Paul Street was to remind himself how far they had all fallen short of their youthful ideals. It was almost impossible to believe that the battered, compromised group of lumpy, middle-aged people were once the hot and sexy young stars of the

Hopkins psychology program, the young radicals who started a revolutionary People's Free Clinic, where they offered an alternative to the kinds of square psychotherapy that were going on at Phipps Clinic at Hopkins Hospital. How they didn't believe in just sitting in a chair and listening to people's problems, how they thought that was a cop-out, an artificial environment that put a huge wall between the therapist and his patient. How they realized that much of so-called mental illness was due to the very thing Jesse was talking about . . . working in dead-end jobs, feeling there was no hope, being trashed by bosses who had no interest in your self-esteem, and in fact had just the opposite interest—they wanted to keep a woman like Jesse down so they could control her. And how once they, the young rads, knew these things, they couldn't remain simple shrinks anymore, just doling out little Freudian insights. No, they had to become revolutionaries who wanted to change not only psychology but the capitalist world, which created a certain kind of "mental illness" to begin with.

When he was done, she looked at him wide-eyed and said, "You're my hero, baby."

Bob didn't know what to say. It was such a pure expression of her love for him that he blushed.

"Well, he said. "That was long ago."

Whatever her educational shortcomings, the usage of the past tense wasn't lost on Jesse.

"And what about now?" she said. "You still have patients and work in the community, don't you?"

"Oh, of course," Bob said. "I just meant that the historical moment . . . the big surge was back then. Now things are different."

"But still good, right?"

"Fine," Bob said. "Things are just fine."

His irritation was aroused again. She was fishing, just like before. She wanted to know exactly *how* good. How long would it be before she asked to see his financial statements? Tomorrow? Two weeks from today?

And what lie could he tell her then? Nothing. He'd be through. This lovely woman, naked in his bed, would walk out and not only would her loss kill him, he'd be . . . God, he'd never thought of this before . . . he'd be a laughingstock to all his pals at the Lodge.

He could just hear them: "Poor old Bob. First he loses his clinic, then his wife to that schmuck Rudy, and now Jesse Reardon walks out on him. And *he's* going to help other people learn how to live? What a joke."

No, he couldn't lose her. Not after losing everything else. He couldn't go back to the old dead life. Not now. Not when fate had cast her into his hands. Surely, God, or whatever power ruled the universe, wouldn't give him a woman like Jesse only to have her leave him.

It was, he thought, a test. A real test of his ingenuity and manhood. You wanted a woman to love and to love you back. Well, here she is. Great-looking, sexy, and talented, and she loves you.

Now how will you support her? How will you keep her around?

# CHAPTER EIGHT

Emile Bardan was back from his trip to England, which he described as a nightmare. He looked it, too. His spiky hair, always a wreck, now was like a tangle of worms and there were dark tea bags under his eyes.

"He was there," he said, scratching his left wrist. "Colin Edwards was there and he kept coming after me. Oh man, it was terrible. He literally came up to me . . . and said right to my face that he was going to steal it. What the hell am I going to do?"

Bob didn't know what to say. During the last few happy weeks Emile had been the last thing on his mind.

"Just because he said he would steal it doesn't mean he's actually going to," he tried.

Emile flashed him a contemptuous look.

"Give me a break, doc," he said. "Edwards will try to steal it. It makes me feel so damn helpless."

The same way it makes me feel, Bob thought. But he had to make a try.

"But you're not helpless," he said. "When he says something like that to you, you can tell him you've hired guards and notified the police, and if anything happens to the mask, he'll be the first person arrested!"

Emile laughed with disdain.

"Please," he said. "You think I haven't said that a thousand times? See, that's what he wants me to do, engage him in talk, you know? Start yammering about how he'll never get it, how I've got guards all over my office, my house, what kind of locks I've got on the safe, and he'll never be able to break in. That kind of thing."

Bob nodded his head, but something Bardan said struck him in the strangest way. Had Emile just accidentally told him where he kept the mask? Hadn't he said that his office was in his house?

"You see, Doc," Emile went on. "Colin is a monster. I have these dreams about him now."

"Tell me about them," Bob said.

Emile shifted uncomfortably in his seat and sighed heavily.

"Okay . . . I dream that I'm in bed just about to fall asleep. The door opens and Edwards is coming toward the bed. I mean, I can't see him, but I know it's him and he's all wet, covered with mud and seaweed, and he's coming right toward me . . . and in his hand is this knife. This huge steak knife and it's all wet, too. And he gets near me, and I'm sure, absolutely sure, he's going to plunge the knife into my back. But he doesn't. He has this box, and instead he opens it and leaves it next to the bed. And then he's gone."

Emile Bardan started to cry. Bob pointed to the box of Kleenex on the table next to him. Emile plucked one out of the box and blew his nose.

"I look down at this box and I don't know what to do. I'm afraid to open it, you know? But I can't not open it. So I reach down and there's this little clasp, and I pull it open and look inside, and there it is. It's there, inside."

"What is?" Bob said, gently.

"It's a head. A human head, all wet and drenched with leaves and mud, and I pull it out by the hair and look at it and it's him, my old friend, Larry Stapleton. His eyes are gone. They've been eaten by maggots and his nose is half eaten away and his lips are black, his teeth knocked out. It's horrible."

Emile shook and cried bitterly.

"I put the head back in the box and then I wake up."

"Very powerful," Bob said. "What does it suggest to you?"

Emile shook his head and wiped the tears from his cheek.

"Well, it's not all that subtle, Doc," he said. "Once you know the truth, you'll see that. Larry Stapleton and I were very close friends. Larry was a Brit and was from a very wealthy family. Colin knew him, as well...it's a very small world...and he wanted Larry to invest in his business. In fact, he took Larry to his country house for the weekend to talk him into it. I know all this from friends of Larry who were up there with them. They went hunting, drank champagne, and had it on with some of the local girls...and then Colin got down to business and asked Larry to invest in his company. Larry declined and then he dropped the big bomb. He told Colin he intended to back me in my business instead. Colin went crazy. They had a terrible row. Then they made up...at least Larry thought they had...and they went out on the river for a row. No one knows what happened exactly, but somehow the boat capsized and my friend Larry Stapleton drowned that afternoon. Killed by Colin Edwards, I'd stake my life on it."

"Did the police investigate?" Bob said.

"Sure, but there were no witnesses to the actual drowning. In the end it was marked down as an 'accidental death by drowning,' but I knew, hell, everyone knew, what had really happened. Edwards was always impulsive, had a terrible temper. He still does, and if you cross him he'd just as soon get rid of you. So now you understand my dream, right?"

Bob shifted in his seat. The story had taken a turn he wasn't at all prepared for.

"You see," Emile Bardan said, dabbing the tears off his cheeks once again, "I'm not only afraid he's going to take the mask, but that he's going to kill me when he does."

"Why didn't you tell me this before?"

Emile shrugged and shook his head.

"I was barely aware of it, I suppose," he said. "I mean, I've always known, but not known, if you know what I mean. Murder is something that happens to other people."

"Yes, I know," said Bob. "But why would he bother to kill you? It's the mask he wants, not your life."

"Not exactly," Emile said. "He wants control. He wants to have complete freedom. You know what Edwards was in college? A utopian leftist. I was always a centrist politically, but not old idealistic Colin. He believed in a new world, and all that. A real fanatic. But when he couldn't get it, oh man, you just don't know. Those are the worst kind, Doc, the ones who have the big dreams. It's the same with the artists in the world. I love painting and I love sculpture, but the people who make it, the ones who won't compromise or play the game, they're the ones you have to fear, because they don't really give a shit about people. They live for 'ideas' or 'beauty' or 'God' or some other abstraction. They're bad news. A guy like Colin could kill me tomorrow and never lose a single night's sleep over it."

Bob looked down at the rug. For a second he'd felt that Emile Bardan had been describing him, not Edwards.

"Time's up for today," Bob said, looking at his watch. "But I think we've done some important work."

"Yeah, I think so, too," Emile said. "Hearing myself talk about Edwards, I just realized something."

"What's that?" Bob said.

"If he comes after the mask, and I'm around, what I have to do is shoot him in the fucking head."

"A very bad idea," Bob said.

"Maybe, Doc," Emile said. "But outside of this bastard I have a good life. And I don't intend to let the son of a bitch do to me what he did to Larry. I mean, what would you do?"

"I'm not at all sure," Bob said. "But I don't think that it'll come down to shooting a gun."

"I hope not," Emile said, as he went out the office door. "But if the bastard comes around, I'm going to shoot first."

Bob slumped down in his chair. The session had left him exhausted and shaken. He thought about Emile's version of Colin Edwards. Was it possible the man was actually a killer? Maybe it was true and, if so, perhaps Emile Bardan was eminently sane.

And then he thought about what Emile had said to him. You had to fight if you loved something. But how much would he risk now that he was in love? How far would *he* go to protect his new life?

Bob was due over at Jesse's in an hour. Then they were going to Victor's restaurant down at Harborplace for Lou Anne's birthday. Christ, Bob could already see the bill there. He'd have to put it on his card, which was already ridiculously overextended. But what choice did he have?

He locked the front door behind him and took a walk toward the harbor. As he neared the pier the wind whipped up, pushing him back. He put his hands in his jacket and pushed forward. The cool air refreshed him. He looked at a big freighter anchored eight or nine miles out, and heard a ship's horn in the distance. He loved it here. He could think, open his mind, and then suddenly there was something coming to him . . . something he felt that had been there for quite a while . . . maybe months . . . but up till now he hadn't been able to really picture it.

But he could feel it coming now.

He felt the wind whip off the water, the sea spray hitting his face, and then he had it. He saw and felt it as clearly as he could see the tide and the steam coming from the freighter's stacks.

The thought was so clear, so vivid, that he laughed out loud and did a little dance, a kind of a jig, on one foot.

How could he have not seen this before? Because he had never considered this answer before. It was almost like stories he'd read of scientists who were blinded by an old paradigm. They couldn't solve the problem until they came up with a whole new question. What was that book they'd all read years ago? Kuhn's *The Structure of the Scientific Revolution*? Yes, that was it. It was just like that. You had to attack an impossible problem by changing the way you saw the problem to begin with. And that, finally, was what he'd just done.

Bob walked down to the water's edge and sat down, kicking his legs up and down against the seawall.

They thought he was a bumbler, Mr. Good Guy, the kind of nerd who could never get in step with the real world. An adolescent who never grew up, really . . . lost in kiddy dreams of impossible utopias and doomed to live a life of lonely martyrdom. But that very image—the loser, the amateur, the hopeless utopian—was going to be the very thing that made it easy for him. Because no one would suspect him. No one. He was too dreamy, too soft, too *nice* to pull off anything as brazen as stealing from his own patient.

But they were wrong, all of them, because that was precisely what he planned to do. Steal the mask from Emile and sell it to Colin Edwards.

How much could he get? He had to do some research. But if the mask was really priceless, why not two, three, even five million dollars?

And once he had the money, he'd wait a year or so, just in case anyone *did* suspect him, then take Jesse away with him to—to—hell, to any place they both wanted to go. Rome, Florence, Greece, Mexico . . . Spain. . . . He'd always wanted to see Barcelona.

Just the two of them traveling, eating and drinking, making love.

Living for pleasure, until they found the right place and settled down.

But how would he deal with the guilt? Wouldn't it gnaw at him, tear him up inside?

That was a problem, of course. There was no getting around it. But somehow he had a feeling that he'd handle it just fine. Hadn't he spent thousands and thousands of hours helping people at his old free clinic, which the city had closed for "lack of funds"? Hadn't he given therapy to old people and blacks and immigrants from El Salvador and Chile for a fraction of the cost he might have charged?

Hadn't he, of all the old gang at Hopkins, been the only one who lived out their dreams of being downtown shrinks for life, living among the people who really needed both therapy and a radical perspective on their lives?

So hadn't he accrued points, thousands upon thousands of points, like a kind of moral good cholesterol that could be charged off against this one bad act?

Besides, if he had that much money (millions!) he could use some of it to help the poor, but *really* help them. Not just give them his useless pep talk, but a grant. The Bob Wells Grant to Deserving People. People Bob singled out as worthy of his help.

A single mother who was trying to put her kids through school. A struggling artist who couldn't paint because of poverty. A handicapped man who wanted to start a clinic for other handicapped people. Yes, why the hell not? He could be a kind of modern Robin Hood!

All he needed was a plan, and some help. What did second-story men call their gang? A crew. That was it. He needed a crew of guys. . . .

And he knew right where to start. Ray Wade. His old friend, Ray Wade, he of the six-inch sideburns and the fifties DA. Ray Wade, whom he'd have to watch like a hawk, but who wasn't all that bad of a guy. Slick Ray would help him put together the right crew.

But before contacting Ray he had to do some work on his own. He had to find this Colin Edwards and see if he really did want the mask. That was the first piece of business. Bob threw his head back and laughed.

It was terrible what he was going to do. It went against everything he'd ever learned, everything he stood for. By all rights he should be sick to his stomach for even thinking about betraying his patient, becoming a criminal.

So how come it felt so right? How come he was standing here by the pier, freezing from the cold winds, and laughing his ass off?

Because he was, for the first time in more years than he cared to think about, standing up for himself. Fighting back. And nothing felt better than that. Besides, Emile Bardan was a rich man. In the end, he'd probably be better off without the damn mask in his life. He'd move on, forget the whole thing. And hell, he must have insurance on the goddamned thing. So really, the only loser was some crooked insurance company, people who, if you really thought about it, probably deserved to get ripped off.

Really, it was a win-win situation.

One little move. One little crime and he and Jesse would be set for life.

This was good, Bob thought, as he walked toward Jesse's. This was the best idea he'd ever had and the truth was, moral qualms aside, he couldn't wait to get started.

# PART II
## RAIN OF STONE

# CHAPTER NINE

Practicing psychology was such an ambiguous profession. He was never sure how much he'd really helped any of his patients or, to be honest, if, even after years of therapy, he'd helped them at all. In fact, he was pretty sure that there were at least a few patients who'd gotten worse under his care. But crime . . . crime was like . . . well, business. You stole something, you sold it to another guy, and you reaped the rewards. It was straightforward, American. You didn't have to justify your profession by saying that somewhere along the line maybe you'd done some good. You had your reward sitting there in front of you. Cash! And plenty of it! And in the end, Bob told himself, wasn't this what people really valued? Power? Money? No matter what else they gave lip service to.

So he would do it at last. Lay his absolutist morals aside—okay, temporarily aside—and make some real money. But that led him directly into his first problem.

What was the mask actually worth? Somewhere in his patients' notes, Bob found that Emile had said it was "priceless." But what the hell did that mean? For the next three days, Bob traveled to various public libraries to use their computers, so no one could trace the searches back to his home.

What he found out was a little disheartening.

Utu was known in ancient Babylon as the ruler of heaven and earth, a god who "lived to render justice" and "who dealt out swift punishment to those who broke the law." From his shoulders he "issued bands of light," the "light of justice," and in his hands he carried a "many-toothed saw," presumably to hack the limbs off criminal offenders.

Jesus, Bob thought, just his luck. He finally has a shot to cash in big but he's got to offend the god of justice himself. He shut his eyes and envisioned Utu coming for him like ... like ... Leatherface from *The Texas Chainsaw Massacre*, a screaming power saw aimed at his neck. The very thought of it made him break out in a sweat.

Of course, he told himself seconds later, the whole idea of Utu was absurd. Just some primitive way of keeping the citizenry in check. It wasn't like he was really up there in the sky watching Bob, getting his new Skarie Skill saw ready to hack him to bits. Bob only felt nervous, he was sure, because the whole thing— betraying the trust of his patient, stealing a valuable work of art— well, all of that would be enough to make *any* honest man nervous. And especially Bob, who had always been so intent on doing the right thing, the moral thing, as though God were watching him, keeping tabs on his efforts. That was it. He'd always had this feeling he was being watched, graded by the Big Teacher in the Sky, so now he was simply transferring his feelings of the Big Moralistic Sky Daddy from Jesus and Karl Marx to Utu.

Of course, that's all it was.

What he had to do was literally say, Fuck all that. Fuck Jesus in the sky, and fuck old Big Daddy Karl, and fuck Utu, too. Yeah, that was it. Fuck Utu and the whole nervous-making "god of justice" bit.

After all, where was the justice in his wife leaving him for Rudy fucking Runyon, the old fraud? Where was the justice in a guy like George Bush becoming president of the United States? No, wait, stealing the presidency from Al Gore? Where was the justice for the millions of Negroes who had been slaves?

But the hell with all that. Forget justifying what he was going to do. He had to be practical, find out what the fucking mask was worth. Like any real criminal would.

He ran a Google search and found that the mask was sold by one Lawrence Stapleton to an "undisclosed buyer" in 2003, and that it was, indeed, "considered priceless."

An "undisclosed buyer." That must be Emile.

But there it was again. "Considered priceless?" Christ, how many times in movies and novels had he seen the word "priceless" used? Usually by some ascot-wearing, crooked art dealer in forties movies, Clifton Webb maybe, a golden cigarette holder in his trim hand. "Yes, my good man, that etching is priceless." But in those movies guys like Webb always knew exactly how much money "priceless" really meant.

Bob, on the other hand, had no idea. "Priceless" might mean one million, it might mean twenty. How the hell did he know what to ask?

He ran another Google search, looking up "Utu," and after an exhaustive effort found that the mask had been purchased for between nine and ten million dollars in 1956.

Bob felt his heart start racing. Nine and ten million dollars? The thought was too much for him. He couldn't imagine walking up to Colin Edwards and demanding that much. The guy would laugh at him or maybe just shoot him in the head.

No, what he had to do was to find Edwards and convince him that he could deliver the mask at a price. So the question then wasn't *really* how much was the mask worth, but how much did Bob and Jesse need? Bob was much more comfortable when he thought of the heist in that way. Why, it was almost a Marxist solution to the problem. "To each man according to his needs." So how much did they need, then?

How about two million?

Two million dollars.

Strange, but only yesterday, two million dollars sounded like a tremendous amount of money. Back in the sixties and seventies, two million dollars was all the money in the world. But now, with a fabulous-looking woman like Jesse, and a third of his life left, two million suddenly seemed like, well, chicken feed. Especially, when you considered that this was it, the big shot, his *only* shot.

Okay then, how about three? Three was better. "Three" had a solid sound about it. Much better than "two." But what about relocation? Christ, moving to wherever it was they decided on. Say, Mexico, for example. For years he had thought about leaving America to live in San Miguel de Allende, but after a few looks on Google at the housing market in old San Miguel, it was obvious the place wasn't the artists' paradise it once had been. Christ, some of the whitewashed bungalows, with the rose trellis walls, were now going for five or six hundred thousand dollars. The days when a starving painter or poet (or retired shrink) could move down there, get himself a groovy little bungalow, and hang out at the Instituto de San Miguel attending free openings and guzzling the free chardonnay were gone forever. No, three million dollars wouldn't last that long there, especially since it might be hard to find any kind of decent work. And what if he and Jesse moved to Mexico and hated it there? They very well might despise the rich, retired squares who hung in such a place, trying, at sixty-five, to become the painters and poets they didn't have the guts to be when they were young. God, if that happened they'd have to move again. Which would mean an even greater expense.

To hell with it, Bob thought. Three million wasn't going to work in Mexico.

And if Mexico was out, so was Costa Rica. Of course, Costa Rica was much cheaper, but it was also much less developed. He was used to a certain amount of action and where would he find it down there? Who the hell would his playmates be? Machete-toting guys named Juan who hung at the jungle bodega? And what would Jesse do all day, hang out with the sloths in the trees? Become a nature nut who went out with tourists to see the coatimundi or the howler monkeys? Face it, he was too old now to start over on some beach with a bunch of moronic peasants and parrots jabbering at him. They'd be worse than his patients.

No, three million wasn't going to make it and there was no way he was being selfish or greedy here. The truth was just a lot more complex than he'd ever considered. He had a younger woman now, one who thought she was moving up the food chain by latching onto a big-time shrink as a boyfriend. She wasn't going to dig some place where the chief social activity was taking a canoe trip down a river to find the Sacred Caiman.

That meant that the very third world countries he had always fantasized about retiring to were totally out of the picture.

Face it, he was an urban guy and he needed an urban environment. Well, most of the year anyway. What they really needed were two homes. A city home and a little hideaway, a shack by the sea.

And the price of houses being what they were in any place that anybody who was anybody would want to live was going to be exorbitant.

Three wasn't going to make it. Hell, you buy the two houses and boom, you're broke. It was going to take four, at least four.

But then there was the car problem. For years he'd driven a piece-of-shit, ancient Volvo, like the good, nonmaterialistic lefty he was, but he couldn't expect a young girl like Jesse to share this sentiment. She wanted to have a fashionable car, one she'd be

proud to drive around in, and hell, to be perfectly honest, he
wanted her to have a cool car, too. As an older man with a younger
woman he had to keep her happy. She wasn't going to be into
making sacrifices for "the people." Hell, she *was* the people. She
was from funky Beckley, West Virginia, and she'd done all the
"sacrificing" she was ever going to do with Dwight. She loved
Bob, he was sure of it, but he was a meal ticket, too, and that was
cool. It made him kind of a patriarch, okay, a patriarch without
kids, but a great older man nonetheless. A man with a mysterious
past, a man with a swell-looking blonde babe, a man with two
houses and cool cars. Maybe a two- or three-year-old Jaguar would
do. For her. But he *also* had to have a car. Maybe a slightly battered but still great-looking Porsche.

So four wasn't quite right, either. Nah, it would have to be five.
Five million was the price and the truth was, he wasn't really sure
if they could get by on that.

But he didn't want to price himself out of the market.

No, five was really rock bottom. He had to get five or he'd have
to find another guy to buy the damn mask. Whoever that might
be. And he had to think about that, too. Jesus, there was a lot to
consider when you became a criminal. It wasn't an easy gig. Not
at all.

Emile had already let it slip that his office was in his house. That
was good. And that the mask was in a safe within the office. Probably behind a painting or something, or perhaps on the floor. In
any case it shouldn't be too hard to find it. But before you could
get to the safe you had to get by the guards. Two guards. And
then there was the alarm. Somehow you had to detach it, something he knew nothing about. But even assuming you could get
rid of the alarm, sneak by the guards, and find the safe, how the
hell would you ever crack it? In movies guys listened to the

tumblers on some kind of microphone and they just knew. Well, Bob could stand there listening for twenty years and have no idea what he'd heard. And then there was the little problem of finding this Colin Edwards person. And making the deal with him. Not to mention somehow actually collecting the money. After all, what was going to stop Colin Edwards from taking the mask and giving Bob a suitcase full of newspapers? Or for that matter, giving Bob counterfeit money? How the fuck would he know the difference?

Wait, he was moving too fast again. The first thing he had to do was find Edwards and make the deal.

How to do that? On the off chance that all this would be resolved in an easy fashion, Bob tried calling information in the Baltimore-Washington area, but there was, of course, no listing for the man.

Okay, forget it. Don't beat up on yourself. How best to proceed?

Ask Emile about Edwards? Pry a little. And how would he do that?

"Excuse me, Emile I was just wondering where this Edwards fellow lives? I'm thinking about stealing the mask and . . ."

No, that wouldn't do. Emile must never think that he had contacted his enemy.

Okay, then what did he know? Only what Emile had told him. That Edwards drove a silver BMW, that he sometimes parked near Emile's house in order to mock or unnerve him. That was it. He'd set up a post, like a spy on reconnaissance until he saw the silver BMW, and then . . .

He'd have to improvise.

First, he had to lie to Jesse again. He'd tell her that there was more financial work that needed to be done. He'd have to meet with his accountant tonight. Maybe for a few nights. He hated lying to her, but he reminded himself that the ends surely justified the means.

Because if he was going to keep her around he had to have the money.

That was the simple truth of it all. Lie now. Make love later. Everything else was just idle conversation.

# CHAPTER TEN

The only problem with Bob's plan was that after two weeks of casing Emile Bardan's house, he still hadn't seen Colin Edwards or any of his so-called crew. He had tried watching the house from a stoop down the street, from the back alley, and from the roof of a burned-out row house directly across the street from Bardan's place, but he hadn't seen one suspicious character the entire time.

Bob's middle-aged back hurt and his stomach rumbled from eating junk food. His fallen arches were radiating little circles of pain. Plus, he was tired, really tired, and discouraged. He thought of a line of one of his patients, a black kid who'd gotten involved in gangs. When he didn't like somebody, he said, "Dissed and dismissed," and that was how Bob felt now. Shut down before he'd even begun.

But he had to fight through that. Get positive again.

He told himself that the stakeout wasn't a total loss. He'd found out quite a bit about Emile's habits. Every Friday night Emile made the rounds of the local art shows, and ended up at the Havana Club, an illegal gambling casino out on the Ritchie Highway. From there, Emile went home with a Cuban woman named Laura Santiago. She lived on the opposite side of town, way out in the county, so Emile didn't get back until the next morning. During that time, he left two guards at his place, one downstairs and one up on the third floor. Obviously this was where the safe was. But how he was going to get past two armed guards was anybody's guess.

By the end of the third week, Bob became depressed. Obviously his stakeout was a flop. He'd have to find the guy some other way. But how? He'd already tried looking up Edwards on the Internet and found nothing. Maybe Edwards had lost interest. Gone off to steal some other work of art? Then what? Bob stayed up late, working on the computer, trying to find another buyer. There were a few names that kept coming up in all the stories about the missing mask. One was a man named Tommy Asahina, a Japanese collector.

The guy had served time for swindling investors in a securities and exchange scam. Maybe he would want to buy the mask. But calling him was to make himself vulnerable. Bob didn't really want to start a bidding war. He just wanted to do this not-so-simple transaction and then disappear from the world.

By the last day of the fourth week, Bob had nearly given up hope. Sighing unhappily, he shoved his binoculars into his jacket pocket and headed on home. All his plans were on the rocks and he had no clear image of where he might go from here. He had to come up with some other plan, maybe push Emile to tell him where Edwards was now. That was risky as hell, but it was all he could think of.

Weary and aching in every joint in his body, Bob shuffled along down the street, heading back to his own neighborhood. Some damn crook he'd turned out to be. He couldn't even find the buyer, much less grab the prize.

He turned down Aliceanna Street, trying to keep all the negative thoughts out of his mind. Every rookie criminal must go through times like this, he told himself. It was how you responded to a crisis that determined if you were going to be a great villain or just another cheap little punk. What he had to do was keep his hopes up . . . stay positive. What he had to do was . . .

Bob's train of thought was interrupted by something he saw in front of him. Not a half block away there was a man sitting on his stoop, a guy wearing an expensive dark suit and a three-hundred-dollar haircut. His shoes were so shiny they reflected the streetlight that glowed in front of Bob's house.

Parked at the curb in front of the man was a silver BMW.

"Bob Wells?" the man said, with the trace of an English accent.

"Yeah?" Bob said.

"Colin Edwards," the man said, standing. "A pleasure to meet you."

Bob walked a few more steps and reached out to shake Edwards's hand.

"Sorry," Bob said. "I'm not sure I know you."

"You don't," Edwards said. "But you want to, right?"

"Maybe," Bob said, taken aback by Edwards's total confidence.

"Oh, come on now," Edwards said. "You've been casing Emile's place for the better part of a month. I've been watching you the entire time. You must have something you want to discuss with me."

Bob felt his stomach lurch. It was all well and good to stalk the man, but to learn that Edwards had been aware of him the entire time was unsettling. It made him feel like . . . well, like what he was, a rank amateur.

"Okay," Bob said. "Let's walk."

"Sounds charming," Edwards said. "I love this area of your town. The brick houses, the narrow streets, the local fishmongers. Reminds me of my old neighborhood back when I was a mere lad."

"Where was that?" Bob said.

"Liverpool," Edwards said. "Dear old rotting, rat-infested Liverpool. Of course, the Beatles made it all seem charming. The Fab Four and their bar mates, all of that. But, trust me, it was and still is a hard place."

"Like Baltimore," Bob said.

"A lot like it," Edwards said.

They turned left at Broadway and walked past closed and abandoned stores, toward the harbor.

Edwards took a theatrical sniff of the air.

"Ah, nothing like the smell of salt air and machine oil," he said. "Started that way myself, you know, ordinary seaman and wiper. Went all over the world on freighters. Learned to speak eight languages and found myself interested in art. Eventually, I made it to Oxford. Had to pull a few strings to pull that off, but I never cared for university life. Too dull, predictable. Snobbery. Quit school and got into the import/export game, made a killing and began to collect. Been an exciting life, but very competitive."

"Really?" Bob said. He had to admit rather liking Edwards's tone. It was smooth and confident, so unlike those of his harried patients.

"Oh yes," Edwards said. "That's something the average person doesn't know. They think of an art dealer as a refined gentleman who wears a vest and goes around buying pictures, in between attending polo matches and getting the old Bentley reupholstered. But that's bollocks. People who collect art are wealthy, single-minded, and ruthless, y'know? Some of them are downright dangerous."

"So I understand," Bob said.

"I can only imagine what Emile has told you," Edwards said, lighting a Gitanes. "Let me guess. He said that I tried to get his friend Larry Stapleton to back me and when Larry turned me down, I took him out to the raging sea and drowned him."

"Something like that," Bob said.

Edwards laughed and shook his head.

"That's wonderful," he said. "The man is a complete fabricator. Really, you can expect anything at all to come out of his mouth. Anything but the truth, that is."

"And what is the truth?" Bob said.

"Simply, the exact opposite of what he told you. I was the one who was the working-class boy who had worked my butt off. Emile's company was slipping and Stapleton knew it. While they were out rowing on the river, he told Emile that he was withdrawing his money from his house and backing me instead. Emile lost his temper, there was a row, and Larry 'fell' overboard. Of course, Emile swore that he'd tried to save him, but everyone knew better."

They turned left down Thames Street, by the old Merchant Marine Building.

"Love it here," Edwards said. He started to walk out on the dark dock. Bob looked at the cold, oily water lap against the pilings. Who was he to believe? Emile or Colin Edwards? Somehow, he couldn't imagine the diminutive Emile Bardan losing his temper and smacking his old friend with an oar, but perhaps it didn't matter. Even if Edwards was a killer, he wouldn't hurt Bob now. Not when he obviously wanted to hear what he had to tell him. Bob ventured out on the old pier.

"Now," Edwards said, when they were halfway out into the wet darkness. "Let's talk turkey. Are you going to help me get my mask back?"

"Oh, it's *your* mask?" Bob said. "I suppose you're going to tell me that Emile stole it from you?"

"That's right, my friend," Edwards said. "I bought the mask from a private owner, one year ago. I had the provenance and the bill of sale. The mask was under lock and key in my manor house in Sussex. I won't bore you with the small details. Suffice it to say, Emile bribed one of my guards, broke into my safe, and stole it."

Edwards strolled obsessively around the end of the pier.

"So you see," he said, "this Emile, he's not the quiet little victim he seems to be."

"So you say," Bob said.

"So I do say," Edwards said. "And how sayeth you, Bob Wells? Are you going to team up with me, restore the sun god to its proper place in this skewed universe, and make yourself a rich man in the process?"

"That would depend on you," Bob said. "But I think I can be of service."

"How?" Edwards said.

"I'm going to get the mask, quietly, without fuss. And then I'm going to sell it to you," Bob said, scarcely believing his own words.

"What makes you think I'm going to let you do that?" Edwards said.

"Because you don't know where it is," Bob said. "If you did, you'd already have it."

"Even so," Edwards said, "I can merely grab Emile off the street and torture the information out of him."

"But you wouldn't want to do that," Bob said. "Emile has guards with guns. There's no guarantee that someone wouldn't get hurt, maybe even killed. At the very least there would be a big scene, which would draw a lot of attention. I'm your best shot. Believe me."

Edwards glowered at him, and even in the darkness Bob could feel the force of his malignant will.

"Fine," he said, controlling himself. "I'll pay you two hundred thousand dollars for the mask. Not bad for a night's work, hey, Doc?"

Bob saw a chunk of loose concrete at his feet. He picked it up and threw it out to sea. It sank without a trace.

"I must have misjudged you," Bob said. "I thought you were serious. I'll have to go see the Japanese collector, what's his name? Asahina? I bet he'll make a more reasonable offer."

Edwards moved toward Bob and grasped for his throat, but Bob quickly slapped his hand away, then pushed him back with a quick palm to his chest.

"Touch me again and I'll break your face," Bob said. Edwards stepped back and Bob was pleased by the surprise on his face.

"I did my homework, Colin," Bob said. "Asahina wants the mask as badly as you do. You want to get into a bidding war, it's fine with me."

Edwards's eyes darkened as he stared down at Bob.

"How much do you want?" he said. All the playfulness was gone from his voice.

"Six million dollars," Bob said.

"That's ridiculous."

"Asahina won't think so," Bob said. He turned and started to walk back to the city, half expecting a knife in his shoulder blades.

"Three," Edwards said.

Bob kept walking. Each step was heavier than the last.

"Four, then," Edwards said.

Bob stopped, turned around.

"Five," he said. "You can turn it around and sell it for twenty, so don't fuck with me."

Edwards stared at him with such fury in his face that Bob could barely meet his gaze. Finally, after a long period of silence, Edwards nodded.

"All right," he said. "Five it is."

Bob had to restrain his wild emotions. He felt like leaping for joy. Instead, he walked coolly forward and offered Colin

Edwards his hand. The Englishman took it, but there was anger in his eyes.

"How do you plan on pulling this off?" Edwards asked. "Hypnosis? 'Look into my eyes, Emile'?"

"That's my business," Bob said. "But you don't have to worry. I know what I'm doing."

"Fine," Edwards said. "I'll call you tomorrow and we'll arrange a meeting place. There's one more thing, though. As you may have guessed I'm not always as good-natured as I've been tonight. If you try and fuck with me in any way, I'm going to kill you and your girlfriend."

"Fuck you," Bob said. A rage blew through him that was so intense that it was all he could do not to reach for Edwards.

"Better chill out," Edwards said. "Stealing is best done with a cool head. Talk to you tomorrow, Wells."

He flicked his cigarette into the bay, then turned and walked down the pier.

Bob stood watching him, his body humming with adrenaline. All the aches and pains he'd felt earlier, standing watch, were gone. He'd done it, made a deal with the devil and gotten exactly the terms he'd wanted.

The only small problem he had now was that he had no crew and absolutely no idea how to get the mask away from Emile Bardan.

# CHAPTER ELEVEN

Ray Wade had been a criminal for as long as Bob had known him, which was fifteen years. But unlike most of the other street thugs, hustlers, second-story men, and other wags who hung around Elmer's bar on South Bond Street, Ray had style and intelligence. He dressed like a "drape," Baltimore's term for a juvenile delinquent back in the 1950s. His thick black hair was combed straight back; he wore a black T-shirt, black jeans, and ancient motorcycle boots. He drove an equally ancient Indian 1500 cc motorcycle, and he usually had a woman (or "babe-ette," as he called them) riding on the back. He wasn't strictly a womanizer, though, for he fell madly in love with each new girlfriend and had married at least three of them.

The reason he couldn't stay married was not only that women found his lithe body, big muscular arms, and killer smile impossible to resist, but also because his heart belonged to Mommy.

His mother, Dorsey Wade, was sixty-two years old and lived three blocks away from Ray on South Lucerne. Ray was her only son, though she had three daughters she couldn't stand. As far as Dorsey was concerned, nothing her handsome boy ever did, including a three-year bit in the Maryland State Pen for auto theft, was wrong. On the other hand, Bob thought, as he looked for a parking place down the street from Dorsey's house, nothing any of Ray's wives or girlfriends did was right. She hated them all. Bob had learned all about this when he'd played briefly with Ray in one of his blues bands, when he was in his thirties, and Ray was the "kid" who played bass and sang, and damn well, too. They had renewed their acquaintance back in Bob's poker-playing days, those bad times when he'd lost most of his life's savings. But he didn't blame Ray. In fact, Ray had often warned him he was out of his depths.

Bob was about to ring Dorsey's row house doorbell, when he heard a scream of fury coming from the upstairs bedroom.

"Goddamn you, Raymond, I tole you," she said. "I tole you I dint want you to take that cedar chest home with you."

"Hey, geez, Mom," came the plaintive reply. "You said Angel could have the chest just last week."

"I did not say anything of the kind, Raymond," Dorsey answered. "I would not let that whore have even a coaster set, much less a cedar chest."

"Whoa, Moms," came Ray's voice. "Don't be calling Angel a whore, okay?"

"Why not?" Dorsey shouted back. "It's a well-known fact that she screwed half the police force."

"Goddamn it, Mom," Ray said. "I'm not going to take much more."

"Did 'em all in their patrol cars, is what I heard," Dorsey said.

"Shut up, Mom, you old skank," Ray said. "I love Angel."

"Oh man. Well, count me out on this one, Raymond," Dorsey said. "I'm not coming to this wedding. No sir. By the way, you better use a rubber, Raymond, 'cause Angel baby could give you a good dose."

"Goddamn you, Mom," Ray said. "She's not like that anymore."

Jesus, Bob thought, this might go on indefinitely. He rapped on the door, hard enough to rattle the glass in the storm windows.

"If 'ats 'at whore of yours, don't let her in," Dorsey said. "I love her name . . . Angel . . . ha ha ha . . . what a joke *'at* one is."

"Shut your trap, Mom," Ray said. "Or I'm gonna come in there and slap some sense into you."

"Listen to you," his mother said. "Threatening the very person who gave you life."

"Be right there," Ray said, as he came hustling down the steps.

The charming smile on his wide face said he fully expected Angel Harkins and when he saw that it was only Bob, Ray looked somewhat crestfallen.

"Dr. Bobby," he said. "Man, I forgot we had a meet."

"It's important, Ray."

"Don't worry," Ray said. "I'm more than ready to get out of here. Mom's on the warpath."

He looked upstairs and gave a yell.

"Me and Bobby are going out, Ma," he said. "You want me to bring you something from the store, babe?"

"Yes, honey," she yelled. "Get me a Payday and some Nerds, will you?"

"Sure, Ma," Ray said. "See you later."

" 'Bye, sweetie," she said in a cheery voice.

"Come on," Ray said. "Let's go, before she gets started again."

"Don't bring that whore, the so-called Angel, back here with you," Dorsey cackled as Ray shut the door.

They walked up Lucerne Avenue, past a couple of kids who were chasing a little white dog with broom handles, and went into Patterson Park.

"Well," Ray said calmly, "what kind of sinister shit do you have in mind, Dr. B?"

"Hardly sinister, Ray," Bob said. "But I think you'll find it interesting."

Bob smiled and as they continued walking across the green park, he told Ray Wade the story of Emile Bardan, Colin Edwards, and the priceless mask of Utu.

"That's quite a tale, Doctor," Ray said when Bob was done. "I can't believe you're really considering becoming a bad guy."

"Me, either," Bob said. "But what the hell. It's just this once."

Ray laughed and shook his head.

"I always said you scratch a saint and you're gonna find a sinner," Ray said. "And how much would we collect for this hard night's work?"

"Five million dollars," Bob said. "Of which you get one." He had considered lying to Ray, to keep his end down, but he didn't want to become overly greedy and have it bite him in the ass.

Ray's eyebrows shot up in dual exclamation points.

"Wow," he said. "I wasn't expecting anything that exceptional. This would be, possibly, the score to end all scores, so to speak."

"Precisely," Bob said.

"But I usually get half," Ray said.

"Yeah, I know," Bob said. "But this is my score, my one and only. And I've already put a lot of time in getting the information. Not to mention I'm risking my entire career and good name if it goes wrong."

Ray looked at him with sleepy eyes.

"I can appreciate that," he said. "Okay, solid. One it is."

Bob was shocked that Ray was rolling over so easily. He'd expected a struggle on the split.

"You're sure that this Utu mutherfucker is actually in his home office? In a safe," Ray said.

"Yeah," Bob said, "I'm sure."

"What kind of safe? Wall or floor?"

Bob felt foolish. How had he managed to miss out on that little detail?

"I don't really know," he said. "But it's not like his office is all that big. Should be easy to find it."

"So you say," Ray said. "Look, you pull a job, you gotta get in and out fast. Every second you spend hunting for shit . . . like the safe . . . is one more moment you can get busted."

Bob felt his face redden and his breath get short. What kind of an imbecile was he? But Ray, who was sometimes surprisingly tender, patted him on the back.

"Probably a floor job. Most of the walls in Canton are too narrow for a safe. Lemme ask you this. Is the guy gonna be home when we go in?"

"No," Bob said. He then explained how every Friday night Emile went to the Havana Club and spent the night with Laura Santiago.

"That's good," Ray said. "What about guards?"

"Two," Bob said. "Upstairs in the back and down on the first floor."

"Hmmm," Ray said, blowing two jets of smoke out his nose. "We're gonna need some more help."

"How many guys? I want to keep this thing small."

"Sure you do, Bobby," Ray said. "But we got the guards and we got a safe. I've blown a few of them, but for this we need a real specialist. We also need an alarm expert."

"Jesus," Bob said. "Can't *you* just cut the alarm?"

"Sure," Ray said. "If you want the red light and alarm to go on at Southeast Station."

"Then how do you beat it?"

"Jam it. Loop it, so it outthinks itself. But that's not my thing. We're also going to need a driver."

"I'll drive the getaway car," Bob said.

Ray could barely repress a laugh.

"You? Who the fuck are you, Dale Earnhardt? You can't drive no getaway car."

"Why the fuck not?" Bob said. "Nobody is gonna be chasing us."

"You don't know that," Ray said. "Look, Bobby, you came to me because I'm a professional, so don't start backsliding into amateurism. You ain't driving the getaway car, and that's all she wrote. You're gonna meet us afterwards."

Bob felt a little rage whirl through his stomach.

"No way," he said. "Either I go in or I get somebody else to do this with me."

"Hey, you don't know anybody else," Ray said, laughing. "See, on a heist you only take in guys who do a specific job. What's yours?"

"Okay," Bob said. "Let me ask you the same question. What's yours?"

"That's different," Ray said. "Think of the heist as a bunch of guys building a house. My job would be, like, general contractor."

"Well, you should think of me as the guy who hired you," Bob said.

"That's funny," Ray said. " 'Cause that would make you the owner of the house, which means you'd be robbing your own joint."

"Forget it, Ray," Bob said. "I'm going in. I'll stand guard."

"The problem is, on a job like this, with real guards in the house already, you gotta take in a piece. You ever shoot a gun?"

"Many times," Bob lied.

"You're lying," Ray said.

"I shot guns down the country when I was a kid," Bob said. "With my grandfather. Pheasants and rabbits."

"Yeah, but did they shoot back?" Ray said. "Okay, maybe I'll make an exception. You can come in. You'll be like an assistant guard. What about video cameras?"

"He's got them," Bob said.

"Then we wear masks, along with our gloves. We gotta knock out the guards, too. You down for that?"

Bob shook his head.

"There's got to be another way," he said. "I don't want any violence."

"Perish the thought," Ray said. "But this is a heist, Doctor, and throughout criminal history, armed guards have been known to resist, sometimes in a violent manner."

"Fuck history," Bob said. "No violence."

"Okay," Ray said. "Maybe we stand outside on the street and say, 'Hey guards, come out and play!'"

"Ray," Bob said. "You got any other ideas? Or do you just want to stand there and mock me, like your mother mocks you?"

Ray's thick neck jerked back as if Bob had slapped him in the face.

"That's playing dirty, Doctor," he said. His tone wasn't amused anymore.

"Sorry," Bob said. "But let's cool it with the attitude and just get the deal done."

Ray scratched his head and walked around in a tight little circle.

"Okay," he said, "I know a totally nonviolent way. Really, Dr. Bob, if Martin Luther King had been a thief, this is what he would have used."

"What is it?" Bob said.

"Gas," Ray said. "But it's expensive. Might cost two or three grand."

"What kind of gas?"

"Halothane and fentanyl cocktail," Ray said. "Knocks them right out. We go in wearing gas masks."

"How long are they out?"

"Six hours, at least," Ray said. "No problem."

Bob walked around the old iron bench. He remembered when he was a kid his dad chasing him around it. What would the old leftist Jimmy say if he could see this? His son, a common thief. Though he didn't think he believed in God, Bob suddenly felt that Jimmy was right above him, perched in a cloud, looking down on him. And he wasn't happy.

"You ever used this gas before, Ray?"

"Yeah, once," Ray said. "In a little caper over in D.C. Worked great. I think gas is just the thing."

"But how do we get it inside the house?"

"Let me worry about that," Ray said. "But that brings up another problem."

"You going to have to hire a gas man?" Bob said in a dejected tone.

"Not to administer the gas. I can do that. But you see, the stuff comes in a liquid form. We gotta find a guy who can change the liquid to gas."

"Let me guess," Bob said. "He doesn't come cheap."

"Afraid not," Ray said. "Ten grand at least."

"Jesus," Bob said. "I shoulda held out for more money."

"Renegotiate," Ray said.

"I can't," Bob said. "This guy doesn't play that way."

"Well, what can I say?" Ray said. "Those are the facts. You need a good crew and they don't come cheap. The safe and alarm guys I can get to take a back-end deal. The ten Gs for the gas you gotta put up front."

Ten Gs? Could he even raise ten Gs?

"Okay," he said. "Man, it's a lot of dough, but I'll get it."

Ray nodded and assumed a mock-humble pose.

"Listen, Bobby," he said. "I don't usually administer gas. But I'm willing to subjugate my individual ego for the good of the team."

"That is *so* kind of you," Bob said.

"I know," Ray said. "But that's my nature. And a man shouldn't fight his own good nature, wouldn't you say so, Dr. Bobby?"

Ray punched him in the arm and laughed.

"And how much are we going to pay the crew?"

"Well, Cas, the safe guy, he's the best in town, so he's gonna want a percentage of the gross."

"No fucking way," Bob said.

"I might be able to get him to take a flat fee, but he usually wants points."

"Jesus," Bob said. "What about the alarm guy?"

"Tony? I can get him cheap," Ray said. "Like maybe a yard and a half."

"A hundred and fifty dollars?" Bob said. "Say, that's more like it."

Ray shook his head.

"Bobby, what planet are you living on? A hundred fifty thou."

"You're nuts," Bob said, spluttering and turning around in a circle. "These guys are fucking highway robbers."

"You got that right," Ray said. "But you want the best, you gotta pay for 'em. Which brings me to another small point. Since you are the employer and I the mere employee, you gotta pay the crew outta your end."

Bob shut his eyes and saw his ideal retirement villa in Rome disappear and turn into a tin hut in Manila.

"All right," Bob said. "That's okay. But no points for either of these guys."

"I'll see what I can do. Let's talk tomorrow," Ray said. "Now I gotta go get Ma's Nerds before she goes nuts."

He reached out and shook Bob's hand and his grip was like a vise.

"You're gonna be a rich man soon, Bob. Where you gonna live?"

"I don't know," Bob said. "I can't move anywhere, right away. And neither can you. It'll cause too much heat."

"True," Ray said. "But after all the heat's dissipated, where will Dr. Bobby and his new girlfriend set up Shangri-la?"

"I don't know," Bob said. "Maybe Mexico."

"Really?" Ray said, laughing. "That's good."

"What's so fucking funny?" Bob said.

"Makes sense," Ray said. "You spend your whole life trying to help the poor, so when it comes time to move, you move to a poorer place than here."

"The place I'm going to move to down there isn't poor," Bob said. "It's a very cool city."

"Oh, sure," Ray said. "But it's still Mexico. I been down there, and even the rich places are poor compared to the majesty of Baltimore. So is your plan to, like, use the money to, like, help the people or something? A middle-aged Robin Hood thing?"

Bob felt himself blush. Of course, he had been thinking that very thing. But hearing it from Ray's mouth made it sound absurd. And after the crew was paid off, there would be precious little left, surely not a cent to give away.

"No," Bob said, using a cynical tone. "I'm all through with that. The helping thing is over for me."

"That's too bad," Ray said. "So what are you going to do then, Bobby, start eating caviar off a woman's breasts every day? Walk around the campo wearing an ascot and carrying a walking stick?"

"Sounds good, minus the ascot," Bob said.

"Interesting," Ray said. "This will be a real interesting experiment. Maybe you'll be like one of them rare leopards."

"What kind is that?" Bob said.

"The kind that can change their spots," Ray said.

"I don't know for sure, either, Ray," Bob said, "but I can't wait to try."

# CHAPTER TWELVE

So far, Bob thought, as he stood up onstage at the Lodge waiting for the band to launch into "Working in a Coal Mine," the hardest part of being a rookie villain wasn't the criminal side of things at all, but the straight side. It was hard, really hard, to fake interest in, say, some meatloaf Jesse made from a special recipe that she'd gotten from her old aunt Gen in West Virginia when he was dying to hear from Ray about meeting the crew. It was hard to get into Lou Anne's funny tale of how clumsy Dave had been when they'd recently tried to learn salsa dancing when Bob was worried about the gas they were going to buy and whether or not it would actually knock out the guards. It was tough even to play rock 'n' roll, concentrate on music and chords and all the people dancing in front of him on the barroom floor when he just wanted to be out of there. To be so close to being free, rich, a man of power made his everyday life all the more unbearable. And his anxiety showed in his sloppy musicianship. He was playing badly, missing his fills, screwing up his leads. Not that anyone noticed at the Lodge. Old Finnegan, Young Finnegan, Tommy Morello, Lizzie Littman, crazy Gabe DeStefano, the boat poet . . . they were all out there in their funky hats and blue jean jackets and biker leathers, and now a bunch of younger guys and girls, all of whom had started to come because of Dave's reviews. And just a few weeks ago, Bob was digging it, really feeling great about it all . . . his town, his hood, his community. But now that he had the shot, the shot to make, Jesus, millions, now it had all started to seem old to him. Feelings he didn't want to have . . . he'd always hated people who cast off their old friends when they got some dough. But maybe, he began to think now about his attitudes about such matters as instant wealth, maybe they'd been kind of unearned attitudes. Having had no money or any real chance for any, his attitudes had become set, and hardened at a certain (he now suspected) adolescent level.

Because being on the cusp of wealth, he had to admit that some things about his old gang were more than a little annoying. The way they reacted to any new person or idea with the same old street attitude. The way Old Finnegan thought people who weren't from Highlandtown, or hadn't driven a bike, were all fags. Bob had always filed Old Finnegan's attitude under the heading "colorful," but suddenly it didn't seem so colorful anymore. And the way his younger brother always repeated everything he said . . . like if Old Finnegan said, "Asshole," about some perfectly decent, educated guy, Young Finnegan would say, "Total asshole." Bob had found that kind of funny, too, local color and all that, but now he had to admit that maybe he was sick of local color. Sick of the Lodge, sick of playing old rock songs, like they were the hallowed text of some great epic poem when all most of them were was just simple rhythms and dumb teenage lust lyrics written by a bunch of third-rate hacks.

How had he not seen all that before?

Because, Bob thought, he had never dared to think bigger before. Because without the opportunity, why allow yourself to think of finer things, wider horizons?

All it would do is break your heart.

But not anymore. No . . . now he could dream about . . . well, about anything, any place, and it didn't have to be the impossible dream. No, he and Jesse could go there and he could drive any car he wanted . . . so suddenly cars became an interest . . . when he had always sworn that a car was a mode of transportation, nothing more. Because old Man o' the People Bob couldn't afford a new car . . .

And food. God, all his life he'd said how happy he was eating the local delicacy crab cakes and drinking National Bohemian beer at the Lodge, but now he had to admit that he was bloody sick of crab cakes, and couldn't stand watery, tasteless Boh when he could have great beers . . . anytime he wanted.

He was sick of leftovers, he was tired of being practical, and had started to truly hate common sense.

He wanted glory, excess, self-indulgence. Wanted it so badly that he found himself snapping at everyone around him. It was like he couldn't stop himself. He'd tell himself to chill out, that these were his old pals, for chrissakes, but dreams of luxury, of ease, of being catered to (instead of him catering to the hapless poor) poisoned every exchange. It had gotten so bad if someone came up to him and merely said, "Hi Bob," he felt like taking their head off. "Hi Bob? What the fuck do you mean, 'Hi Bob'? Do you know who I am? You fucking third-rate artist moron? I'm Bob fucking Wells and soon I'm going to be able to buy and sell you a thousand times over, asshole!"

Of course, Bob never said those things. But he felt them with a fury and self-righteousness that shocked him. All these years he had worked for peanuts, waiting for the world to wake up, and now he knew without a doubt that the world had passed him by, and goddamn it he wanted revenge. Revenge on them all . . . though he knew, of course, in his right mind that none of it was his old pals' fault. The fault lay within himself, but knowing that didn't seem to do any good.

He was filled with belated ambition and a monster resentment. And he figured the only thing that could really stop it for good was to get his dough and get the fuck out of Baltimore. Christ, he wished Ray would get things ready. He could barely stand another minute of his old life.

Jesse and Bob finished up "Coal Mine" and then Bob saw Dave and Lou Anne walking up the steps to the stage. For a second that confused him. What the hell did Dave want anyway? Fucking Dave was starting to get on his nerves, too, and Lou Anne with her perpetual Miss Upbeat smile. Christ, she was a little too much. Lately she had talked about becoming a nurse, and thanked Bob for being an "inspiration to her," which Jesse and Dave had seconded, hugging him, and the whole thing had made him kind of sick to his stomach. He didn't want to be a fucking inspiration anymore to anyone. "Inspiration" meant martyr, and he'd had a lifetime of that sad shit.

But here were Dave and Lou Anne, walking across the stage:

"Dave," Bob said. "My man."

"Bob," Dave said. He put his arm around Bob's shoulders and leaned into the mike.

"Hey, everybody. Is this a great band or what?"

The kids cheered and shouted and a couple of them fizzed beer on one another. Bob looked out at their bald heads and suddenly wanted to scream random obscenities at them, but instead smiled and held up his guitar.

"I just want to make a little announcement," Dave said, pulling Bob close to him with one big arm and Lou Anne with the other.

"Miss Lou Anne Johnson and I have gone and done it. We sneaked down to city hall today and tied the knot. Dave McClane is now an old married man, and happy as hell about it, too."

A huge cheer went up in the crowd. Dave held Bob close and Jesse came over and joined the little knot of hopefulness. In spite of all the poison in his system, Bob felt a wave of sympathy and happiness for his old pal.

"All right," Jesse said, in the mike. "We love these guys!"

"Yes!" came the cheer back.

"I got my man!" Lou Anne said into the mike and the kids cheered again.

Dave hugged Bob tight, his sweaty cheek rubbing against Bob's, and Bob suddenly felt that he couldn't breathe. He wanted to push Dave away, off the stage if necessary. If he would only let him loose.

Then Dave released him and was back at the mike.

"I just want to say that this is a great and wonderful day for me. I'm here at the Lodge, my favorite place in the world, with the woman I love and my best friend, Bob Wells, and his fantastic girlfriend, Jesse Reardon. And I just want to say that now that this old rebel has fallen, I wonder how long it's going to be until the two people I love best follow us down the aisle?"

Bob felt intense embarrassment. He loved Dave, he really did, but Dave didn't respect boundaries. He wanted them to be like teenagers forever, best buddies who went through all of life's passages together. It was charming in its way. But it was tiresome, too . . . Bob thought about the money . . . the money that would get him out of here. Away from the tired old Lodge and, at least for a while anyway, away from frigging Dave.

"Hey," Bob said, taking the mike, so Dave couldn't say anything else. "This is totally great. Everything you said to me, Dave, comes right back at you. Jess and I love you and Lou Anne and all of us love the Lodge. I propose a toast to the newly married couple. Here's to two great people. The best! To Dave and Lou Anne!"

Then Bob and Dave and Lou Anne and Jesse all put their arms around one another, and bowed as the band worked up a drum roll, and Bob stared out at the people who had been his friends for years and saw them all as one gape-mouthed, sweat-stained, many-headed animal, like some mythological beast from a fairy tale, and it was all he could do not to leap off the stage and run screaming out into the street.

# CHAPTER THIRTEEN

A week after Bob first proposed the heist to Ray, he met his crew at Elmer's bar on South Bond Street, at the bad end of the Key Highway. He'd been by the place a thousand times and always felt a shudder of distaste and, face it, fear. The joint had been a biker hangout in the fifties and sixties, then turned into a kind of hippie/doper bar in the seventies and eighties, and now had devolved into something too sleazy to name. Bob looked around at the cobalt blue concrete walls, the ancient pool tables with their ripped-out pockets, and filthy, stained-glass windows, relics of the hippie thing, Bob guessed. The grill was at the end of the bar and, judging from the smell, Bob thought that maybe they were serving roasted rat. The bartender was a transvestite redneck named Mary Poppins who sported tattoos on both his/her muscular arms. Bob found himself staring at the hissing snakes and other demons that moved like shadows when Mary flexed.

"You looking for Wade?" Mary said.

"Yeah," Bob said.

"Inna back." Mary pointed and the snake looked as though it might strike at Bob's face.

He sat in a worm-eaten booth next to Ray, who had come to the party dressed in his usual black shirt and black Levi's. Across the table from them was the big safe expert, Cas Jankowski. Cas wore a red shirt with black penguins on it. He ate a monstrous triple burger with double fries and worked on his second schooner of beer. His massive body had a serious triple layer of fat, but one look at his enormous wrists convinced Bob that he was nobody to fuck with.

Sitting next to him was a ferrety-looking guy named Tony Hoy. Tony was a diminutive half-Chinese man who wore an open shirt so he could show off his curly chest hairs. Around his neck he wore a thick gold chain with a pendant hanging off it.

"Ray tells me you're a head doctor," Tony said.

"That's right," Bob said. "I—"

"So tell me something, Doc," Tony interrupted. "Why is everything so fucking lame?"

"Why don't you tell me," Bob said.

Hoy looked at Jankowski and the big man smirked.

"All right, I will," Tony said. "No matter where you look, things are less than they used to fucking be."

"Take the NFL," Cas said, absorbing another fry. "Few years ago when the Ravens won the Super Bowl, that was exciting, but since then there has been a . . . falling off."

"The team's rebuilding," Bob said. "I think they're going to win the Super Bowl again."

"Really?" Tony said.

Ray was working on a mayonnaise salad sandwich with a shrimp hiding somewhere in it. He looked at Bob and laughed without making a sound.

"But I'm not talking about building or rebuilding," Tony said. "I'm talking about, you know . . . bad shit. The feeling that the world is slipping by, the kind of thing where even if say Johnny fucking Unitas came back to Baltimore tomorrow, it wouldn't amount to shit."

This was met with a general stunned silence. In Baltimore, Johnny Unitas was a secular saint and it was generally agreed if God ever did come back, he would have number nineteen on his back and be wearing black high-tops.

"That's a very harsh thing to say," Ray said, shaking his head. "Very, very harsh."

"Tell me one thing's as good as it used to be," Tony said.

"Pussy," Bob said, trying to keep the party upbeat. "Pussy's still good."

"But not as good as before," Tony said. "When I was a young man it was a great mystery, right? Now pussy is, like, on the Internet. You can do a Google search for pussy and come up with ten million sites. You can click a key for it, just like Domino's."

"But wouldn't that be, like, a good thing?" Bob said.

"No way," Tony said. "Supply and demand. When there's that much going around, where's the mystique? Now you get e-mails with girls doing horses. Nah, there's a relaxation of standards. I think it's the decline of the fucking West."

"Well, there's a lot of truth to what you boys say," Ray said. "But I know one thing that's as big a kick as ever."

"And that would be?" Tony said, with a belligerent stare.

"That would be bypassing a guy's alarms, entering his house, cracking his safe, taking away his shit, then fencing it off for a considerable pile of cash. That's still as big a rush as it ever was."

Tony hesitated a second, then smiled with his big white teeth.

"You are a hundred percent right," he said. "Thank you, Raymond. You've restored my faith in the criminal subculture."

"Yeah," Cas agreed. "So when do we go?"

"Soon," Bob said, surprised at himself for jumping in. "But before we do, we have to get the deal straight. I'm offering you guys fifty thousand apiece. That seems like good pay for one night's work."

Tony and Cas exchanged a look and then both of them glowered at Bob.

"Let me explain reality to you," Cas said. "I get a hundred grand on a big heist like this. And a percentage. Usually five percent. Reason is, I'm the best. Now you're gonna ask what that means exactly and I'm gonna tell you that it means I open the tumblers without having to use nitro, you see? You get a guy who uses explosives and you might blow the shit out of your mask in there. You don't want that, and you don't want to use some punch-and-peel joker using a cheap-ass hammer from fucking Pep Boys who is gonna take two hours, do you?"

"Not at all," Bob said. "But I know a guy over in D.C., an ace safe guy, and he does it by manipulating the tumblers. Uses high-tech equipment, has his own scope."

Ray raised an eyebrow. He hadn't expected Bob to know anything at all about safe cracking. But then he hadn't been with Bob to the library for the past five days doing his homework, either.

"Good luck," said Cas. "That can take maybe forty-five minutes. You want to sit in the guy's house that long, be my guest."

"No," Bob said. "It doesn't take forty-five minutes. I'd rather use you, Cas, but if you're stuck on a percentage, I'm going to have to go with the other guy."

"D.C. guys are all assholes," Cas said. "They don't even live where they grew up."

"True, but I guess I can live with that," Bob said. "Fifty thou. You in or out?"

"I don't know. . . ."

"I definitely get a percentage, usually six percent," Tony said. "You don't want to hire some second-rate alarm man, risk the bells and whistles going off inna gendarmes' station house, now do you?"

"Same deal for you," Bob said "I was a psychologist down at Jessups, so I know three security systems guys who served time. Any of 'em will do the job. So what do you say?"

Tony looked at Cas. They looked away, down at the table, then back at each other.

"Sixty," Cas said.

"Yeah, or go spread the news to D.C.," Tony said.

Bob sighed and looked frustrated.

"Okay," he said. "You guys are tough. Sixty each."

He reached across the table and shook hands with each of them, trying to keep a straight face in the process. But inside he was ecstatic. All that morning he'd had a serious attack of the jitters just thinking about facing career criminals. But now that he was sitting here in this sleaze bar, he was cool, just like he had been years ago when he was Bobby the Street Guy. If he got through this in one piece, he really ought to write a monograph based on the premise that social activism was a wonderful training ground for a second career in crime.

"I have four clean SIGs for us," Ray said, lighting a Camel.

"I use a thirty-eight police special," Cas said. "I don't fuck around with no SIGs."

"You're using the guns I got us," Ray said, staring hard at him. "They're clean."

Cas looked at Ray, but then quickly down at his plate.

"Okay, Ray-Ban," Cas said. "We'll play it your way."

"Good," Ray said. "I also have the gas we need and the masks. Do we know where we make the exchange?"

"I find out tomorrow," Bob said.

"Okay, then. That's all for now," Ray said. "We're gonna meet again in two days. Then we go. I'll call you."

The four of them shook hands again and slid out from the booth.

"You coming, Ray?" Tony said. "We're going down to Glen Burnie, to the fights."

"Not tonight, Tone," Ray said. "I gotta discuss a few things with Bob."

"Okay," Tony said. "Later. Nice meeting you, Doc."

"Yeah," Bob said. He liked saying "yeah." You could say it in a way that made it sound like "a real pleasure to meet you, as well, shithead." Being a criminal was big fun. Like being in a movie, only better.

When the other two partners had gone, Ray shook his head.

"You're a natural, Doc. You handled those two real well."

"Thanks," Bob said.

"Only one thing," Ray said. "Don't try to handle me. Our deal is firm."

"Right," Bob said. "Totally firm."

"That's good," Ray said. " 'Cause I hate guys who try and rip me off. It's almost a physical thing, like an allergy. I get this itchy feeling everywhere, and then I go nuts and just start fucking people up."

"Got it," Bob said.

"Good," Ray said. "You bring the ten Gs for the gas?"

"Yeah," Bob said. "Right here."

He pulled an envelope out of his pocket and slid it across the table to Ray.

"One more thing, Bobby," Ray said. "If by chance your boy, Emile, comes back early that night, all bets are off."

"What do you mean?" Bob said.

"I mean, Emile could end up very dead," Ray said. "We're not into being ID'd."

"Hey, wait," Bob said. "No killing my patient."

Ray laughed and lit a cigarette.

"That's not so useful, Doc," he said.

"What's not?"

"Thinking of Emile as 'your patient.'"

"Oh no? How *am* I supposed to think of him?"

"More like 'your victim,'" Ray said.

Bob grimaced.

"That's cold."

"All right then," Ray said. "Think of him as 'the mark.' 'Cause that's what he is. You wanta be good in this business you gotta, like, suspend your normal human feelings for the 'mark.' You get into that 'he's a human being, too' shit, things could go downhill for you and for me, real fast."

"Thanks for the tip, Ray," Bob said. "I'll try to remember to be as cool-blooded as possible."

"That's a good idea," Ray said. "The thing is you're gonna feel some guilt. But you can, like, lose a lot of it if you concentrate on being professional. You get me?"

"I think so," Bob said. "I feel better if I think about it as a job well done."

"That's it," Ray said. "You're a fast learner, Bob. You're gonna do just fine."

He reached over and gave Bob a friendly, almost fatherly pat on the cheek. Bob was still wary of Ray, but he felt they'd opened a door. They were actually becoming friends.

# CHAPTER FOURTEEN

A day after his successful meeting with his crew, a newly confident Bob Wells walked with his buyer Colin Edwards up Gay Street. Edwards was dressed in a tan linen suit, looking every bit the successful art dealer that he was. As Bob strolled along with him, it was easy to imagine himself buying a new closet full of fine threads, stylish shoes, and silk ties. Of course, he'd always turned up his moral nose at fashion, but for the first time he wondered if that was only because he'd never had any reason to look fashionable. Who cared how anyone looked in Highlandtown?

Edwards, however, wanted to talk about Baltimore. . . .

"I'm really falling in love with your old town," he said. "The buildings have such character. And the Dundalk Marine Terminal. That's really terrific. Baltimore is still an unspoiled place, you know? You're a lucky man to live here."

"People who aren't from here always say that," Bob said. "That's because they don't know how small the place can be, how prejudiced. You live in one neighborhood and go five blocks away, the next neighborhood hates your guts. Why? Because you don't live there, they don't know you, and they hate and fear anybody they don't know."

Edwards laughed.

"But that's wonderful," he said. "It's tribal. What do you want, Bob, the whole world to be exactly alike? That's the alternative, you know. Every place is like every other. All the people have a patina of sophistication they got from watching television. They don't value anything really, though, except ass-kissing celebrities. They're dead, zombies. People in Baltimore are alive in an ancient, tribal way."

Edwards was starting to piss Bob off. The last thing he wanted to hear was how bloody lucky he was.

"You like it so much, stay here," Bob said. "Give up your globe hopping and settle down with a nice Catholic girl from the 'hood. Visit her family every Sunday for dinner, join the Knights of Columbus, and spend every night in the local bar talking about how shitty the Orioles are."

Edwards shook his head.

"No, it's too late for me," he said. "I'm a citizen of the world. But don't think it's all that great, Bob. Because it's not. The people I know don't care whether I live or die. They're sophisticated, cool, and stylish, but inside they're empty. If we had to battle terrorists tomorrow, who would you rather have by your side, some cosmopolitan jet-setter or the guys in your neighborhood? I know who I'd choose. Your Baltimore guy, he'd fight to the end. For you and him, because he's your mate. You're a lucky man, Bob, working here, having close friends. I'm telling you, hanging out here has really made me miss old Liverpool. You ought to stay right here, Bob. Take trips, see the world, but don't dig up your roots. You do that, you'll never be at home anywhere again. I know."

"Yeah . . ." Bob said. "Thanks for the tip. Now if you don't mind, I'd like to get down to business. Where do we meet?"

Edwards smiled and pointed at the big brick building directly across the street from them.

"Right there," he said.

Bob looked at the fortress of a building, with its old and shattered windows.

"The American Brewery Building?" Bob said. "That's all closed up."

"Not anymore," Edwards said. "Don't worry, we're covered. It's a perfect meeting place. Fifth floor at one A.M."

"I'll be there," Bob said.

Bob looked at Edwards's intense gray eyes. They looked, he decided, like a frozen carp's.

"See you then, Bob," Edwards said. "And don't forget my mask."

"You don't have to worry about that," Bob said. "Tell me, just for fun, Colin. You're giving me five million. How much are you selling it for?"

Edwards gave a slit of a smile and shook his head.

"That would come under the heading of 'things you don't really want to know,' Bob. I've got to run now. Diplomatic party over in D.C. G'night."

He pressed his cold hand into Bob's and then turned and walked toward East Baltimore Street, where a sleek, black limousine was waiting for him. Bob watched him get in and speed away.

Yeah, Bob thought, Colin loved old Baltimore. As long as he could hop in his limo and speed off to D.C. As long as he could get in his private Learjet and land in Paris.

Well, in a few more days, he'd be able to afford a limo. Whenever he liked. The thought made him flush with pleasure. No, he was going to be fine. Edwards was just indulging in a kind of verbal masturbation. In reality, a guy like him would last five minutes in "Charm City" before he was bored out of his mind.

Bob had had a whole lifetime of the neighborhood clans, the small potatoes romance of the 'hood. He wanted out, he wanted sophistication and beauty and sexiness, the whole wide world that he'd missed. He'd be just fine in New York and Los Angeles and Paris and all the other rich, decadent places.

And if he did get homesick, he could always sky back to old Baltimore, eat a crab cake, drink a National Bohemian beer, catch an Oriole game, and then get the hell out again.

That would be all the hometown this hometown boy would ever need.

# CHAPTER FIFTEEN

From the back alley, behind a wall of honeysuckle vine, Bob watched as Ray Wade hit the remote button. They were dressed in the uniforms of the Baltimore Power and Electric Company, gas masks half on, the goggles sitting on their foreheads making them look like World War I aviators.

There, partially hidden by Emile Bardan's hedge, was a canister of gas painted in earth tones. From the canister there was a black wire, which entered the house via the crawlspace door just under the pantry at the rear of the house.

"Gas is activated," Ray said.

"How long will it take?" Bob whispered.

"Not long," Ray said. "Anyone in that house will be asleep in about nine minutes."

Bob's cell phone vibrated and he quickly answered it.

"Yeah."

"You start it up yet?"

"Just now."

"How long?"

It was Tony Hoy, who was stationed on the other side of Emile's house. Once the gas was activated, he and Cas would open the ladder, and with Cas holding it steady, Tony would climb to the roof where he would deactivate the burglar alarm. This meant he had to climb a ladder right in front of both a first- and second-story window. If one of the guards happened to somehow stay awake he'd be dead meat.

"Nine . . . no, about eight minutes," Bob said.

"You sure?" Tony said.

"Yeah," Bob said.

"Guess what Cas is doing?" Tony said.

"Jerking off?" Bob said.

"Eating a sub," Tony said. "Fucking guy ate three oyster subs from Captain Harvey's today. Always goes on a binge when it's showtime."

Bob felt his stomach churn wildly. Wasn't there some kind of code of professionalism among thieves? No eating on the job?

"Got the ladder ready?" Bob said.

"Oh yeah. Man, I hope that gas works."

"Yeah," Bob said. "Me, too."

He took a quick peek over the bush and saw a small piece of the metallic ladder sticking up over the bushes.

"Your ladder's visible," he said.

"Sorry, boss," Tony said.

Bob felt a stunning rush of happiness. "Boss," Tony had called him "boss." This was his "crew" and he was "The Boss."

"How much time now?" Tony said.

"Not long," Bob said. "Chill."

Good advice, now if he could only take it himself. His chest pounded. He tried not to think of the words "heart attack." What if someone came along and saw them? He looked around, but didn't see anyone.

After what seemed like an eternity, Ray spoke.

"That's it," he said. "Everybody is wasted in there."

Bob hit the preset button on his cell phone and waited.

"Yeah?" Tony said.

"Go," Bob said.

He watched as Tony and Cas went barreling into the yard, through the gate. Cas quickly set the ladder against the side of the house. Tony climbed it so fast he looked like a primate.

Ray smiled tensely in the darkness.

"Wait till you see how quickly he disarms the alarm," he said. "You're getting your money's worth."

Bob shifted his weight from one foot to the other, his nerves screaming inside him. He hated it out here in the alley, but if they headed into the backyard they'd activate the motion sensor lights and maybe even the burglar alarm.

He took out his binoculars and saw Tony on the roof. He was working on the fuse box, about two feet away from the high-tension wires. For the first time Bob realized the affinity between criminals and athletes. They were both about physical performance under pressure. No wonder the public liked clever criminals so much more than they did psychologists. They risked more, and they were physically brave. Psychologists had more in common with, say, movie critics and other wimps.

Even standing in an alley next to a can of rotting trash, Bob felt glamorous. He shut his eyes and imagined a young woman, someone in her twenties, checking him out: so cool, so composed, waiting in the alley with a SIG Sauer in his coat pocket. Compare that to a nerd sitting in an office saying, "Hi, Elmo. Tell me all about your mom."

"Get your gas mask on," Ray said. "Time to rock 'n' roll."

They found the first guard, a big black man, snoring on the kitchen floor. He looked peaceful, and they quickly relieved him of his automatic weapon. The second guard, a Latino, was sprawled in a less comfortable way, right on the second-floor steps. His head had hit the edge of the step when he fell and there was a bit of a bump on it. In spite of himself, Bob felt sorry for him and had to restrain himself from waking the guy up and offering a towel wrapped around some ice cubes. Ray took the second guard's pistol out of his holster and dragged him to the landing.

After tying and gagging both guards, they raced up the steps to the third floor and quickly found the floor safe under the right corner of an expensive maroon rug.

Bob wanted to stay there with them, where the action was, but dutifully headed down a narrow hall to the master bedroom, which overlooked the street. His job, the only reason Ray had relented and let him come inside, was to keep watch on the front of the house.

He looked out the front window. The street was empty.

He started to sit back down on the bed when he was jolted out of his skin by his vibrating cell phone.

Jesus, who the hell would call him now? Of course, he wasn't going to answer it, unless . . .

He looked down at the display and to his shock and surprise he saw Emile's cell phone number.

What should he do?

Not answer it. Right, of course. Emile was out at the Havana Club, dancing and seeing his girlfriend.

But what if he wasn't?

Bob looked at a little door, which led from Emile's bedroom to a small balcony covered with dying plants.

Where the hell was Emile? What if his girlfriend was sick and he was coming home?

Bob slid out on the balcony, crouching down so no one could see him from the street. He quickly took off his gas mask, then answered the call.

"Hello, Emile?"

"Doc? You there?"

"Right here," Bob said in a shaky voice.

"Listen, Doc, I just need to talk to you a second. You have a minute?"

"Of course, Emile," Bob said. "Where are you?"

"I'm over at the Havana Club," he said. "I just started having a really bad feeling, Doc."

Bob swallowed to keep the panic down in his stomach.

"Tell me about it," Bob said.

"It's like he's here, watching me," Emile said.

"Have you actually seen him?" Bob said.

"No. But I thought I did. I'm having a tough time telling what's real and what's not."

"Of course," Bob said. "You've been under a very great strain. That makes perfect sense."

Bob was suddenly swept away by a surge of warm feeling toward his patient. Even though he was robbing him, he still felt sort of protective toward Emile. He didn't want him to suffer, not unduly, anyway.

"Listen to me," Bob said. "Look all around the room."

"Okay," Emile said. "But I'm getting a sick feeling. That he's going to try and finish me off tonight."

"Are you looking?" Bob said.

"Yes," Emile said. His voice was small and scared. Bob felt a wave of guilt so strong that he nearly vomited.

"And what do you see?"

"The band, the dance floor, people eating, drinking."

"Right," Bob said. "And no sign of Colin, right?"

"No," Emile said. "No sign of him. Ah, he's not here, Doc. I'm just a screaming paranoid."

"Not at all," Bob said.

His back hurt from stooping by the huge, dead balcony plant, so Bob stood up and looked at the street below.

There, on the opposite side of the street, three stories down, a man walked a dog. What if the guy happened to look up at him? Bob crouched back down and his back began to ache again.

"I'm sorry to bother you," Emile said. "Hope I didn't disturb you, Doc."

"Not at all," Bob said. "I suggest you and your girlfriend dance and, though I don't want you to overdo it, have a couple of drinks and relax."

"You don't think I should just go home and crawl into bed?"

"No!" Bob said. "I mean, the thing about anxiety is if you try to run away from it you legitimize it to yourself, which, of course, only increases it. But if you face it head-on, and deal with it for what it is—just a feeling, not a reality—then you back it down."

"You make it sound like a person," Emile said.

"It *is* like a person," Bob said. "Fear is a bully. You back a bully down, he loses his power."

There was a pause. Bob looked inside down the hallway. Still no sign of them.

"Okay, Doc," Emile said. "I get it. I really do. Thanks a lot. I'm starting to feel better."

"No problem," Bob said. "I'm glad I could be helpful. Now you go have a Cuba libre and enjoy your night." He felt that generally he'd given Emile excellent advice. In most cases, where the phantoms *were* illusory, staying and facing up to your demons *did* disempower them.

Tonight, of course, was an exception.

Bob flipped his suffocating gas mask back on and took a step inside. Just as Ray Wade came walking in from the back bedroom. In his hands was a black carbon-and-steel box. Silently, he held the box in the air over his head, like a boxer displaying his championship belt.

Bob moved forward and Ray placed it in his hands.

There was a glass window on one side of it. And there, staring him in the face, was Utu the sun god, seeker of justice and vengeance.

Bob felt his heart skip a beat.

The eyes were carved in such a way that they seemed to stare *through* his own eyes, leaving them craters of ash. The face was strong and cruel. He felt, suddenly, that the mask was passing judgment on him.

The thought sent shivers through his body and he quickly handed the box back to Ray.

"We did it, Doc Bobby," Ray said. "Now let's get the hell out of here."

# CHAPTER SIXTEEN

It had started to rain. As they drove in Ray's '79 Camaro I-Roc to the old American Brewery Building, it came down in driving sheets and pounded on the windshield. Suddenly, rookie criminal Bob began to worry about 911. Was he out in the rain catching his death of cold? And what about Ethel Roop and all his other patients? Did they need him? Would they miss him? Maybe his kindness and insights were all that kept them from falling apart?

He suddenly felt sick to his stomach. What was he doing here in this car with these men? He had a stabbing impulse to leap out of the car, go to a church, confess the whole caper, and beg the priest for forgiveness.

"I heard you back there on the phone, Bobby," Ray said, barely able to see through the windshield. "Really threw me for a minute. Thought you might be calling our local gendarme, Officer Garrett."

"Get serious," Bob said.

"But I gotta say, given the caller, I think you played it just right," Ray said.

"Hey," Tony said. "Giving a guy therapy while you're breaking into his pad? I never heard of anything like that before. That's exceptional villainy. I think Dr. Bobby should maybe get a special bust in the Hall of Shame."

"Exceptional villainy," Cas said in the backseat.

"I gotta agree with you," Ray said. "It should read like, 'For his originality and brilliance in the midst of his first criminal outing. Rookie Crook of the Year. Dr. Bobby Wells.'"

"And you say the guy's thanking you at the end of the call, for what? Being there for him?" Tony said.

"Yeah," Bob said, trying to get with the twisted happiness of it all. "Kinda like that. He was very grateful."

"That's fucking great," Ray said. "You were very cool under fire, Bob. I would have to say that it augurs well for your new career."

"Augurs extremely well," Tony said.

"What the fuck is an 'augur'?" Cas said.

"Jesus, you are ignorant, Casmir," Ray said. "It isn't a thing. It, like, foretells the future."

"Really?" Cas said. "And I thought it was a fucking tool that bored its way through shit."

"No, Cas," Tony said. "*You* are the fucking tool."

This drew laughs all around. Bob didn't bother telling them that "augur" and "auger" were two different words, and that Cas was right. Why ruin their fun? But still, the crew's retrograde vocabulary skills and casual cruelty bothered him almost as much as their failure to understand that he didn't feel all that great about fucking over his patient.

That was the crummy thing about humanism; it kind of stuck to you even when it wasn't useful anymore.

Ray parked the car in the old American Brewery parking lot, and for a second Bob felt as if they were just a bunch of working stiffs headed in for the night shift.

They slipped through the barely opened side door and up the old steps, stepping over old hot dog wrappers, condoms, and a seemingly endless supply of beer cans, liquor bottles, and home-made crack pipes.

"Sure it's the fifth floor?" Ray said.

"Positive," Bob said.

Cas groaned, but kept up the pace.

When, exhausted and panting, they finally made it to their destination, Ray opened the door and looked inside.

"Don't see anybody," he said.

"Maybe we're here first," Bob said. He held the mask in his hands, looked down through the glass window, and felt a strange and sinful smallness. It was almost as though Utu was staring into his ulcerated soul and passing a harsh and overwhelming judgment.

"You gonna stand out there in the hall, Bobby?" Ray said, politely holding the door for him.

Bob managed a weak smile and joined the rest of them inside.

The room was huge and filled with old conveyor belts and dead refrigerators. Bob looked around and saw broken windows. A rat scurried into a hole in the wall.

"Anybody here?" Tony said.

"Of course," said a voice from the dark corner.

Tony and Ray swung their flashlights that way and saw Colin Edwards approaching them, a shotgun in his hands. He looked dapper, Bob thought. Next to him there was a boy in his mid twenties with acne and blond shoulder-length hair. He held a tan suitcase and a .44 Magnum.

"Is that the mask, Bob?" Edwards said.

"It is," Bob said.

"Let me see."

"The money first," Ray said.

Edwards looked at Ray's SIG, which was pointed at his well-coiffed head.

"Of course," he said. "Show them the money, Rafe."

Rafe moved forward one step and snapped open the case. There in his hands were packages of hundred-dollar bills.

"Hey," Cas said. "That's a lot. Tony, I think maybe we're being robbed."

"Yeah," Tony said. "How come all we get is a lousy sixty grand?"

Ray turned and aimed his gun at Tony's head.

"You both made your deals," he said. "You want, I can cancel them now."

"That's all right," Tony said.

"It don't seem fair, though, Bobby," Cas said.

Bob felt a lance of pain. He hated cheating good-natured Cas. He was about to say, "Well, you've both done such a good job, maybe we could tack on a bonus. How does twenty-five grand apiece sound?" But before he could get the words out of his mouth, Ray had turned around and was giving Cas a terrifying look, all crazed eyes and bared teeth. The color drained out of Cas's face as he shrank back into the darkness.

"Now the mask," Edwards said, handing the shotgun to Rafe, who took it after laying the briefcase on the floor next to him.

Bob handed it to him, and Edwards's left hand trembled with eagerness. He hit the release button on the side of the box and the glass window popped open. Carefully, Edwards reached into the box and removed the mask.

He turned the mask over in his hands, once, then again. He placed it over his face and peered at Bob through it.

"Boo," he said.

"Hey," Ray said. "Give us the fucking money and you can play with it all morning."

Colin Edwards shook his head. It was, Bob thought, as though he were aging right there in front of them.

Then he threw the mask of Utu to the brewery floor, where it smashed into a hundred pieces.

"No," Bob yelled. He fell to his knees, scooping up bits of the sun god's broken face.

"What the fuck?" Ray said. "Why?"

"Because," Edwards said, "that's not the real mask. It's a fake!"

He snapped his fingers and from the corner came two more men, one a fat boy wearing plaid golfing pants, the other a Polynesian, as wide as two Hummers. Both of them were carrying automatic rifles.

"Drop your guns and tell me where the real mask is," Edwards said, "or we'll shred all of you."

Ray looked at Cas and Tony and Bob and all four of them dropped their guns to the floor.

"It can't be a fake," Bob said. "You're wrong."

"Trust me, it is," Edwards said.

"I don't understand," Bob said.

"Well, let *me* explain it to you then," a voice said.

Behind them the elevator doors opened and Emile Bardan walked into the room. In his hand was a .38 Colt automatic. As he moved toward them, the blond boy turned and aimed his Magnum at him. Emile shot him in the forehead; Rafe fell at Bob's feet.

Emile grabbed Colin Edwards around the throat and used him as a shield.

"I wouldn't suggest anyone else try anything so foolish," he said. "Everyone drop your weapons. Or I'll shoot Colin in the ear."

Colin said, "Do as he says."

Edwards's remaining boys dropped their weapons, while the blond boy lay on the floor, leaking a ribbon of velvet red blood.

"Hi Doc," Emile said. "How are you?"

Bob, still on his knees, with the shards of the fake mask in his hands, felt his stomach heave, his heart pound.

"You set me up?" Bob said.

"Looks that way," Emile said.

"You planned this from the start?" Bob said.

"Not *right* from the start," Emile said. "It was harder than that. In fact, I almost gave up the game a couple of times. But it turned out you were the right man after all. Smart, but not too smart. Underpaid and bitter. Your two patients, Ethel Roop and Perry Swann, were very helpful in filling me in on your marital and financial difficulties. And I also knew that Colin would probably get in touch with you to enlist you in his nasty little plans."

"You bastard," Bob said. He tried to get to his feet, but Emile kicked him in the face. Bob fell back, his lower lip split and bleeding.

Bob got to his knees and tried once again to stand. But Emile Bardan had other ideas.

"Stay like that," he said. "I like you on your knees. At last we have the proper power dynamic in our relationship."

He turned and looked at Edwards.

"Colin, old man," Emile said. "How decent of you to bring all that money for me."

"Well, since you're the better gamesman, you certainly deserve it," Edwards said.

"Thank you for saying so," Emile said. "You know, Colin, I thought about selling you Utu, but this way is so much better. I get to keep the real mask *and* your money."

"But not for long," Colin said.

"Really?" Emile said.

"Of course. I'll hunt you down, Emile, and then you'll wish you'd never been born."

"I don't think so," Emile said. He shot Colin through the chest from only two feet away. Edwards flew backward and sagged against the wall. He looked up at Emile, groaned, then all the passion drained from his face as he slid down the wall and died.

Emile looked down at Edwards and sighed.

"Look how flat he is now," he said.

He was right, Bob thought. As the blood drained from Edwards's chest, his body turned from puffed peacock to plastic pancake.

"Now," Emile said. "Give me that money, please."

He reached for the suitcase, but the fat boy in plaid smashed it into his face. Bob watched in horror as they all dove for their guns. He told himself that he, too, should be going for his, but he couldn't bring himself to move. Instead, he crawled into the wall space on the other side of the ancient refrigerator and watched as the shooting began.

Ray shot Emile in the shoulder, hitting an artery. Blood spurted out like water from a fire hydrant on a hot day. Then Cas tried to shoot Emile in the back, but slid in a puddle of Edward's blood and shot Tony Hoy in the chest. Tony had a look of horror and great surprise as he fell to the floor. Cas turned then and shot the big Samoan in the right eye. This drove the Samoan mad and he shot wildly back at Cas, hitting him in his massive stomach, which spouted a geyser of blood. The fat boy shot Emile in the other arm, which caused him to drop the suitcase full of money and start running for the exit door. Ray shot the fat boy in the right ear. Falling, he shot Cas in the ass as he was screaming, "Emile's getting away!"

Bob watched in horror as chunks of bone, gristle, blood vessels, and cartilage spewed across the room. Cas fell a few feet in front of him, holding his stomach, and the big Samoan lay down, holding what might have been a gelatinous piece of eye. Tony was already dead, pancaking out on the floor. Only Ray remained unscathed.

But not for long, as the fat boy shot Ray in the back, causing Ray to turn and shoot him in the mouth, sending teeth and bloodied gums flying onto the factory floor.

"Bob," Ray said, grimacing. "Watch the money. I'm gonna get that little shit Emile."

Ray started to run to the steps, but then remembered the elevator and limped toward it.

"I can surprise him on the first floor," he said.

He pushed the door shut and Bob saw a green down light go on. That's when the bomb exploded.

The blast hit the elevator doors and blew out into the room. Bob felt himself flung upward like a rag doll, and an awesome wave of heat pushed him backward right into the refrigerator door. He opened the door and stood behind it, using it as a shield.

In front of him he saw wounded men catch fire. The blast decapitated both Cas and Tony, who were flung into each other in midair, as though they were professional wrestlers. On the other side of the room Rafe lost both arms, then burned, his dead eyes staring down at his flaming torso.

The Samoan was sent flying up toward the ceiling, his Hawaiian shirt aflame. He came down on top of the old conveyor belt, itself curled and bent from the heat. His huge, legless body was splayed over the belt. Bob scanned the room for the legs, but he could only find one of them hanging off the top of an ancient air-conditioning unit that bulged out of a glassless window.

The blast had started fires in several spots in the room and Bob knew at once that he had to get out. The only part of his body that he was able to move was his hand, which now crept forward in front of him, his fingers moving like a spider's, and magically, without Bob knowing how or why, his body followed. For a second he wasn't sure what he was doing; then he knew.

He was picking up the suitcase full of money, which was still sitting there, right in front of him. The sides of it were charred, a little like himself, he thought . . . ha ha ha. Yes, he and the suitcase there together . . . charred twins . . .

He pulled it to him and laughed harder.

What an odd thing a human was. So fine, a miracle of engineering when all the arms and legs were in the right spot, and so ludicrous when mutilated and dead.

Bob heard himself screaming now, wandering across the floor, trying to avoid a huge, gaping hole. The floor, like the heads, no longer connected by logic to its walls.

Nothing connected to nothing, Bob thought.

Shit just floating out there. Could be an eyeball . . .

Oh God, God, God . . .

He was crying now, trying not to look in the blown-out elevator at whatever had become of Ray. Bright, cool Ray. Hipster, tough, cruel Ray, who lived with his mom. All of those character traits now described a mass of blood and guts inside the elevator. Pink, distended bowels hung off the walls like some kind of blown-apart Mexican piñata, but with no candies.

Instead, the candies were in his hand and he'd better run, run down the steps before the ceiling caved in. Nothing in here, see, neither building nor people are structurally sound anymore, oh no . . . no no . . . nothing is for sure . . . a ceiling could cave in, a nose could melt . . . ha ha ha . . .

So run, Bob, run. . . . He was talking to himself in the third person, a trait he always hated when athletes were being interviewed on TV ("That's right, Darius know how to bound!"), but now somehow thinking of himself in the third person was the only way he could keep going.

He was Bob and Bob had to run down the steps, clutching the money like a favorite teddy bear, run and run, Bob, down to the third floor.

Where suddenly . . . oh, this was too weird . . . the steps ended.

The blast had twisted the steps so badly that there was nothing but a hole there . . . a hole with about a five-foot gap to the next flight of stairs. And down in the gap was darkness. Christ, the basement must be thirty or forty feet down. . . .

You fall down there and who knew what would happen. If the fall didn't kill you, it would probably break your spine, which, Bob thought, was perhaps what he deserved.

But the leap didn't seem too bad. If he could just get a little head start. Go up a few steps and then get a good jump. Oh yeah, it was a piece of cake, really.

He hustled back up the steps, clutching the briefcase, and was getting himself set, doing his one-one-thousand, two-one-thousand, three-one-thousand thing, when he heard it.

Heard the crying and then the screams.

Bob stopped for just a second thinking that what he was hearing wasn't real at all. No, not a chance, not real at all (was any of this real? No, yes, maybe . . .), then yes, yes, it was real, and he ran back up to the third-floor landing and he saw a door ripped off its hinges. The very foundation of the building must have been twisted. He peered inside and saw a hallway leading to a flat of offices. The cries had stopped now. He didn't know which one to look in. He tried the first one. An old office with a couple of battered desks and no one inside. The suitcase of money still in his hand, he went back to the hallway and tried the second door. He looked inside a huge warehouse room, not unlike the one upstairs. There, by the far wall, were two kids, a boy and a girl, maybe seventeen years old, and the girl was kneeling over the boy's body like he was dead, and she was holding her ears and screaming, and for a minisecond Bob thought he should run, run far away from them. Leave them there. They'd be okay after all. Bob couldn't really afford to *be seen* with these kids, too many questions would be asked, too many questions he could never, ever answer about the mask and melting elevators and most of all about the dead bodies upstairs, and the nifty little briefcase full of money in his hands.

He had to go back out there to the landing, and he had to make his little jump and get the hell out of there and forget the kids.

But the girl was leaning over the boy and crying and above her there was this cracked ceiling and maybe the boy was only minutes away from death, and maybe Bob could save him, but why should he? He had his shot here. He had the money for chrissakes, and wasn't that what this was all about?

He ran back out on the landing. Looked out a broken window. Below him was a Dumpster with piles of old boxes on it. Probably been that way for years. If he dropped the briefcase down there, behind it . . . if it didn't open when it hit, he could retrieve it when he got outside.

But what if it did open? The money floating away in the wind like in *The Treasure of Sierra Madre.*

Oh no, he couldn't bear that. He couldn't bear the thought of it.

The girl was crying louder now and saying, "Please. Somebody help us. Pleeease." Her cries pierced his heart. And he hated her for it. Wanted to go in and slap her in the face and scream, "Do you know what I've been through to get this money, you little bitch? Do you know how many people I got killed? Why the fuck should I stop for you? You'll never be anything anyway. You and your boyfriend will just grow up to be two more disappointing adults, who sell out your early promise if indeed you have any. So why the fuck should I give up five million bucks for you?"

But when she screamed again, there was something so help-less, so touching in her voice that he couldn't turn away.

And so there he was with his arm out the window, and the suit-case there, hanging by the side of the building, and then, in spite of the voices screaming "Sucker!" in his head, he let it go. And watched it slide down the building and crash and land on some cardboard boxes just behind the Dumpster. He could still see it, lying there, shut . . . and he thought of Ray, so recently departed, already headed for hell, and laughing at him now . . . Bob Wells, the would-be barbarian, who gave away his fortune to help two white-trash kids in trouble. Trouble Bob himself had gotten them in.

The girl, whose name was Leslie, was suddenly hugging him and screaming, "Ronnie's dead. Ronnie's dead. Oh God," and Bob was now gently disengaging himself and he was checking Ronnie's pulse and he saw that Ronnie wasn't dead at all, but damn close to it. He saw, too, that Ronnie was bleeding from his left arm and Bob found himself ripping off his shirt and applying a tourniquet and yelling at the girl that they had to get Ronnie out of there because the roof above them was falling and would drop right on them.

And somehow, he and Leslie, who he now noticed was really rather sweet and cute and not white trash at all but Latina, were carrying Ronnie Holocheck down the steps of the third floor of the American Brewery Building, down the crummy steps and over the condoms and crack pipes, and back to the hole, the gap, the maw of blackness forty or fifty feet down to the basement. Bob saw the hole and heard the sound of crackling above him, and the girl said, "Oh God, we're going to die," and Bob said, "No, no, we're not," and picked up the boy on his back and said, "It's easy. We're going to jump that little crack here in the steps now." And the girl looked at him like he was insane and said, "I can't make it," but Bob had the skinny boy over his shoulder now and Bob, jacked up now with fear and anger, got in her face and screamed, "The fuck you can't! You're gonna jump over that crack, right fucking now!" But she only shook her head and made a mewing sound, saying, "I can't. I just can't." And for a second Bob felt helpless, but then thought of Utu, his horrible stare, and he stared at her with his mask/face, his eyes blazing, his mouth contorted in a terrible grimace, and he screamed, "Listen, you little bitch, you either jump over that fucking hole or I am gonna throw you down it. Do you hear me?!!"

Her terrified eyes were locked on his and suddenly she began to nod her head in fearful agreement.

"Okay," she said. "Okay, okay, okay."

And now bits of plaster and concrete were falling down on them like stone confetti and Bob felt the boy slip a little and bolstered him up on his fifty-year-old, creaking back.

"This whole place is coming down. Go!" Bob said.

He watched her back up then and start toward the crevasse with long, loping strides. Then she was up and sailing over it. She made it over to the other side, with room to spare, and her forward motion carried her into the far wall, where she bounced a bit but came up fine, in shock and awe that she'd made it.

Then she turned and looked back at Bob, and he hoisted the boy on his shoulder and got himself ready. He remembered all the running he'd done when he'd played lacrosse. All the times he had jogged nine and ten miles. But now he was fucking old, his legs weak, and he knew it, his left knee was already buckling and what if he and the boy went down the hole?

Only forty feet down or so, maybe they wouldn't die. Maybe they wouldn't be that lucky.

But what choice was there? What shot standing here in the building that his own crew, no, his own little evil mind had blown to bits?

He couldn't make it. He couldn't do it. He thought of praying to Christ, but there was no way. He wouldn't know how. It had been too long and he had defamed the church he grew up in too many times to call on it now.

Then he looked at the kid and suddenly he remembered the way he used to feel when he saw someone helpless or hurt. He used to feel this kindness and compassion for them, but even more than that he used to feel that he couldn't let them down.

And he remembered something his father had told him: "If you can help someone and you don't, that's a sin."

God, he hadn't remembered that for the longest time.

But having thought it now he knew it was true. He had to run with the boy on his back and he had to make it over the gulf.

He ran down the remaining steps, telling himself he could make it, he would make it, he had to.

Then he took off, the crevasse yawning beneath him. He felt the boy lurching from his shoulders, he felt his body being sucked down, down, down. . . .

He had to make it. He had to stay up. He had to.

# PART III

## RAIN OF LIGHT

# CHAPTER SEVENTEEN

It was funny.

The rain had changed form twice. First it came from the heavens as water, then it morphed into concrete, hard chunks of flaming concrete ingots that fell toward his head. And now there was a third kind of rain, a rain of white light, so harsh that he was sure his face was melting. He blinked, gasped for air, tried to speak.

"The kids," he said. "The kids."

He blinked again and realized that someone was shining a flashlight in his eyes.

"He's coming out of it," a voice said.

He squinted up at the terrible white rain of light and saw a woman in a white coat staring down at him. Her glasses seemed to be melting, like a Dalí pocket watch.

"Mr. Wells," she said. "How do you feel, Mr. Wells?"

How does he feel? He doesn't know. Only that there's this terrible pain in his head, like someone has stuck a straw inside of it and blown it up. And why are they asking him about himself anyway? The kids, someone has to get the kids out of that place. Don't they see that?

"There are these kids," he said, pleading with them. "You gotta get them out. Two kids!"

"The kids are okay, Bobby. Thanks to you."

Another voice from the other side of the bed. He turned his head slowly, so slowly, with the greatest effort. It was like a slow-motion camera shot that seemed to take forever and the pain in his neck was like someone had carved a trench in his skin.

"Baby," said the voice.

Bob knew that voice and that sweet smile beaming down at him.

"Jess," he said. "Jess . . . the kids . . ."

"They're all right," she said. "Leslie told us, Bob. She told us all about it. How there was a bomb in the building and how you went inside and saved them."

"I went inside?" Bob said, and for the briefest of moments he thought it was true. He could almost see himself taking a late-night walk through the fog and rain. Right by the American Brewery Building. He lay there and watched himself watching the bomb go off up on the fifth floor. Yes, he could really see it now. Dr. Bob Wells, dramatically racing up the steps, no, *fighting* his way up the steps as the debris came hurling down all around him. He could feel the first wave of fear, telling himself, go back, go back, but then somewhere up on the second floor, dodging giant chunks of flying concrete and broken pipes, he heard the sound of the kids' screams. "Help us! Help us!" And what kind of man could *not* respond to that? Of course, he had to go on. He had to. And he had, hadn't he . . . hadn't he . . . gone up the steps, no matter that any second the building might crash in on him? And the girl was screaming, but Bob had been undaunted, right, un-vanquished by fear . . . hadn't he?

And then like somebody had clicked off the computer, it was over. His little fantasy was finished and he remembered it all, the way it really went down, and his feeling of disappointment and revulsion was so great that he had to vomit and he was barely able to signal to the woman in white, who somehow grabbed the basin and held it out for him, and then he was throwing up his dinner and, it seemed to him, his own heart, as well. And why not throw it up, he hadn't used it for so long?

"Bob. Bobby, are you okay?"

Jesse was holding his hand and Bob fell back on the bed, as the woman in white handed him Kleenex so he could wipe off the stench. He knew it was merely a cosmetic thing because he would never be able to wipe off that stench, never, ever. The stench of greed, the stench of murder. There was only one path for him, it was obvious. He would find Detective Garrett and he would confess. He would sit in a room and tell them all what had really happened and Garrett would crow in triumph, finally getting even with the son of a bitch who'd broken his nose all those years ago. But that was okay, because what he had done was all wrong and their triumph would be his ritualistic cleansing. And he would never hurt anyone again. In jail he would become—the thought almost tickled him—the saint of the prison. Yes, the wise old con who took care of the younger ones, the guy they called Doc, with the rimless glasses and the fancy Johns Hopkins education.

Bob fell back on his pillow, shaken and weak.

Then Jesse was there, putting her head lightly on his chest and saying, "You were a hero, Bob. You saved them all."

God, she believed it. And then above her, coming from some corner of the room that he hadn't been able to see, there were Dave and Lou Anne. And they were smiling down at him, too, their faces full of love and beaming admiration.

"Bobby," Lou Anne said. "You are just too much, darling. You're my hero."

Dave had tears of happiness in his eyes.

"Bob," he said, "you did it, buddy. You came up big."

And despite the pain and anguish inside of him, the desire, the nearly overwhelming desire to confess, Bob Wells turned on his best "aww shucks, 'tweren't nothing" smile.

"You saved them all," Jesse said. "You saved the kids."

And then Bob heard himself saying, quietly, with lovable modesty and humility: "Yeah, Jess, I guess I did. I guess I did."

He lay there in the darkness, the pain much better now that they'd given him the Vicodin. In fact, there was no pain at all, either in body or mind, which was a curious sensation. Because when Tony and Cas's flying, dismembered heads came floating back to him, when Ray's bloody stump drifted up out of the primal ooze, he expected to feel pain, lots and lots of pain. But there was no pain with the synthetic opium coursing through his veins. The images were there, all right, but they floated toward him like in some corny old horror movie, *The Heads from Beyond the Grave*, and he was grateful for the temporary release from guilt.

Guilt he knew he would feel, tons and tons of it.

And that reminded him of the goofy conversation he'd had with Ray that day at Elmer's. "Say, Ray, how much guilt do you think I'll have?" And what was it Ray had answered? "Depends on the job. If it's a job well done, that tends to lower the guilt ratio," or something like that.

But Bob had forgotten to ask the second question, which would have been, "But what if the job *isn't* so well done? What happens then, Ray? For example, what if this whole thing was a setup and, like, there's a bomb there and it goes off, and basically you and all the other guys are blown to shit? How much guilt am I going to feel then, Ray? Can you answer that one, huh? Can you, Ray-Ban? Can you? Huh?"

Like an eager little kid anxious to find out from Daddy-o that every little thing is going to be just fine and dandy.

Yes, it turned out that he'd had all that wrong, as well. In the fucked-up, mixed-up family that was the crew, it wasn't Bob who was the father figure. Uh-uh . . . it was Ray. Bob was merely the bright honors student who had gone wrong, the youngest brother who had squandered his potential but still had enough juice to convince lesser mortals that he had a foolproof plan.

It was almost funny. He had wanted to be the Cal Ripken of crime, but he was just a rookie who'd had a good first half of the season and ended up back playing in the Delmarva D League.

He'd blown it for all of them, and yet . . . and yet, he thought, suddenly selfish (easy to be selfish on Vicodin), he hadn't lost everything. Not yet. No, not yet.

Behind the Dumpster was the briefcase with five million dollars inside.

His money, yes, his money. Hadn't he paid for it in blood? If he could just get out of bed. Bob tried to sit up, but the pain in his head and his neck was so great he nearly blacked out.

Jesus, what could he do? He could just see some guy coming by, some old bum hanging out, drinking cheap wine or doing a pipe back there behind the Dumpster, and finding it. His money, his five million . . .

He tried again to climb out of bed, got his upper body halfway up, then fell back on his pillow, unconscious.

He lay there for the longest time, drifting in and out of consciousness, all the time hearing a little beat in his head:

"Get the money. Get the money. Get the money."

He fell into sleep once and then felt himself wake up, the red nurse's light on above his head, the smell of disinfectant in the room, and then he knew that someone was watching him, someone over by the window.

Someone with large, sad eyes, a balding head, deep wrinkles in his cheeks, and a little slash of a mouth. And another one who looked something like a baboon with a tie.

Detectives Bud Garrett and Ed Geiger of the Baltimore Police Department.

"Hey, hero," Garrett said.

"Officers Garrett and Geiger," Bob said. "What time is it?"

"About four A.M.," Garrett said. "We're working nights this week."

"Yeah," Geiger said. "Just thought we'd come by and see a real-life hero for ourselves."

"I just did what any man would have done," Bob said.

"A modest hero, too," Garrett said.

"I'd expect nothing less from brave Dr. Bobby," Geiger said.

Garrett moved closer to Bob's bed and his face reflected the night-light. It reminded him of a funhouse giant that had terrified Bob when he was a kid.

"Look, Garrett," Bob said. "I don't know how you got in here, but if I push the button and get the night nurse, you'll be right out on the street."

"That's true," Garrett said. "But you won't do that."

"No? Why's that?"

"Because you want to seem like a good citizen. A Good Samaritan. You get me tossed, it might make us police think of you as bad news. If you had me thrown out of here, I might think, for example, that you had something to do with all the bodies we found on the fifth floor."

"Bodies?" Bob said.

Garrett smiled and turned to his partner, who had crept up just behind him.

"That's good, huh, Ed? The nice soft way he said that. 'Bodies?'"

"Yeah," Geiger said. "It had a nice, surprised quality to it. Only one thing gave him away though."

"Look, Garrett," Bob said, slurring his speech from his cotton-mouth. "I don't know what you're—"

"You rubbed your nose," Geiger said. "You said 'bodies' real soft and innocent-like. But you rubbed your nose like this, right after you said it."

Geiger rubbed his nose with his right forefinger. Bob forced down a gulp of air. *Had* he rubbed his nose? He was pretty sure he hadn't. But what if he had?

"You like me rubbing my nose so much, Geiger, I'll do it for you again," Bob said. He rubbed it again. Garrett laughed.

"That's good," Garrett said. "Why don't we talk bodies, Bobby? Why don't you tell me who was upstairs on the fifth floor?"

"Gee, I'd like to," Bob said. "But I don't know anything about . . ."

"Uh, uh, uh," Garrett said. "You don't want to say that. You want to be helpful, because when you're helpful you don't get the lethal inject for murder one."

"Murder?" Bob said. "Everybody around here has been talking about a bomb. Surely you don't think I set off a bomb, do you, Detective? Explain to me how that would work. Let's see, I set off a bomb, to do what? Blow myself up? Then I had a change of heart and saved a couple of kids?"

Bob knew he was saying too much, but he couldn't resist a chance to bait Garrett. He still had his radical father's old hatred of cops.

Garrett smiled and wagged a finger at Bob. A finger that seemed to come out of the past, back when a cop's finger had a certain mythical and moral dimension.

"See, the problem, Bobby, is that some of the bodies we found had holes in them. Not from the bomb blast but from bullets. We figure that some people were up there, one of them being Ray Wade, who everyone knows is a pal of yours, doing some

nefarious shit. And one of the players brought a bomb, which he
had in the elevator."

"The elevator?" Bob said. "Why would there be an elevator in
that old building?"

"Worked off a portable generator," Garrett said. "For the jani-
torial crew. They're cleaning the building up. So they can turn it
into a museum."

Bob felt a huge desire to rub his nose and to rip the Vicodin
drip out of his arm. Jesus Christ, what if the janitors came tomorrow and looked down into the Dumpster?

"Well, maybe you ought to ask the janitors about the building," Bob said. "Maybe one of them saw something, but I didn't.
I was just taking a walk . . ."

"In the rain?"

"Yeah," Bob said. "And I was singing in it, too."

"That's another good one," Geiger said. "You're gonna do really well."

"What do you mean?"

"In prison," Geiger said. "They say that the guys who do the
best are the ones with a sense of humor. That would be you, Dr.
Bobby. You've always been a clown. Hey, when you get down the
Cut maybe you can be in, like, the prison talent show. That's assuming you tell us all about what you and Ray Wade and all the
other stiffs were doing up there before we find out from another
source. See, once we do that, then you'll be in for murder one,
and they don't allow the death-row inmates to take part in the
Christmas pageant."

"You're scaring me to death, guys."

How he hated cops. How he wanted to get out of the bed and
rip their faces off.

"I'm feeling sleepy, if you don't mind," Bob said.

"I don't mind a bit, Bobby," Garrett said. "I hear they're letting you out of here tomorrow. Maybe you'll feel more like talking to me when you're back home. Hey, maybe then I can talk to your girlfriend. She might be able to help us help one another, huh?"

"Fuck you, Garrett," he said. "You leave Jesse alone or I'll get a lawyer and nail you on a civil suit."

"Shocking, Dr. Bobby," Garrett said, as the two detectives headed for the door. "Is that any way for a hero to talk?"

"Good night, hero," Geiger said. "We're really gonna look forward to having you down to interrogation real soon."

They disappeared into the hallway. Bob could hear them laughing as their footsteps receded to the elevators.

The shits . . . they knew . . . they *knew* he was bad. And they'd be waiting, but to hell with them. He had to somehow get some sleep. Tomorrow, no matter what he felt like, he had to grab the money.

# CHAPTER EIGHTEEN

For all of Bob Wells's adult life he had harbored the secret desire (and until a few years past, the secret belief) that one day all his good works would be recognized by the City of Baltimore, the State of Maryland, and then, suddenly, his fame would catch fire and would spread wildly, until he was celebrated around the world.

It would start humbly with the local media coming to his door to canonize him. They would be in awe at his purity of purpose, his total commitment to the poor, the indigent, the lame and the halt, the blind and the deaf, the suicidal and the mad.

They would come and they would bow down in obeisance. They would see that you didn't have to go to India to find a true saint. There was a local saint right here in funky old Baltimore, a guy who rivaled them all when it came to goodness.

Having heard the news, the mayor and the city elders would decide to give him Bob Wells Day, with a parade and a float, covered with sick winos and junkies and beat-to-shit unwed mothers, exhausted homeless people hanging off the sides.

A band would play, speeches would be given down at the Inner Harbor, and from there the national media would pick up on it. Overnight Bob would be not only locally famous, but universally acclaimed, as well.

He had been so good for so long. Why, it had to happen, didn't it?

It was only when he chugged past fifty that Bob finally realized that the answer to that question was a collective shrug of the shoulders. Not even a "no" writ in thunder. The world couldn't even work itself up to that much passion regarding the sainthood of Robert Marshall Wells.

To put it bluntly, nobody cared.

And so Bob had seen the truth. He was like some obscure artist who works and works and struggles and really masters his craft and is never discovered, ever, his life a meaningless toil for absolutely no reward.

Instead of Bob Wells, a living example of good-eventually-rewarded, his life would be emblematic of another kind of universal truth:

Bob Wells, an example of the ultimate absurdity of human existence.

This would be his fate. Bob would be Captain Anonymous. Unheralded and unsung.

"For all your good work, Bob, today, a very special day, we give you (trumpets blare) . . . nothing. A sack of shit. Zero. Zip. Nada."

Until now, that is.

Until Leslie and Ronnie told their inspiring story to none other than Dave McClane, who wrote up the piece while Bob was asleep, and printed it in the *Baltimore Sun* under the headline, "The 'Saint' Saves Two." It was Dave at his thirties agitprop best. No cliché lay unwritten as he heaped praise on his old pal, telling of Bob's hard early years fighting against city hall and then going on to itemize all the other wonderful things Bob Wells had done, without "asking for or even wanting any recognition." Bob was "old school," the kind of "real man's man who didn't need to brag or publicize his accomplishments," just like the modest "greatest generation of World War Two."

Bob read the piece in his hospital bed and didn't quite know what to make of it. It was so emotional, so full of fiery (if cornball) passion. Not the type of thing the *Sun* usually ran at all. Maybe Dave had pictures of the editors with barnyard animals or something. In any case, Dave had gotten really worked up, getting quotes from guys at the Lodge, which all sounded too good to be true. Bob's bandmate Curtis had said: "In this age of hype and phoniness, Bob Wells is the real McCoy." To which Dave added: "People want to know how he did it, ran into a burning building and made the impossible leap with a hundred-and-sixty-pound teenage boy on his shoulder, but in downtown Highlandtown they already know. They know that Bob Wells was able to run up those steps precisely because his entire life has been an act of selfless heroism. Not as dramatic as the rescue he made yesterday perhaps, but equally courageous and heroic. Bob Wells, a real-life, honest-to-God hero, who is at this moment unconscious from the terrible beating he took in yesterday's impossible and brilliant rescue, is a man this reporter is proud to call his friend."

Bob was pleased, of course, but wondered if the emotional piece would be seen as even credible. Wasn't it all a little too much? As Jesse wheeled him down the hospital corridor, Bob found himself wishing that somebody else had written the piece, someone less emotional, who could have given the whole event the dignity it and he deserved.

One more bad joke on him, Bob thought bitterly as Jesse rolled him toward the door. He finally does something semiheroic and the guy who writes it up is too much of a hack for anyone to believe him.

But, about this, as about so many other things, Bob was dead wrong.

For as Jesse pushed him out of the hospital in his wheelchair, Bob suddenly saw the camera trucks. There were five, six ... good Lord, eight of them in the Johns Hopkins Hospital parking lot. And there were reporters, clustered against the doorway, microphones in their hands, their cameramen behind them. God, he even recognized some of them. There was Stormy Terrell, from channel 13, *Eyewitness News*, and there was Johnny Moorehead from channel 11, and there was, oh man, who was the one sticking the microphone into his face? Oh yes, she was Lake Harper from *The Morning Show*. Man, she was really cute, a pixie's face, and she was smiling at him, like she was madly in love. And there were radio guys and print journalists, one long-haired guy, must be from the free *City Paper*, and as Bob cleared his throat, he swore that he wouldn't be like *some* celebs who didn't talk to the print journalists, no sir, not Bob, he would talk to them all.

Jesse pushed him down the steps and he heard them yelling, "Bob! Bob, you saved two kids! How did you make it over that crevasse?"

And then, incredibly, Jesse was saying:

"Bob can't answer questions just now. He's just gotten out of the hospital! Step back, all of you!"

Bob jammed on the handbrake on the wheelchair, turned, and glared at Jesse. What the fuck was wrong with her? Not talk to the press? For God's sake, that's all he wanted to do! He'd talk until his voice had turned to sandpaper and he had to use sign language. This was his golden moment. This was his *shot*! Had she gone mad?

"Whoa, hold it, Jess," Bob said, holding up his palm. "We have a duty here. Now if you'll just hold on, I'll try to answer everyone's questions. Regarding the jump across the crevasse, I don't exactly know how I did it. I mean, I saw that it was huge, but I also saw that there was no other way, and I just set my mind to it, you know? I said, 'We have to get over. If we don't, we die.' Maybe you could say . . . a really terrifying fear of death compelled me to jump."

The reporters all laughed. They liked that, he could tell. A self-effacing, good guy. A real American hero. What a story!

"Bob, you've given your life for others," Lake Harper said. "Don't you ever feel, well, bitter, that you've not been recognized more by society?"

Not only was Lake adorable but she was smart, too. This was the money question, and she'd offered it up as a home-run lob.

Bob squinted and looked into the camera. He gave a slight shake of his head, as if he was so modest, so kind, that the mere mention of "personal glory" was something so foreign to him that he could barely understand what she meant.

"Acknowledgment?" he said. "I look at it another way. See, I figure I get nothing *but* acknowledgment. When I help an un-wed mother get over her problems and face life with a positive attitude, man, that's acknowledgment. When I help a home-less person get that job he or she hasn't had in twenty years and they invite me for Christmas dinner, hey, that's serious acknow-ledgment, and when I help a kid on drugs get clean and make something of his life, that's the greatest *kind* of acknowledgment. And yesterday, when I saw the looks of gratitude on those two kids faces, hey, that's all the acknowledgment any man needs. Right?"

Lake Harper looked down at Bob and he saw the love in her face. He had done it with that speech, all right, laid waste to them all. The reporters actually were speechless for a few seconds until they gathered themselves and fired away another round of ques-tions. This time it was Stormy Terrell, the hottest anchorwoman

in town, rumored to be leaving the city to go to work at CBS in
New York.

"Bob," she said, just like they were old friends, "what will you
do now?"

"I'll just keep on trying to help people, I guess," Bob said.
"That's what I do, after all."

"Then there's no truth to the rumor that you're talking to book
publishers about your life story?"

"No," Bob said, truly shocked. "Not that I know of."

(Oh God, he thought, let it be true. Please, let it be true.)

"Well, I heard three publishers are anxious to talk to you."

"That's very interesting, Stormy," Bob said, "but I seriously
doubt it. I'm just an ordinary guy doing what he loves to do."

"More like an ordinary hero," Stormy said.

Bob gave her his best modest smile and signaled for Jesse to
move on.

"Wait, wait," came the cries from behind Bob. "Just a few
more questions, Bob. And we want to talk to Jesse, too."

Bob looked up at Jesse, who beamed her loving smile down at
him.

"Stop and talk to them," he said.

"Jesse?" one of the faceless print reporters called. "Is it true
that you and Bob are going to be married?"

"No," she said. "Why ruin a good thing, darling?"

Huge laughter. God, she was great. A born performer.

"Jess, is he really this humble guy at home?"

"Absolutely," Jesse said. "The only place Bob's not humble is
in bed."

More laughter. Bob laughed, too. Fantastic. Now he would be
known as a sexy saint.

"Time to go," he said. He made a face part grimace and part
smile, the kind that said he was dealing heroically with his pain.

Jesse wheeled him across the parking lot, toward their car and the waiting Dave McClane.

"Hey guy," Dave said.

"Dave," Bob said. He wanted to jump out of the chair and hug old Dave for the piece he'd written, but he suddenly understood that their relationship had changed. They were no longer two losers wasting the afternoon at American Joe's tavern.

Not anymore.

Now Bob was a hero and Dave was his Boswell.

It was amazing, really. Because of Dave's savvy in writing the piece, both of them had completely reinvented their lives.

Bob felt a huge surge of gratitude toward Dave. Thank God for old Dave's loyalty, his faith in Bob's greatness.

Tears sprang to Bob's eyes.

It had finally happened. Bob was somebody in the world at large.

Thanks to his dear old pal . . .

It was all he could not to throw his arms around Dave, thank him profusely. But, of course, that wouldn't do.

He was a hero now. He had to play the part of one. Modest. Kind. Understated, like the saint Dave had made him out to be.

So instead of hugging and kissing the man who had pulled him from the mulch of obscurity, Bob offered Dave a manly, understated handshake.

As the press snapped the picture and the TV cameras whirled just behind him.

"Good to see you, Dave," Bob said. "That was a fine piece."

"You earned it, Bob," Dave said, smiling, his eyes shining with admiration.

Bob nodded in an old-fashioned Gary Cooper way, then let Dave and Jesse help him out of the wheelchair and into his car. And as he fell into the passenger seat (giving another little clenched-teeth grimace of pain so the cameras could catch it), Bob suddenly felt the clean rush of saintliness.

He was a real hero. Of course he was. Hell, as much of one as, say, Jessica Lynch, who hadn't done a damn thing but get caught and raped, and as much of one as any football star murderer or billionaire basketball crackhead. Why beat himself up about his "authenticity"? That kind of thinking—rigorous honesty—why, that was for the old world, and the old Bob. America wasn't about that anymore, if indeed it ever was. That kind of thinking was for losers. So was the whole guilt trip, too. Why, in this world, the real world, you were as you were perceived to be, and Bob was perceived as a hero. Only a schmuck or some kind of overearnest graduate student of Ethics 101 would question the validity of his new fame and fortune.

And besides, Bob thought, as Jesse slowly rolled out of the lot—and as Bob gave all the reporters a George S. Patton-esque thumbs-up, which would be shown that night on the *News at Eleven*—just think of all the thousands of good things he'd done over the years, helping the poor, the downtrodden, the disenfranchised. The truth was he was an artist, a special kind of artist, who didn't use paint or words, or play music, but rather an artist who used humanity as his canvas.

He was, he thought, as they eased out into the traffic, a kindness artist. Like a metaphysical Johnny Appleseed, he moved from place to place, dropping dabs of kindness and insight.

And now, at long last, the world would be able to see his life's work.

That happy thought brought tears to his eyes.

His miserable life had come to something after all. He was finally being recognized. And God, he was loving every minute of it. Bob Wells, American hero. At long last.

\*  \*  \*

On the bright spring morning Bob arrived home his phone never stopped ringing. It was, he thought later, as if all the calls he'd been waiting for his entire life were taking place in one day.

There were calls from the *Washington Post,* calls from a paper in Richmond, Virginia, and finally, as the day ended, calls from *The New York Times* and, sure enough, a publisher called Pavilion Press in New York City.

As Bob waited for it to get dark enough to go retrieve his money, he answered them all. He told his life story over and over again, adding nifty little touches each time. For the *Post,* he said that he'd muttered a little prayer just before his fateful leap. For the Virginia paper, he mentioned his father's name and his own jogging, "which gave me strong legs."

But he saved the best for *The New York Times.* He mentioned that he was a "religious man . . . quietly and privately religious . . . that there were 'certain spirits' he communed with and these spirits aided him when the chasm looked insurmountable." That was just the right thing for a hero. A low, steady flame, which he could turn up in time of peril. The *Times* guy loved it, and the piece practically made Bob out to be a male Mother Teresa.

The editor, Jane Bennett, from Pavilion Press, was the best of all. She said that they wanted to do a book with him and put it in their new Real Heroes line. She actually articulated the very thought Bob had wondered about so many times: "Why should jocks and movie stars be the real heroes? They don't do anything for mankind." Right, Bob thought, damn right. He agreed to go up to New York in the next few weeks to meet with a ghostwriter who would interview him and actually write the book.

"As long as it's real," Bob said, not only playing the modest hero but actually feeling that way as he spoke.

"Absolutely," Jane said. "We don't write a thing without your 'input.'"

Yes, that was great, fantastic. Input. They wanted his input!

He hung up in a delirium of happiness, only to receive another call.

This one he could not believe. A producer from the *Today* show named Lori Weisman called. She sounded hysterically excited about "meeting Bob."

"I just think what you did, why, it's so amazing," she said. "We live in a world now where each act of heroism gives the rest of us strength to carry on. I mean, I think your story could be a real inspiration to all of America, Bob."

Bob heard her words and realized that this was truly it, the apogee of his success. His great dream was coming true. Television interviews! On the *Today* show! He would be part and parcel of the national colloquy. He, Bob Wells, was going to be on network TV!

"That's fine," he said, trying to sound cool and calm, as though this kind of thing was swell but not his real focus in life. "But I can't spend too much time in New York, because, well, I can't leave my patients."

He looked at Jesse, who was walking through the room, and she gave him a complicit smile. She understood that he was playing it up, and why shouldn't he, after so many years of being invisible.

There was a long silence on the phone then, during which Bob thought he might have overplayed his hand. Maybe she was thinking, What a phony asshole.

But when she came back on the phone she was even more breathless than before.

"That's so great," Lori Weisman said. "That's the spirit we want to catch, and I don't think you can do that, catch the real you, in the studio. No, I think I need to come down there. Bring the camera crew and film you as you minister to your people."

For a second Bob couldn't get his breath. They were going to come to him? Like he was some celebrity.

"You mean, come to my house and hang out?" he said, realizing he sounded lame, but too stunned to care.

"Absolutely," Lori said. "Listen, Bob, when I read Dave Mc-Clane's pieces about you, I knew this was a huge story. It's the kind of thing people need now. In a world of Enron phonies and fucking perv priests and greed and suicide bombers, we all want to hear about a good guy who puts other people first, you know?"

Bob could hardly speak. At last, at long last they finally understood him and the world would hear his story. It was so wonderful . . . he could barely breathe.

"So can we come down, Bob?" Lori said.

"You bet," he said. "But as far as filming my patients, well, we'd have to ask their permission. I mean, I can't compromise their treatment."

"Of course not," Lori said. "We'd get them all to sign releases. How's the day after tomorrow sound?"

"Fine," Bob said. "Great."

"We've heard from Dave McClane that you and your girlfriend play in a rock band. Any chance you could play that night?"

"I guess so," Bob said. "I mean, you'd have to call Link, the guy who runs the Lodge, but I think he might be able to work it out."

"Great," Lori said. "Bob, I think this is going to be really terrific. I can't wait to meet you."

"Same here," Bob said. "Thanks for calling."

"No," Lori said, her voice suddenly bulging with emotion, "thank *you*, Bob. It's easy to get cynical in this world and I think our viewers are really ready for a real hero."

"Gee, thanks," Bob said, and hung up the phone.

"Bob, you ought to get up to bed," Jesse called from the kitchen. "You'll wear yourself out."

"I'm okay," Bob said. "Just a little headache."

He reached into his pocket and took out the bottle of Vicodin.

Suddenly, he was struck with a terrible fear. What if while Lori was here, the cops told her that there was some question regarding Bob's involvement with a mass murder on the fifth floor?

Neither Garrett or Geiger had mentioned his name in the article about the bombing, but they were lying in wait. It could happen at any moment. Why, instead of a piece glorifying him, the whole thing could come out as an exposé.

Bob fell back on the couch. It was getting dark. Maybe, if these well-meaning reporters dug into his past, they'd find out that he hung out with Ray Wade. Maybe they could even connect him to the crime. What if they talked to the bartender at Elmer's? Had anyone seen him in there? And what of Cas and Tony's relatives? Did they know about him? Would they come forward and tell the cops the truth? And where was Emile Bardan? Would he come back and kill Bob in his bed?

Then he took a deep breath and reminded himself that he was okay. So far no one had anything on him. What he had to do was take things one step at a time. Isn't that what he always told his patients?

One step at a time. And the first step, the step he had to do right now, was to go get the money.

He lay there on the couch until Jesse came out of the kitchen.

"Bob," she said, "you really should get your rest."

"I know, Jess," he said. "I'm just fine here. I need to think through a few things, that's all. You go up. This has all been hard on you, too, baby. You need your sleep."

"Okay," she said.

Then she looked at him in a curiously cold way.

"Bob," she said. "You know they found these bodies upstairs from where you saved the kids. And one of them was Ray Wade. I have to ask you this . . ."

Bob looked up at her with the most earnest of his shrink faces.

"You want to know if I had anything to do with those guys?"

"Yes, I do," Jesse said. "I have to know."

"No," Bob said. "That's the answer. I saw Ray as a friend, but you don't really think that I would have had anything to do with his business dealings, do you?"

"I hope not," Jesse said. "I sincerely hope not."

"Don't you believe me, Jess?" Bob said.

"I want to," she said. "But you told me you were attending a seminar up at Hopkins that night. So how'd you end up taking a walk by the American Brewery? At one o'clock in the morning."

"I came home and couldn't sleep," Bob said. "You know how I am, tossing and turning all night. I lay there for an hour, then said 'to hell with it,' and got up to take a walk. Usually, after a walk, I sleep just fine."

Jesse managed a smile.

"That's true," she said. "There's another question I have to ask you, Bobby."

"Sure," Bob said. "Shoot."

"Well, I know you jumped over the hole in the floor with the boy on your back, but how did you get over it the first time?"

"What?" Bob said. He really didn't understand the question. "What first time?"

"When you came into the building," Jesse said. "How did you get over the hole to get to the kids you heard screaming?"

Bob looked at her with astonishment. She really was sharp . . . thank God she was on his side.

"Well, that's the weird thing," he heard himself say. "You see, when I first went into the building, the hole wasn't there yet. But while I was inside trying to wake Ronnie up, there was this huge, thunderous roar and the whole damn foundation just collapsed. So when I came back out . . ."

"The hole *was* there," Jesse said, finishing his sentence for him. "That's what I thought, Bob. It's just amazing."

"And it's all true," Bob said. "Have a little faith in me, Jess."

"I do, Bobby. You know I do."

She bent down and kissed him on the forehead.

"Don't stay up too late," she said.

"I won't, baby," Bob said. "Now you go get some sleep."

Though it killed his battered knees and made his headache worse, Bob ran through the back alleys, over potholed cobblestones, past piles of trash as he made his way toward the American Brewery Building.

All the way there he heard the voices in his head: What if it's gone? What if it's gone?

The thought tortured him and his head throbbed all the worse for his fears.

Finally he came to the huge, old brick building, which loomed over him in the dark. He saw the yellow crime tape around the whole place. Good God, that had somehow never occurred to him, that they would search the whole building, inside and out. They might already have found the suitcase, sitting there behind the goddamned Dumpster.

Or maybe they left it there, empty, of course, to see who would come back and fetch it.

He wondered if they would have a guard hanging around the building now, just waiting for him to come. Bob began to berate himself. Christ, he'd been a fool, an idiot to save those kids. He'd gotten a few minutes of fame and glory, but the money might be gone. And there was Garrett, too. What if the guy was following him? Bob looked around the streets, at the alleys and the bar across the street called Mike's. Detective Garrett could be sitting right in there, just waiting for him to come. . . .

Maybe he should just leave the money. He was getting famous, right? Maybe his book and life story would be worth so much that he just shouldn't risk it.

Yeah, right. You're going to leave five million dollars sitting there, after what you went through to get it?

Bob felt a chill in the air, coming off the bay.

Time to go, hero.

Time to get paid, as dead Ray used to say.

He ran around the back of the building, staying close to the walls, trying to blend in with the shadows.

He walked over the condoms and pieces of charred concrete and then he saw it, the Dumpster. Same as it was yesterday. Great piles of cardboard on it. They hadn't gotten to it yet. . . .

But what if some bum . . . some guy . . .

Shut the fuck up.

He had to look, he had to look now. . . .

He slid back behind the Dumpster, reached down in the darkness. It should be right here.

And was.

Just like that. Easy as pie. He had the briefcase in his hand.

But was there anything inside?

He knew he should wait, wait until he got it in his house, but he couldn't stand it.

Bob stepped out into the light and clicked open the case.

It was there. Money . . . piles and piles of neatly wrapped hundreds.

Oh, Jesus Christ on a crutch, he was rich . . . rich, rich, rich.

And don't forget famous, famous, and soon to be even more famous.

And then he heard it, a car coming, a siren screaming. Where the hell was it? Just a block away on Gay Street and heading this way. A trap? Had they just been waiting for the rat to come and pick up the case?

Bob turned and ran, across the battered, filthy lot next to the building, sliding on the gravel as he hit the alley, and then he was flying through the alley . . . his knees creaking, his body wracked with pain from his heroic leap. But he was moving fast, faster than he had in years, and the briefcase was in his hand and he wasn't ever going to stop until he got home.

# CHAPTER NINETEEN

In the back of his basement, Bob sat on an old lawn chair and opened the suitcase. There it was . . . all his . . . all that money.

M.O.N.E.Y.

Five million dollars.

He took out a few of the packets, rubbed them across his cheek.

Oh God, he was rich.

He, Bob Wells, the poor guy, the martyr, the former laughing-stock, was loaded.

He loved the smell of the new bills. They smelled like . . . like . . . well, there were no really good metaphors. Money smelled like money and nothing else smelled half as good. Okay, maybe a woman's skin, yes, sometimes that could be great, but the feeling of power, the intoxication of the money, right now, it was way better than sex. Just holding so much of it made him a little giddy, mad. He wanted to get closer to the money. He wanted to inhale it. He wanted to take a bath in it. He wanted to—go ahead, admit it—make love to the money.

What a mad, mad thought . . . but why not? When you had money, anything you wanted became legitimate, didn't it?

Mon, mon, money, moneeeeeey! All for him. Money!

He was like an animal that had finally found his own habitat. All those years of groveling to state officials to get money for the poor. All those years of visiting people in crummy bomb shelters of homes. That was over, history. He didn't need that shit anymore.

It was the world of money, success, and glitter for Dr. Bobby Wells now.

He kissed the packets and felt like a priest observing a religious ritual.

"Yes, my son, you are witnessing a High Holy Moment. The Blessing of the Packets."

He laughed wildly, kissed one packet of hundreds after another.

Oh money, money, money. How do I love thee, let me count the fucking ways.

He took out the packets and covered himself with them. A blanket of money.

A coat of money, a coat that would protect him in his old age.

A coat that would lift him, along with his newfound celebrity, to higher and higher circles of power.

Oh God, he loved it. Absolutely loved it.

He lay that way for a little while, then reminded himself that he had to be practical, together. Many a criminal had been caught wallowing in his newfound dough. He had to play it smart. And he would.

He quickly gathered up all the packets and put them back into the briefcase, then carried it over to his knotty-pine wall. And right here, Bob thought, was further proof that having the money was his destiny, because for years there had been this loose knotty-pine board on the back wall, a board Bob had intended to fix but had never gotten around to. And now he knew why. Because this loose piece of knotty-pine planking was there expressly for the purpose of providing a hiding place for his money. He pulled the board out and felt around inside, and there it was, a neat little hollow that was just big enough to stick the briefcase in.

Well, of course, it was. Because this was all fated.

Bob put the knotty-pine plank back up, then began to beat the nails in with the heel of his shoe.

The money was safe there in the wall, he was pretty sure of that. Safe for a few days anyway.

But what was the next move?

Ray had mentioned a guy he knew, Jake Gimble, a crooked lawyer, who would launder the money for them. But going to see Gimble seemed dicey. Before the bomb blast, Bob had just assumed that he and Ray would waltz in there and see Jake, and because no one fucked with Ray, the guy would treat them both like solid citizens.

But now he had to go see the guy all by himself. How did that work? You went in and gave the guy all your money and what did you get back, some kind of lame bank receipt from the Cayman Islands?

Like, what would it say? "Received from Bob Wells: Five Million (Minus Gimble's Cut) in Blood Money."

And, Christ, what if the guy decided to stiff him? It wasn't like you could go to a cop and say, "Ah, Officer, perhaps you heard about the big bombing down at the old American Brewery, in which quite a few people were blown to very tiny bits? Well, just purely by accident, ha ha, I happened to end up with all the stolen dough and I gave it to this crooked lawyer fellow and he seems to have had the temerity to steal it from me, and I wonder if you could possibly aid me in getting it back?"

Yeah, that would be just great.

He wouldn't have a leg to stand on. Christ, what in God's name was he going to do? Trust the guy? No way . . .

Then he realized the answer. He would have to convince the banker that he was no one to fuck around with. Yep, that was it.

He'd have to go in and see Jakey boy and let him know that if there were any games he'd blow his nuts off.

That was his new power, after all. Since he no longer played by civilized rules, after all, he'd have to be willing to back up his threats.

But could he?

If the guy stole from him, could he be like Scarface and do something . . . something violent?

Bob Wells, the kindness merchant? Do something completely, openly vicious?

The truth was, he didn't know. There was a time, not long ago at all, that he would have said absolutely not. . . . Okay, he had punched Garrett in the nose once long ago in a street fight, but that was just a tussle.

That wasn't gangster stuff.

But kill a guy or badly hurt him over money?

Could he do that?

Now he wasn't sure and the thought tortured him. He had gone through so much to get the money, seen men die. Okay, not the best men in the world, but living, breathing men . . . guys he had started to feel a kind of maggoty affection for. Dead, flaming, their heads on fire . . . images he never wanted to think of again yet would never forget.

He had almost been one of them, but fate had spared him.

But having undergone all that, hadn't he been changed forever?

If someone threatened his money now, money he had gone through hell for, wasn't it his right as a man to protect what was his?

Okay, okay . . . he had stolen it. He'd almost forgotten that. But it didn't feel that way. Why, it was as if the money had been left to him by the recently deceased. Yes, and he was the rightful and legitimate heir to the fortune.

And if some banker tried to steal it from him . . .

For that matter, if Emile Bardan came back, and he might very well . . . what was he willing to do to protect his money, his and Jesse's future?

Would he really hurt his old patient to stop him from grabbing the money?

Forget "hurt." That wasn't the real question. The question became one of killing.

Would he kill Emile to keep the money?

Bob continued to nail the knotty-pine plank back into his wall and felt the sweat run down his neck.

It had all seemed so funny when it had started. Bob remembered doing his little dance down at the pier. It was a lark, a crazy scam. . . . No one was going to be hurt, not even Emile, who certainly was insured for the mask. But now . . . the laughs were over.

Bob had to decide now. How far would he go to protect his new fame, and his money?

And the scariest part of all was he suspected he already knew the answer to that question.

After all, having gone this far, he could never, ever go back to the moldy old land of the poor.

# CHAPTER TWENTY

The *Today* show people came to Baltimore just as they claimed they would. Bob made sure Dave knew all about it so that he and Lou Anne could be in the show, too. Bob had worried a little that Ethel Roop and Perry Swann wouldn't want their stories aired on national television, but this only showed how out of the loop he was. Not only did they want in, they couldn't *wait* to tell their stories to Lori Weisman. Bob stood by stunned, as Ethel Roop described her "battle with flab," even pinching her chunky thighs on camera, so the whole world would know exactly how gross she was. She said all the right things about Bob, what a great shrink he was, how much he cared, how amazing his insights were, things she had never said before, things Bob doubted she even believed. The truth was he felt that he'd failed with her and he was pretty sure that she felt the same way. But none of that seemed to matter now. She was, after all, on a major television show; the script called for a hero, so a hero Bob would be.

The same went for Perry Swann, who had once flat out called Bob a "fake" and a "jerkoff," but who now told the cameras that Bob was "the only man I'd ever confess my sins to. Because he took the job as seriously as a priest." Bob wasn't sure that was such a compliment, given the quality of priests these days, but

Perry radiated such sincerity that Lori Weisman said, "Beautiful. Right after the show they're probably going to fucking canonize you, Bob."

The same went for all the old black women Bob saw every week. Lutitia Morgan, the ninety-year-old woman who sang spirituals for Bob, said, "Dr. Bobby is the onliest white man I would ever trust."

Dave, of course, got on camera and positively gushed about Bob.

"Bob is the kind of guy whose whole being is bound up in helping other people. And what does he get for it? Nothing. Sometimes less than nothing. Sometimes a kick in the teeth! But it doesn't stop him from being a great guy."

Frizzy-haired, hip Lori Weisman lapped it up. She interviewed Bob outside his house as Jesse watched from the neighbor's stoop alongside Dave and Lou Anne.

"How do you manage to keep your equilibrium, your balance, when you see longtime friends like Rudy Runyon making money, while you, frankly, have so little?"

Bob smiled his modest smile and gave Lori Weisman his best Gentle Ben look, then did a variation on the speech he'd given when he was coming out of the hospital, ending with his "I consider myself one of the luckiest men on earth" line. He almost added, "Thank you, Lou Gehrig," but managed to resist.

When he was all done there was a reverent silence, and then Dave said, "Bob, that was beautiful, man." And Lori Weisman nodded and said, "Yes, it was. It's going to play beautifully, too."

Bob blinked and shrugged a little as if he had no idea what she was talking about. "Play." What does that mean?

Then he added:

"I hope it didn't sound pompous or anything. I sort of got caught up in the moment there. Guess it's my dear old dad's influence. He was a union man and a hell of a speech giver."

"Oh, really?" Lori Weisman said. "Tell us about him a little, while we walk around your neighborhood."

"Really?" Bob said, as he began to walk toward Patterson Park. "You think anyone will care?"

"Oh yeah, they're going to care," Lori said. "Trust me, after this piece comes on the air, your whole life is going to undergo such an amazing change. Wow, we may have to do a follow-up piece in a year to see how you handle fame and celebrity."

Bob made a shrug face and then looked over at Jesse.

"He'll do just fine," Jesse said. "Bob knows exactly who he is."

"We'll see," Lori Weisman said. "I just hope I'm not creating a monster here."

There were laughs all around at that one. Imagine sweet, caring Bob Wells, a monster. What a thought.

That afternoon Lori Weisman and her crew arranged a lunch down at Bertha's Mussels, the Fells Point bar and grill where Jesse worked. They shot her serving the lunch crowd and interviewed her about her relationship with Bob. She said that Bob was the "realest person she had ever met, and the kindest." Then a few minutes after Bob arrived, Leslie and Ronnie, the kids whose lives he'd saved, showed up, fully recovered. They tearfully greeted Bob at the bar and all of them hugged and kissed one another, as the cameras rolled.

"We're not going to try and interview you right now," Lori told the happy gang. "We want it to be real. Just go for it. Reality, I mean."

The three of them ate mussels, drank pints of beer, and Leslie said, "They say he's a man, but I know better. There's no way he could have jumped over that hole without wings. I say Bob Wells is an angel."

She cried and Lori Weisman smiled as the camera caught it all.

* * *

As Bob, Jessie, Lori, and the cameraman, Danny, left Bertha's around 7:00 that night, the big moon hung over the little shops on Broadway and Bob really felt like the luckiest man on earth. Here he was surrounded by two charming women, the cameraman recording his every word and gesture. No doubt about it, his fortunes were on the rise, and at home, stashed away in the wall, was a cool five million dollars.

Of course, there was still the specter of Emile Bardan out there somewhere, but maybe he'd never come back. Hey, maybe he'd already died of his wounds. Not that Bob wanted him to die exactly, but if he had, well, wouldn't it be the result of his own evil intrigues? Of course it would. Any sensible person would say so.

And if he did come back . . . Bob felt that somehow he would handle him. It was almost as if a lucky star was shining down on him at last. Maybe, Bob thought giddily, it was all due to Utu. The god of vengeance and justice was on his side. Now there was a goofy thought . . . but when you were riding high like Bob, such thoughts weren't merely demented. No, when you were famous, celebrated, and rich, such thoughts were poetic, or at the very worst, eccentric.

The three of them chatted happily as they walked home, when suddenly from the alley next to Oriole Liquors, Bob heard a groan.

"Terrorists," the voice said. "They're coming. . . ."

Bob stopped and listened again.

"Terrorists," the voice said.

"There's somebody back there," Lori said.

"Yeah," Bob said. "And I know who it is. Hang on a minute."

"Be careful, honey," Jesse said.

Lori looked at Danny.

"You have to get this," she said.

Bob headed back into the dark alley, waiting for an attack and 911's trademark kick in the balls.

"911," he said. "You back here, Nine?"

"Get away from me," a drowsy voice said. "I got a knife. You fucking terrorists."

Bob turned and saw the cameraman behind him.

"Don't shine the lights yet," he whispered.

"Don't come a step closer," 911 said.

Bob's eyes had grown accustomed to the darkness. There, in front of him, lying in a heap next to a Dumpster was 911. In his hand was a broken bottle. He thrust it out, but looked more hapless then menacing.

"Nine, it's me, Bob Wells," Bob said.

"Dr. Bobby?" 911 said.

"Yeah. How you doing, Nine?"

"I'm fine," 911 said. "What's that behind you?"

"That's a friend of mine. From TV."

911 squinted past Bob.

"That a terrorist?"

"No, Nine, a cameraman?" Bob said. "He wants to take your picture. Me and you. How about we go get some food somewhere? Like McDonald's?"

Just then, Danny the cameraman shone the camera light into 911's face.

"No," Bob said.

911 let out a terrible shriek, leapt to his feet, and lunged at Bob with the broken bottle. Bob, having been through this a hundred times before, deftly swept his hand aside and watched the bottle go crashing to the ground. Then he turned 911 around and pulled his arms back in a full nelson.

A few seconds later, Bob had kicked the homeless man's feet out from under him and had him pinned on his stomach on the ground.

The stench from his clothes was terrible, but Bob didn't notice. He felt a terrific kindness and compassion sweep through him, the way he had felt almost all of his life when he had to tussle with street people.

"Now calm down, Nine," Bob said. "When was the last time you had something to eat?"

"Two days ago," the haggard, desperate man said in a small, helpless voice.

"I see," Bob said. "Would you come with me now? To McDonald's?"

"Okay," 911 said.

"I'm serious, Nine. No kicking people. Okay?"

"Okay," 911 said. "Can I get supersize fries?"

"Man, this is really good," 911 said, devouring a Big Mac and revealing two great gaps where his front teeth had fallen out. "Thanks, Dr. Bobby."

"That's okay, Nine," Bob said. "After we finish here, I'd like to get you down to the shelter. And then maybe get you to an AA meeting. What do you say?"

"I don't know about them AA meetings," 911 said. "They got terrorists in some of 'em."

Lori Weisman shot Bob a quick look. Jesse gripped his hand under the table, as Danny shot the scene.

"Not this one, though," Bob said. "Lower Broadway kicked all the terrorists out."

911 looked at Bob with a measure of doubt in his eyes.

"You sure?" he said.

"I'm sure," Bob said.

Suddenly, 911 gave Bob a sweet smile.

"I love this guy," he said, looking at Lori.

"Everybody does," Lori said.

Jesse squeezed his hand and Danny caught it all.

After his Big Mac and his massive amount of fries, 911 was tired and dreamy, and went off with his little entourage to the Broadway men's shelter with barely a peep of protest.

"Now don't forget the AA meeting, Nine," Bob said.

"Okay," he said, looking just past Bob's head, at whatever phantoms tortured him. "I been there before, you know?"

"That's good," Bob said. "How many days did you have?"

"A whole year once. And I had a job working for the Department of Recreation as a swimming coach over at Patterson Pool. But some of the terrorists over there had me fired."

"I heard about that," Bob said, feeling happy inside. "But they're all gone now. You could do it again, Nine. Hey, what's your real name anyway?"

911 looked down at the table and cupped his hand around his mouth.

"I don't want them to hear," he said.

Bob put his head close to 911's.

"Barry," the homeless man said. "Barry Lansing."

"Cool," Bob said. "Maybe we should start calling you Barry, huh?"

"You think?"

"Better than a number, Barry. Wouldn't you say?"

"Yeah, okay," Barry said.

Barry smiled at Bob and then looked at Jesse.

"He don't give up on nobody," he said.

Jesse smiled sweetly and took Bob's hand.

"I know he doesn't," she said.

Suddenly Bob felt like he was going to cry. He couldn't bear Barry's kindness and gratitude. He had a crazy impulse to fall down on his knees in front of him and confess everything.

"Hey," Jesse said, looking at her watch. "We have to get moving. We've got to play some rock 'n' roll tonight."

"Cool," said Barry. "But I'm a little tired now. I think I'll go in there and go to sleep."

He hugged Bob and then quickly walked up the steps to the shelter. When he reached the top step he turned and saluted.

"I'm sorry for kicking you that time," he said. "I thought you was a terrorist."

"That's okay," Bob said. " 'Bye, Barry. Get to that meeting, okay?"

Barry Lansing nodded and smiled as if he was struck by his name. Then he turned and walked through the old doors into the cavernous shelter.

"It's amazing," Lori said. "He sounded completely okay for a minute there."

"That happens," Bob said. "I remember when he was lucid for a month last year, but then he went off again."

"Why?" Jesse said. "What makes him lose it?"

"He's got some real instability. Drugs and booze don't help. But the worst thing is nobody giving a shit," Bob said.

"Except you," Lori said.

There was a real sincerity in her voice, Bob thought. The first time all day that she hadn't been speaking like a tough professional but from her heart. What he did, who he really was, had gotten through to her.

But then, Bob noted to himself, as they grabbed a cab to head to the Lodge, if he hadn't committed a crime against his own patient, Lori Weisman and the *Today* show wouldn't be here at all.

* * *

That night the Lodge opened up for a special performance of Bob Wells, Jesse Reardon, and the rest of the fabulous Rockaholics. Bob Wells rocked and blasted out tasty blues licks on his Les Paul and Miss Jesse Reardon shook her sweet body and sang with every ounce of throaty, dark, purring sensuality that was in her. The cameras pumped everybody up. The Lodge patrons went nuts dancing and showing off for the cameras. Old and Young Finnegan danced on the bar again, with a bunch of biker chicks they'd brought in from redneck Glen Burnie, wild-looking women with bandannas around their heads and safety pins through their ears. Ethel Roop and Perry Swann were there and ended up making a wild dance couple, big Ethel shaking her belly while Perry kept pointing to his crotch, which made Bob a little afraid he might expose himself on the dance floor. But Perry managed to keep control of himself, which Bob took as a good sign. Hell, maybe he was even making some progress. Tommy Morello and Lizzie Littman did a wild dance that ended with them practically having intercourse on the floor, as Jesse blasted out "Hard to Handle." The television cameras really pumped everybody up, not the least of whom were Dave and Lou Anne, who made sure they were right up front catching lots of airtime. They shook and shimmied and did the electric slide two feet in front of the band.

When it was all over, and Dave was helping pack up the speakers and amps, Lori Weisman hugged Bob Wells and looked at him with something like awe in her expression.

"Seriously," she said, "working in television you get a little jaded. But meeting a guy like you—well, it really does something for my spirit."

"Thanks," Bob said. "But that's the whole point of what I do. It's not that I'm some kind of saint. It's that you feel better when you're kind. You feed your spirit when you do good."

Bob heard himself say the last speech with a seeming sincerity and simple honesty that used to be his true nature. Now, however, having given in to temptation, the words seemed to float disembodied from his mouth. They had been true only when *he* was true. Now they were just words, unconnected to any heartfelt part of himself. Words that were no different from a commercial that sold beer or Viagra on television. He had, he realized, gone from being a man of distinction, even though a virtual unknown, to a shill for himself, and the thought made him suddenly dizzy and sick.

"What you just said, that's fantastic," Lori said. "I'd like you to say that for the camera. Oh yeah, there is one more thing, Bob. I have to ask you this so the piece just doesn't seem like one long blow job."

Everyone laughed at that one, except Jesse, who eyed Lori suspiciously.

Bob put his arm around Jesse's shoulder and kissed her neck to show her he wasn't tempted by the sophisticated woman from the big city.

"Well," Lori said, "a couple of local detectives, guys named Garrett and Geiger, contacted me just tonight and said that you were under suspicion in the bombing. That you'd been seen with one of the dead men, a guy named Ray Wade, only a few days before the explosion took place."

Bob felt a great rage starting inside of him. What were they doing, screwing up his moment in the sun? The bastards, the sons of bitches. He looked down at the floor and took a deep breath. When he looked back up, he was smiling, in his friendly and humble way.

"It's true I knew Ray Wade. Years ago, he played in blues bands with me. We live in a funky part of town and you get to know all kinds of people. But the idea that I was involved in some kind of criminal activity with Wade, well, that's crazy."

"But isn't it true," Lori Weisman said, "that you played poker with Ray Wade and some of his buddies and you lost almost all of your retirement money?"

Bob felt a lump forming in his throat. When he looked at Lori Weisman now she wasn't the same friendly and openly worshiping person she'd been for the past two days. No, there was a sharp, hard glint in her eyes.

"That's a lie," Bob said. "I lost *some* of my money and as a result I quit playing cards."

Dave was standing right by the two of them and he couldn't resist chiming in.

"Maybe you ought to ask Detective Garrett why he hassles Bobby all the time."

Lori Weisman raised an eyebrow.

"Do you know why?" she said.

"Oh yeah, I do," said Dave. "Because Bob clocked him in a street battle a long time ago when they were both young. He's always hated Bob because he's an activist and he doesn't kiss any cop's ass."

Lori smiled and shook her head.

"Okay," she said. "That's it for now. If I need any more, can I come back down?"

"Of course," Bob said. "You're one of us now. You can come back to good old Baltimore anytime you want."

"And you'll buy me a crab cake and a National Boh?" she asked.

"Night or day," Bob said. "Right, David?"

"Oh yeah," Dave said. "You bet, Lori, any old time."

They all hugged one another and Bob felt better. He was pretty sure she wasn't going to do a hatchet job on him. It was probably just like she said. She had to put a few negative things in, so it didn't make him out to be too good, some kind of saint.

As Bob and Jesse drove home, drunk and weary from the big media day, Bob felt a kind of bittersweet quality to it all. He had, at last, become a celebrated person in his town and soon he would be known all over the United States, maybe even the entire world, but at what cost?

As he turned down Aliceanna Street, he couldn't help but remember something his mother, Grace, used to say when he was young: "Far better for a man to lose his life than lose his immortal soul." No other quote had ever had such an impact as that one. It was possible that through all the changes he had gone through in his life, this one phrase had been the rock of his beliefs.

And now . . . now he had crushed the rock underfoot, given up his soul for worldly success. For fame and money and power.

It wasn't as though he didn't enjoy it. He'd loved being the center of attention for the past few weeks. It was exciting, fantastic . . . actually being taken seriously, people waiting eagerly for his next utterance.

But there was still the problem of the truth.

He had always been honest, earnest . . . good old Honest Bob Wells. Indeed, he had been such a goody-goody that he was a bit of a joke even in his own neighborhood. And maybe even more than having the money, Bob had wanted to take a vacation from that dogged, patient, and boring little man that he'd always been. He wanted to fly in the face of convention, show himself and the world that he was bigger than any of them imagined.

And he had done it. Okay, he had stumbled through it, escaped by the skin of his teeth, but in the end, did he really deserve all this attention?

No, of course not.

The thought tortured him. He had gotten all the attention for the wrong reasons.

He tried for the thousandth time to tell himself that life was ironic—that he was really getting the attention for the heroic way he'd saved the kids—and beyond that, belatedly for all the good works he'd done in the past.

But no matter how many times he said it . . . he still couldn't wipe out the guilt and horror he felt for hatching a plan that had killed so many men, including his old pal, Ray Wade.

No amount of rationalization could totally wipe away the feeling that he was a fraud. And all this talk of his greatness, all the loud huzzahs from the media, rather than make him feel better, in the end, only terrified him. For if he had quietly sneaked away into the night, there would be no risk of the world finding out just what a creep and phony he was. But now, famous, lauded as a saint . . . oh God, now a fall from grace would be a thousand feet high, with only the street to break it.

And perhaps, worst of all was that he had to keep his sins secret from Jesse. She had a vision of him, now completely reinforced by today's media show, that she had found the last honest man. The guy she had been looking for all her life. An old-fashioned man of dignity and honor.

Even now, as he drove toward a sign, which said ROAD CLOSED DETOUR, he could see her sneaking looks at him from the passenger seat. Her face just glowed with love, admiration, and respect. All the things he would have loved to have won from her honestly, he had, instead, cheated to obtain. And how quickly all those loving, admiring looks would vanish and be replaced by hatred and scorn . . . if she knew what kind of a man he really was.

God, there was the pain of it.

He feared losing what he had cheated to get even though he knew that his old self would have found all his winnings worthless.

He had five million in the basement wall, and yet he felt not like a man of wealth and reputation, but more like a crab scuttling down a windblown Chesapeake beach.

He had gone from helping the people on the bottom to being a bottom feeder. And the thought made him sick.

He turned down Latrobe Street, a street so narrow that his old Volvo could barely squeeze beneath the redbrick row houses, which leaned over them like jagged, broken teeth.

"What the hell's going on, Bobby?" Jesse said.

"I don't know. I'm not even sure this street goes through."

He stopped the car and started to back up.

"That's not going to work," Jesse said.

"Why?" Bob said.

"Because of Mister Softee back there."

Bob looked in the rearview mirror and saw the ice-cream truck blocking their path.

"Christ, it's after midnight," Bob said. "Who gets ice cream at this hour?"

"No one, asshole," came the reply.

Bob turned and looked out the open window and saw Emile Bardan's face staring back at him.

"Hi Doc," Emile said, as he shot Bob in the chest with a dart from a five-thousand-volt air-taser gun.

Bob fell backward, his muscles immediately going into wild convulsions. His eyes were filled with a shower of red sparks. He saw a hand come in the window, a hand holding a rag of some kind. He wanted to push it away, but his arms jerked in spasms and then he became aware of the sickening smell of ether. A few seconds later he was out cold.

Jesse leaped out from the passenger side and started running toward the ice-cream truck. She was only a few feet away when the dart hit her in the back and she fell, convulsively twitching, on the street. Even as out of control as she was, she tried to crawl away, but it was no use. The ether-soaked rag came down on her face, as well. She heard a bell ringing in her head, and within seconds, Jesse lay unconscious on the dark street.

# CHAPTER TWENTY-ONE

Bob felt as though someone had cracked his brain and the odor of ether on his shirt made him nauseous. But neither of these was as agonizing as the pain in his arms and ankles, both of which were bound by packing tape. He looked around and saw a bust of some ancient figure sitting near him. He should know that man's name, Bob thought. All those years of education and he could remember so little.

He looked again and recalled it. Alexander the Great. Yes, the conqueror himself. And how much of *his* legend was really just gossip, lies, innuendo turned into "fact"? Bob glanced around the room and his heart sank.

Jesse lay bound and gagged on the floor across the warehouse room. He couldn't tell if she was breathing. God, he'd never wanted to involve her. Seeing her there, bloodied and covered with alley grime, he felt a wave of shame and self-hatred pass through him. The sensation was so strong it was as though he'd swallowed poison.

And, he thought, in a way he had. He had succumbed to evil and evil was poison. And poison didn't care who drank it. Its job was to kill, not to make moral distinctions. But Jesse . . . good, decent Jesse . . . whatever Emile did to him, he deserved. But not Jesse.

"Ah, I see you're awake," Emile said.

Bob turned his head and twisted around on the couch a little. Across from him, the art dealer sat in a comfortable overstuffed chair, a spiral notebook in his hand. Next to him was a gooseneck lamp, which he now shone into Bob's eyes.

"Good to see you, Bobby," he said. "I've missed our little sessions."

"I bet you have," Bob said.

"No, truly," Emile said. "I especially enjoyed the one over the telephone."

Bob said nothing, but strained against the tape. He could feel it loosen a bit.

"Jesse?" he said. "Is she dead?"

"No, no, no," Emile said. "Not at all. Though she will be soon, unless you give me my money."

Bob said nothing, but squirmed around some more. The money was his only bargaining chip. As soon as he gave it to Emile he and Jesse were both dead.

"By the way, Bobby," Emile said, "I watched your little taping session out in front of your house today. You had the fat woman and the flasher out there. I have to admit, I felt a little residual jealousy. I mean, those two nobodies on national television? And you didn't invite me? I mean, think of the interview I could have given the *Today* show, Bob."

Bob looked a little past Emile. Out of the corner of his eye, he saw Jesse squirming, trying to get free. He had to keep Emile talking.

"If you'd only called and told me where you were, I would have seen to it that you got some airtime," Bob said. He tried to smile a little, to show Emile that he was somehow still in control.

Emile laughed and shook his head.

"I've developed my own little theory about you, Bob," Emile said. "Want to hear it?"

"Why not?" Bob said.

Emile crossed, then recrossed his legs.

"Well, first off, I think you're a victim of serious narcissistic grandiosity disorder. Perhaps it stems from your father, Bob. His saintliness as a union leader gave you impossibly high standards to live up to. The only way you could outdo him was to repress all your natural desires for status, power, and prestige. Then belatedly, after Meredith left you for that fraud, Rudy Runyon, you began to see that this strategy was perhaps not the best way to live a life. Coming to this correct conclusion, a sensible person would have perhaps learned a business, tried to have a meaningful second career to tide them over in their declining years, something like selling antiques on eBay. But not you, Bob. You were just as grandiose as ever, exchanging one extreme form of living, saintliness, for another, criminality. When I dangled the bait in front of your eyes, you jumped right at it. I'll even bet you convinced yourself that it was your destiny. That was all part of my plan, by the way. I knew that you had a power fixation, so I offered you a god. Utu. Someone an incipient egomaniac like you could fixate on."

Bob felt the sting of Emile's words. It was all true, he thought, every bit of it. His eye drifted to Jesse, who was awake and still struggling with her bonds.

"That's a brilliant analysis," Bob said.

"Don't try and flatter me, Bob. That's a weak trick. And it won't save you. There's only one thing that can do that, handing over my money."

"Now who's bullshitting who?" Bob said. "You're not going to let me go, are you?"

Emile gave Bob a devilish grin and shook his head.

"You guessed it, Bob. No, of course not . . . I can't do that. But I can make your death pleasant, a quick bullet, or very, very ugly."

Behind Emile, Jesse had somehow gotten her right hand free. But if Emile turned to check on her, they were finished.

"I don't think I'm going to tell you," Bob said.

Emile left his chair at once and walked toward Bob, smiling.

"Play it your way, Bob," Emile said. "Before I kill you, maybe you'd like to see 'your' mask?"

"You don't have it," Bob said. "You never had it."

"Wrong again, Bob."

He walked over to a wooden cabinet, opened it, and took out a case. He hit a recessed button, the plastic cover slipped back, and Emile took out the mask.

It didn't disappoint. There was something terrifying, fierce, and vindictive in the god's expression. Bob felt a chill. Looking at the mask, he suddenly felt that he was looking at himself, at what he'd become, something garish, ugly, and distorted from his original self.

Bob struggled against his bonds. How he wanted to smash the mask, nearly as bad as he wanted to smash Emile's face.

"You see?" Emile said. "He's really marvelous, but I can tell from the way he's reacting that he doesn't like you. After all, Utu was a god, not a lowly, third-rate psychologist who steals from his patients."

There, Bob thought, he had said it. And Jesse had heard it. Whatever she'd thought before, now she knew what a low and evil person she had fallen for. Bob saw her twisting harder now . . . she had one hand free. Then it occurred to him that hearing what she had maybe she'd get free and not help him at all.

After all, why should she?

Above him, Emile slipped the mask over his face.

"How do I look, Bob?"

"Like an asshole with a mask on," Bob said. But that wasn't what he really thought at all. Emile looked like an avenging god from some place deep in Bob's own unconscious. Something one might see after a night of drinking and taking pills. Someone who knew what he had become, and was here for vengeance.

"Very brave," Emile said. "Let's see how brave you are in a few minutes, though, when you've lost your legs."

Emile reached down from the other side of a large packing crate and picked up a portable power saw. He pulled the rip cord and it sounded like a starving animal.

"See, handy to have these around. We use them to make packing crates. Ship our paintings and sculptures all over the world. And by the way, to keep out moisture and heat, this room is sealed tight. So any screaming you do—and trust me, Bobby, there's going to be quite a lot—won't be heard by anyone except me and you. And Jesse, of course."

Bob felt a fear so great that he nearly passed out. He looked across the room at Jesse, who was now looking up at him, trying desperately to undo the tape around her ankles.

"This is kind of funny," Emile said, kneeling down and holding the power saw inches away from Bob's right leg. "On the way over here I thought about how to do this. I thought about threatening Jesse unless you told me, but a guy like you—who would steal from his own patient—hey, a guy like that might just let me saw her into bits. Besides, Bob, I'm no sadist. I don't want to hurt Jesse. Of course, I'll have to kill her, too, but I promise you there won't be any kinky stuff. Now let's see . . . where do we start? How about right here?"

He placed the saw just over Bob's right calf.

Bob felt the heat of the saw on his flesh.

"No," Bob said, "wait . . . wait . . . I'll tell you."

He looked past Emile and saw Jesse on her knees. The sound of the saw was a blessing. Emile couldn't hear her ripping the tape just a few feet behind his back.

"Now, Bob!" Emile said.

"Wait, wait," Bob gasped.

Bob trembled, acted as though he couldn't get his breath. Behind him, Jesse was moving toward Emile. She'd picked up a hammer from the tool table.

"Now, asshole," Emile said. "Where's my money?"

To emphasize his point, he placed the saw blade on Bob's thigh just above his right knee. Then he pressed down. Bob screamed as blood gushed from the wound, a scream that dovetailed with Emile's groan as Jesse's hammer slammed down on the back of his head. Bob watched as Emile turned around, his face open in surprise and shock.

"Bitch!" he screamed.

He revved up the saw and thrust it out at Jesse, who jumped back, the blade narrowly missing her face. Emile tried to rise to his feet, but Bob kicked him forward and he fell awkwardly on his left side, directly on the saw blade. The teeth dug into Emile's left arm, wiggling crazily, like a live animal.

Blood spouted from Emile's half-severed arm. He got up to his knees, but Bob kicked him in the back again and he fell over. When he tried to get to his feet, Jesse was on him, ripping the mask from his face and bashing his head with the hammer. Bob watched her as she struck him time and time again.

Finally, after what seemed like an endless series of blows, Emile fell back gasping and died.

Jesse turned off the bloody saw and freed Bob from his bonds. She glanced at the bleeding wound on his thigh.

"Does it hurt bad?" she said.

"No," Bob said. "Maybe I'm in shock, but I can barely feel it."

Then they fell into each other's arms on the couch, Jesse sobbing and Bob stroking her head.

"Baby," he said. "Baby, you saved my life."

She nodded and cried, then looked up at him in disbelief.

"Bobby," she said, "the things he accused you of, were they the truth?"

Bob felt his hands shake and his stomach rumble.

"Yes," he said. "I was afraid. Afraid to get old with no money. Afraid you'd leave me."

"Jesus," she said. "Oh God."

He reached out toward her, but she jumped back as if he were a rattlesnake.

"Don't say I made you do a thing like that," she said. "Never say it."

"I won't," Bob said. "I love you, Jess."

She looked up at him and the disappointment and pain in her face made him, for a second, wish that Emile had finished the job.

"We've got to get him out of here," Jesse said.

She turned and pointed to a large packing barrel.

"That ought to do," she said. "So let's get to it, Bob. You take his arms. I don't want to look at his head."

Bob limped from the couch and did as she said.

The hero, he thought, saved by his girl.

# CHAPTER TWENTY-TWO

Cleaning up the mess in Emile's warehouse took only an hour, and crating him up in a barrel and driving him down to the shore took only forty more minutes, but finding the right spot to dump the body was much harder. In movies, Bob thought, the cool killer always just drives to a place and tosses the body in the river or lake. But neither of them had any idea where to go, and they found themselves driving down dirt roads to various possible dump sites, only to find a family of Muslims picnicking at Drake's Inlet and five elderly birdwatchers at a spot not far from Gibson Island. Birdwatchers who might have seen them, and who, if questioned, could possibly recognize them. And what was he to do then? Hunt them down and kill them all?

They finally settled on a marshy area on a remote corner of the Chesapeake, a place called Bogert's Cove, which Bob recalled from his own childhood. Though he hated to spoil that pristine, youthful memory by dumping Emile there, he felt it was the best place available on such short notice. Besides, the old cove wasn't quite as nice as he remembered it. Nobody came there anymore. The lovely marshland, the blue water, the cranes, turtles, and black snakes were long gone. The cove was now used as a runoff for nearby chemical companies, polluters who'd ruined most of the bay. The only live things in the rust-brown water were mutant five-eyed fish and three-headed geek crabs. One more little monster would scarcely make any difference.

Bob parked the car on a muddy road and they struggled with the barrel, carried it through marsh grass and scum water that burbled and bubbled its orange-brown foam over their shoes.

After twenty minutes of hard labor, during which time they twice dropped the barrel, they reached the windy point. Making a mighty effort, they lifted Emile in his round coffin and threw him in. He quickly sank and Bob smiled at Jesse, who couldn't meet his gaze. She walked away, to the east a bit, where the sand met the mushy tide. Bob watched her and tried to tamp down his rising panic. Now that she knew, what would she do? Turn him in? Walk away . . . or maybe kill him in his sleep and take the money? He realized the last idea was extreme, but after seeing her kill Emile, the ferocity and barbarity of her attack, he realized that this was one West Virginia mountain girl who wasn't going to lose a lot of sleep over wasting a bad guy.

Bob watched her walk back from the tip of the land. She looked at him and said: "Time to go, Bobby" in a voice that was impossible to read.

Limping, Bob followed her back to the car.

Bob drove down the Annapolis road, under a canopy of highway oaks. Like two people coming back to the city from a little trip down the Chesapeake Bay. Bob looked at a sunburned couple with two kids in a Chevy and remembered when he had been like them, part of the human race.

His leg had stopped bleeding, but the pain radiated up to his crotch. Yet that was nothing compared to what he felt inside.

Finally, as though she were in tune with him, Jesse spoke:

"You know, Bob, I didn't have to save you."

"I know."

"I was so angry, Bobby. You endangered my life. I had this thought, that what I should do is kill you both. Make it look like you'd done in each other. Then go home and find the money."

Bob found himself laughing.

"But you don't know where the money is," he said. "You'd never find it without me. So you had to save me."

She reached over and smacked him hard in the face. Bob's eyes watered.

"You idiot. Is that what you think? I saved you because I love you. I was just angry, angry that you had betrayed what we had. For money."

Bob said nothing. He wanted to remind her how right at the beginning she had told him she couldn't bear being with another poor man. He wanted to dump it all on her, but it occurred to him that if she hadn't come along he might have done it anyway. Out of bitterness, and a sense of defeat, or maybe because he still had to buy his clothes at Ross Dress for Less, and because he feared having to line up with the other old people in powder blue dress shirts at the early bird dinner at Denny's, where he would eat swill and drink bad coffee for the rest of his loser's life. . . .

They drove on in silence until the city lay before them, and they floated by Camden Yards. Bob remembered going to Oriole games as a kid, not here, but at old Memorial Stadium. He had loved baseball back then. He had loved the players, and the fans, and the hot dogs, and Jimmy, his father. He had loved, God help him, everything. Until he had fallen more in love with ideas. With ideas of how the world should be, and then, then nothing ever measured up.

He wanted to tell Jesse about all that . . . how other people had the same ideas, but when the ideas wore out or proved false or simply not useful anymore, normal people forgot them and went on to live their lives. But he had found that impossible. He had stayed there, in Ideaville, blaming the world for not measuring up. And the waiting, waiting . . . this was the funny part really . . . waiting for the world, the whole goddamn world, to admit that they were wrong. He waited until the day they would come to him, all his old friends like Rudy and oddly enough even Meredith, and they would bow down at his doorstep—his simple peasant doorstep—and they would say, "We were wrong to move to the burbs, Bob. We were wrong to have two-point-two children and to buy gas-guzzling SUVs and get golfing memberships, and to pretend we were still 'spiritual' by going to suburban yoga classes. And we were wrong to play tennis and join shitty Republican country clubs, and to go to sixties parties that turned all of our youthful revolutionary fervor into cornball, shitty Dick Clark nostalgia. And we were wrong to occasionally smoke a joint and turn our mystical visions into one more consumer item, and we were wrong to think that Coke was the real thing, and we were wrong to turn on the poor, and blight the environment, and face it . . . we were fucking wrong and you were dead right about everything. And we fall upon our knees to you, Bob, and beg you, the saint, for forgiveness. We were weak, so very weak. We let the world down, Bob, but worse, we let *you* down."

Yes, Bob wanted to tell Jesse all this . . . but what would she think of such a man? That he had been a fool, that all his kindness and goodness had been mere hubris. (And had it? Had it? That was what tortured him. Was kindness and goodness only a strategy against oblivion?)

No, in the end, he could say none of this. It sickened him to even admit it.

He stayed silent, as the sun came up, and thought of the *Today* show and how only hours ago the world had actually done the very thing he had longed for. They'd beaten a path to his door and told him he was right.

Though for all the wrong reasons.

As they turned down Pratt Street, Bob looked over at Jesse. The light played off her features and her skin seemed to be shining like gold.

"I love you," he said. "I want to marry you."

She turned and tears rolled down her face.

"And we'll live with the stolen money?"

"Yes," he said. "But we can do good with it. We'll move away from here and we'll live well, but we'll also give some of it . . . maybe a lot of it away."

"And what about the mask?" she said.

"We'll keep it for a long time, then sell it. No one has to know anything about it."

She looked at him and shook her head.

"I don't know," she said. "It sounds too easy. Living with a lie like that. Can anything good come of it?"

Bob pulled over to the corner of Broadway and Thames and looked at her.

"You said it yourself, Jess. Nothing good can come from being poor. So if we do good with the money, maybe we can make good out of evil."

"I don't even know how much money . . . you . . . we have."

"Five million dollars," Bob said.

"Good God," Jesse said.

"Five million new chances," Bob said. "Not to mention we now own the mask."

"But I don't want it," Jesse said. "Just thinking about it sitting back there in the trunk makes me nervous."

"But Jess," Bob said, "it's worth maybe twenty million. If we could find the right buyer . . ."

"And if we can't," Jesse said. "If we find the wrong guy just like you did, then what? We walk around on stumps for the rest of our lives?"

Bob felt nervous, crazy. He didn't really want the damn thing, either. Five million was more than enough for an old hippie. But what could he do, simply throw the thing away?

"I have an idea," Bob said. "We'll keep it around until we can figure out which museum it belongs in and then we'll give it back to them."

Jesse smiled at him.

"That's good, honey," she said. "You really mean it?"

"I do," Bob said. "Five million is fine. We don't need any more."

"Right," Jesse said.

She leaned over and kissed him.

"One more thing," he said.

"Yes?"

"Will you marry me?"

He reached over to her, and she turned breathlessly and he wiped away her tears.

"Yes," she said. "I love you, Bobby. Okay? Whatever happens, we're in this together."

He took her into his arms and kissed her. And thought that somehow they had made it. The two of them. The crazy, old ideologue with his dreams of innocence and the blonde blues singer from West Virginia.

And Bob felt happy and solid and he thought that, in time, he would teach her to trust him and he would in turn finally learn to trust the real world.

# PART IV
## RAIN OF BLOOD

# CHAPTER TWENTY-THREE

The *Today* show aired two days after Bob and Jesse had dumped his former patient's body into the fouled waters at Bogert's Cove. Bob and Jesse sat in bed, pillows propped up behind them, and held each other's hand as they watched Bob lionized on national television.

The results were immediate and sensational. Bob received calls from *Dateline*, *Time* magazine, *Esquire*, and *60 Minutes*. Newspapers from around the world, including the *New Delhi Times*, e-mailed him, begging him for interviews. Four publishers from New York City contacted him, and Pavilion Press offered to put him up for three days just to "kick around ideas" for any book he'd care to write. Three television producers called him, convinced that his life would make the "ultimate reality series." But perhaps the most satisfying call of all came from his old rival, the very man who had stolen his wife away, Rudy Runyon, who congratulated him, then invoked their old friendship at Hopkins in an attempt to get Bob to appear on his radio show. Bob listened to Rudy's pathetic ass kissing, then turned him down.

"I'd love to, Rude, but I'm afraid the days you've suggested I'll be flying out to the coast to talk to some guy from Universal Studios. But good luck, buddy, and give my best to Meredith."

At five o'clock the same day, Bob and Jesse received three calls from New York clubs inviting the Rockaholics to come up and perform.

"Bobby," Jesse said, "it's like a dream."

Bob smiled and tried to remember how low, how terrible he'd felt only forty-eight hours earlier, but the entire episode with Emile seemed like nothing more than a blip on his consciousness.

Had it ever really happened at all? It seemed not.

Bob remembered a patient he'd had years ago, an inmate named Shirl King, who had committed three murders. When Bob had asked her if she felt guilty about them, she'd said, "Yeah, unless I fuck a lot. Sex kills all the guilt." That was, of course, a crude and reductive line, but Bob now saw the truth in it. Like sex, fame was such a shot of adrenaline that it literally wiped away bad memories and ugly feelings. He was on top now, and even when he tried (and, of course, he didn't try very hard), he couldn't really work up any great guilt over killing Emile. Or stealing the money. Or the deaths of his crew. He still saw the grotesque images from that terrible night, but they were effectively disconnected from his emotional center.

It was like, some guys had died, it was terrible, but I'm going to fly to Hollywood.

And like, I stole money from a patient, I felt horrible, but now I can do good with the money and the world loves me.

So, in the end, how wrong could it be?

It was all about trusting the process, Bob thought, as he fielded interviews and called Jesse's relatives about their upcoming wedding.

It was amazing how important that seemed to him now. He and Jesse were a team. He had never met a woman with more talent, heart, and guts, not to mention sheer, overwhelming sensuality. This was the love of his life, the woman who had started him on the adventure that had turned his life around 180 degrees.

The woman who had saved his life.

He wanted a great blast of a wedding, and one last wild party at the Lodge . . . then they would check out all their new options and in a year or so quietly move out of town.

Where they would go was no longer a problem. When the world loves you, when you are a success, the world is your oyster.

New York? Maybe . . .

Los Angeles? Possibly.

Maybe they would just travel for a while, sample the world's greatest spots.

They had money, fame, and each other.

Only one thing worried Bob, and that just a little. What if someone found Emile's body? What would happen when his friends (if the son of a bitch had any) realized that he was missing? Would the police come and ask about him? How would he and Jesse handle it? Would they look nervous? Give themselves away?

No, they wouldn't. They talked about it and decided to handle it simply. Emile hadn't shown up for his last appointment. Bob, the concerned (but not overly concerned, patients skipped sessions all the time) psychologist, called his home number, got his message machine, and left a polite message, inquiring if he was all right.

That would be the end of it. After all, why should they suspect Bob?

Bob told himself to chill out, relax. He'd made it. Everything would be fine.

"After all," Jesse said to him one night as they watched a late movie on HBO, "if we could handle killing the son of a bitch, we ought to be able to handle the cops."

That was his girl, Bob thought. Tough, sexy, and capable. Man, what a lucky day it was when Jesse Reardon walked into his life.

* * *

It was the morning before the wedding. Jesse was out shopping on her own and Bob was getting ready to go pick up the new suit he'd bought down at Joseph Bank. It was a modest suit, summer weight, and he was debating whether or not he needed to buy new shoes, as well, maybe a pair of old-fashioned cordovans, when his phone rang.

He looked down at the caller ID and saw Dave's number.

"Hey," he said, happy to talk to his old friend. "How's my best man?"

"Great, buddy," Dave said. "You getting ready for the big day?"

"You know it," Bob said. "Just heading down to pick up my suit."

"Cool," Dave said. "Listen, Bob, before you go, I wonder if you could do me a little favor?"

"Name it," Bob said.

"Well, I kind of ran into these guys from the *Washington Post* yesterday, and they said they really wanted to do an interview with you for the Style section. They usually have their own staffers do this stuff, but since we're old friends and all . . ."

"No problem," Bob said. "I can fall by on my way downtown. Won't take too long, right?"

"Nah," Dave said. "Hey, don't worry. I know I can't expect too much time from the great Bobby Wells."

Bob blinked and felt a wave of anger. Dave sounded a little bitter. Of course, that was only natural. He was probably a little jealous of all the attention Bob was receiving.

"You'll have all the time you need," Bob said, trying to sound generous. "Be right over."

"Cool," Dave said. "I worked up a few questions that maybe they haven't heard before."

"Fine," Bob said. There was no mistaking it this time. Dave sounded a little strange. Well, whatever ... he'd hang in with Dave just as Dave had for him. After all, there was a little matter of gratitude. He wasn't the kind of guy who was going to turn his back on his old pal. After all, Dave had gotten the ball rolling for him. He just wished Dave wouldn't get weird and use that proprietorial tone. Like Bob owed him. That was starting to get a little old.

Dave and Lou Anne lived just a few blocks away in a restored redbrick row house on Boston Street. The place was probably worth quite a bit now, as the area had become fashionable. In fact, Bob recalled, as Dave let him in, he had once been jealous of Dave's property value. Just a year or so ago, Dave had learned that his house was worth about three times what he'd paid for it and had needled Bob about all the money he could make from selling the place.

Of course, Bob thought now, as he walked in and checked out the living room, if Dave ever did try to sell the place, any real-estate agent worth their salt would have to first throw out all this crummy furniture. Dave's taste in furnishing was as bad as his prose. The theme was kind of nineteenth-century nautical, the house being only half a block from the wharf. The living room featured a couple of old deck chairs, which were hard and uncomfortable, and a corner in which every sailing knickknack known to man was on display. Sitting on a battered, old mess table were sextants, spyglasses, binoculars, a navy codebook from the same era, a belaying pin, and a grappling hook. The goddamn living room looked like the set from *Master and Commander*.

"Want a little drink?" Dave said.

"Too early for me," Bob said. Ten o'clock in the morning. Was good old Dave turning into a lush?

"Me, too," Dave said. "But what the hell? Some days you just need a little pick-me-up."

"I can dig it," Bob said.

"Boy, some day tomorrow, huh, Bobby?" Dave said.

"Yeah," Bob said. "Never thought I'd get married again."

Dave gave a little chuckle.

"Boy, things have really turned around for you, huh, Bob?"

Bob nodded his head and sat down in one of the uncomfortable deck chairs.

"It's great you'll make the *Post*," Bob said.

"Yeah," Dave said. "They read my other piece on you in the *Sun* and they realized they want a more personal look at Bobby Wells, all-American hero."

Dave took a gulp of his drink and Bob thought he felt the atmosphere change in the room. Had Dave actually been a little caustic with the "all-American hero" bit?

"So," Dave said, clearing his throat, "might as well get to it, huh? Let's talk about that night. You were taking a walk, right?"

"Yeah," Bob said. "Right. But everybody already knows all that."

Dave took out a small pad of paper and began writing things down.

"I know, but I just have to get the chronology straight. You know how tough those *Post* fact-checkers are. Much tougher than the guys at the *Sun*."

Bob nodded his head and tried out a friendly smile.

"I know this is boring," Dave said. "Going over the same old stuff again and again. Guess you might call it the price of fame. Now you walked from your house all the way to Gay Street. That's a long walk."

"Right," Bob said. "But I had a lot on my mind."

"Of course you did," Dave said. "But see, Bobby, right here is where I might have a little problem. With the fact-checkers, I mean."

There was a long silence. Bob stared directly at Dave and was stunned to see Dave, lovable, old-shoe Dave, staring directly back at him. No blinks. No embarrassed turning away. No deferential cough.

"What do you mean, Dave?" Bob said.

"Well, Bobby," Dave said. "As it so happens, I called your house that night. I was heading on down to the Lodge and thought you might want to tag along, have a few beers. But when I got through to your house Jesse told me you weren't home. So I asked her if you were down American Joe's . . . figured I'd stop by there and pick you up, but she said, no, you weren't out drinking, but were at this lecture series over at Johns Hopkins. So I asked her which one and she said she wasn't sure, but she thought it was all about the new activism, some anti-Bush kind of deal. Well, that struck me as odd. If there were something like that going on I'd certainly know about it. Wouldn't you think, Bob?"

Bob felt his fingertips getting cold and a kind of panic had started roiling in his stomach, like he'd taken a little drink of battery acid.

Frantically, he tried to think of something . . . anything . . . that would cool Dave down, but he could think of absolutely nothing.

"Of course, it's always possible I could have missed the lecture," Dave said, warming to his own voice now. "So I called Hopkins and talked to a woman I know over there, Julia Dietz, who runs the series. And I found that no such lecture had taken place. That struck me as odd, Bob, very odd. But I doubt I would have pursued it if Jesse hadn't picked up on my silence. You know how perceptive she is, Bobby? Well, it turns out she was worried about you, said you'd been out meeting with your accountant, what's his name, Schur . . . a bunch of times lately. At night. She was worried about that, too . . . she even asked me about your savings . . . wanted to know if I knew how much money you really had. Seems she'd heard how you lost all your money playing cards."

Bob looked at Dave with a deep scowl on his face now. He didn't like where this was heading, not at all.

Dave smiled and poured himself another drink.

"Anyway," he said, "I might not have paid any of this much notice, but it so happens Mike Schur was down the Lodge that night with a couple of his buddies and I asked him how you were doing, and he said, 'As far as I know, fine.' Well, when I asked him what that meant, he said that he hadn't seen you for a few months, and in fact, you owed him a bill that he couldn't collect. Well, now, I found that very, very interesting. Seems you were going out at night a lot and lying about it. Tell you the truth, I might have still let it all go, but then the explosion happened, and they found Ray Wade up there and that was too good. So I went down and saw Ray's good old mom, and she told me that you had come around to see Ray a couple of times, and that he had mentioned he had to meet with you about something. Well, what could my old friend Bob Wells want with a guy like Ray Wade . . . that was hard to figure. Until I heard that the same night of the explosion another fellow I know, Emile Bardan, the art dealer, had been robbed of a precious antique mask. Then it all added up. Because I remembered once you'd told me that Emile Bardan was your patient. Your only interesting patient. I did a little more digging and I found out that he'd been arrested a few times for suspected art theft. It didn't take a rocket scientist to figure out the rest. You used your position as his shrink to find out about the mask, then you got Ray and the other guys to rob him . . . then you went to fence the mask at the American Brewery Building, but something went very wrong. How am I doing, Bob?"

There was a long and terrible silence. Bob felt as though something was crawling up his spinal column.

"It's a fascinating story, Dave. Maybe you should write that novel after all."

"But this isn't fiction, Bob. It's all real. I even figured out the motivation. Jesse. You met this great new woman and you had to have money to keep her. But you'd lost all your money. A fact she doesn't know. So what to do? Then Emile came along. . . ."

Bob stared at Dave with such ferocity that Dave finally looked away.

"Oh yeah," Dave said finally. "The two kids, Leslie and Ronnie, that you saved? I don't see them as part of it. They were just in the wrong place at the wrong time, taking drugs and screwing, and Bob Wells, decent man that he is—at heart, that is—saves their lives. I think that about covers it."

Bob twisted in his seat. He heard the roaring inside his head again and for a second he shut his eyes and had a visual image of a whirlwind of fury, like a screaming mouth.

"If you knew all this, why did you write the piece?" Bob said.

Dave gave a nervous little laugh.

"Because you and I are so much alike," he said. "See, you met a nice girl who expects something more out of life, and I met one, too. Lou Anne is a lot like Jesse, Bob. Okay, not as sexy—on the surface, granted. But what she knows in bed more than makes up for that. Anyway, just like you and Jesse, Lou thought that meeting a published writer was a big step up the ladder. But now she sees us eating the same old frozen dinners and having to clip coupons and she's already starting to wonder if she made herself that good a deal. There's plenty of those rich D.C. guys hanging around the Lodge these days. My piece on the Rockaholics saw to that. Lou Anne is getting hit on all the time, and she's not the loyal type, like Jesse. In short, I need money, Bobby boy. So I decided to make you a hero. And it worked. You gotta admit that. It worked better than I could have ever expected."

Bob slowly nodded his head. The roaring was louder now and there was this terrible pressure in his temples. Like a hand inside his head pushing out.

"So what do you want, Dave?"

"I propose that we go into business together. The Bob Wells Hero Business."

"You do?" Bob said. He looked at Dave and felt a strange sensation that this wasn't really Dave talking at all. Not the real Dave, who was as loyal as a Chesapeake Bay retriever. This was somebody else, somebody who had temporarily taken over Dave's mind and body.

"Yes, I do," Dave said, with finality.

"But you have a problem, Dave," Bob said.

"I know what you're going to say," Dave interrupted. "Since I wrote the original story making you out a hero, how can I turn around now and write another story telling the truth? Who would believe me?"

"Yeah, who would?" Bob said.

"I thought about that," Dave said. "And I decided that I don't need to write a story at all. All I have to do is tell Detective Garrett about this, about how I went to see you in the hospital and how I told you what I know and how you threatened to kill me if I talked. They might not believe that either, but Garrett wants you so bad that he'll start investigating Emile Bardan. And guess what? He'll find out that he's an art dealer with a very shaky reputation. Oh yeah, and one other thing, that he's disappeared from his home and his art gallery. Yeah, I found that out just recently. Wonder where he is, Bob?"

"I have no idea," Bob said.

"Well, of course not," Dave said. "But I bet Detective Garrett would find all this very interesting, don't you think? Especially when I tell him that Bardan was your patient. He'll find that very fascinating because he's already put together some fragments of a sculpture of some kind from the brewery floor."

"When did you hear that?" Bob said. His voice rose a little. How he hated Dave now. The phony, the sycophant, the third-rate hack.

"Heard it yesterday," Dave said. "From a good friend of mine who works the crime blotter. They're already getting the idea, Bobby. All they need is a little push in the right direction."

Dazed, Bob stood up, his legs wobbly, his head spinning. He walked toward the far corner of the room. Dave, sensing his panic, stood up and followed him. Bob felt a fire building in his chest. It burned so hot that it made him want to run out the door, go hide somewhere until it went out. But, of course, that wasn't going to work. He would never get away from Dave now.

His back still to Dave, Bob picked up the sextant, rattled it around in his hand, then set it down. He looked at the binoculars. He could just see Dave peering out at the sea at night, pretending he was a nineteenth-century whaling captain. The idiot, the moron. To think that he could be stopped by a third-rate creep like Dave McClane? It was the ultimate insult.

"How much do you want?" Bob said.

Dave moved up behind him, only a couple of feet away, and Bob felt as though he'd suffocate.

"That's a good question," Dave said. "See, I don't know how much you made from the heist, Bobby."

"I didn't make anything," Bob said, trying to sound bitter. "There was a bomb, remember?"

"I do recall that," Dave said "But I know you, Bob. You wouldn't go into this thing without making something out of it. You're too smart for that."

Bob almost laughed. Dave was right again. What a smart and clever bastard Dave was.

"How much do you want?" Bob said. His eye lit on the old grappling hook. It was polished and sharpened. Cap'n Dave always took care of his relics.

"Well, since I don't really know what you made," Dave said, "I have to look at it another way. How much is your freedom and your new life worth to you, Bobby?"

Bob reached down and picked up the hook. It was surprisingly light and balanced nicely in his sweating palm.

"How much do *you* think it's worth?" Bob said, squeezing the hook's handle.

"Two million dollars," Dave said. "And a fifty-fifty split of whatever money you make on your book and any movie or television deals we make about your life. Since I made you, I think that's a fair and equitable deal."

"Very fair," Bob said. "Does anyone else know about me, Dave?"

Dave hesitated for a second before saying, "No, of course not."

"What about Lou Anne?" Bob said. "She knows, right?"

There was a short silence before Dave nodded his head.

"Okay," he said. "I had to tell Lou Anne. But she'll never say a word. Not as long as you pay."

"Don't worry," Bob said. "The check's in the mail, Dave."

He pivoted quickly on his right foot, faced Dave, then raised the hook above his head and brought it down with all his force into his old friend's right eye.

Dave fell backward screaming, as blood and bits of eyeball splattered on his shirt.

"Bob?" he said. "Oh God . . . God . . ."

Bob moved in on him, slashing him again, this time through his ear, ripping it in half. There was a brief moment when they both watched it fall to the floor, and then Bob took the hook and sliced it in a sideways stroke across Dave's neck. The blood surged out, flowing down his shirt, making spiderweb lines over his pants.

Dave made a low groaning sound and fell to the floor, the blood pouring out of the severed veins and pooling around his chin.

Bob sat down in one of the hard captain's deck chairs and watched Dave twist and twitch on the floor.

"Sorry, Dave," he said, "but I'm not taking any passengers on this trip."

As he watched Dave die, he waited to feel a surge of pity or unbearable guilt, but instead felt nothing at all.

He took this as a good sign. All his life he had been too attached to the other guy's story to do anything for himself. Well, that was over now . . . he was out there at last, fighting his own battles, on his own destined path.

Bob noticed the smell of the blood. It was overpowering really.

He leaned down and put a little of it on his forefinger. Was it wrong to taste it?

Bob put his blood-dipped finger into his mouth. It was warm, thick, salty, like goose gravy, he thought, though he had never tasted goose gravy, had only read about it in fairy tales.

Bob sat back and watched Dave McClane, his oldest friend, leak his life's blood out all over the wooden floors.

When his body had stopped twitching, Bob pulled himself out of Dave's chair and walked upstairs to the bathroom. What he needed now were some towels. Lots and lots of towels.

* * *

After he cleaned up the mess, moving Dave's corpse into the cellar, Bob realized he would have to hang out for the rest of the afternoon, until Lou Anne came home from the Lodge. He dreaded sitting there in old Cap'n Dave's house. What was he supposed to do all that time? Read a novel? Watch TV? Bob looked at the corner and saw the bottle of booze. God, that was tempting. But what if he got drunk? What if he fell asleep?

No. He couldn't let that happen. The price of crime was vigilance. Wakefulness.

Bob sat down in the hard deck chair and stared blankly at the wall.

"You've done it now," he told himself. "You've really done it now."

It was about seven o'clock at night when Bob heard Lou Anne outside the house, having trouble with the lock. Jiggling it left, then right, as Bob, waiting behind the door, nearly laughed. Somehow it (and everything else) made perfect sense. Of course, she would have trouble with the lock. She was goofy, awkward, and loud Lou Anne, wasn't she?

She rang the bell once or twice, and called out "Dave?"

But, of course, Dave didn't answer. Instead, a smiling Bob Wells did.

"Bob?" she said. "What are *you* doing here?"

Bob saw the fear in her face. Loudmouthed, flashy, and fleshy Lou Anne. Was there any doubt in the world that she was going to talk?

"Dave and I are down in the cellar," he said, shutting the door behind her. "Conducting a little business."

"Oh," she said, dropping her coat and packages on the ugly little Victorian couch. "Well, that's fine. You boys go right ahead."

She started to head to the back of the house to avoid the distasteful subject, but Bob quickly crossed the room and blocked her way.

"Oh, come on, Lou Anne," Bob said. "No need to be defensive about it. Dave told me that you know everything."

"About what?" Lou Anne said, playing dumb. She looked past him, out to the friendlier confines of the small dining room.

"Lou-Annnne," Bob said, in a singsongy way. "We're all friends here. It's a business decision, right? You and Dave know certain damaging things about me and Dave chose, out of loyalty to our old and deep friendship, to keep those things hidden, so that we all might profit. Right?"

"I . . . I guess so," said Lou Anne. "Where is Dave?"

"Like I just told you," Bob said. "He's down the basement, Lou Anne. That's where we're making the deal. You know, blood brothers, cutting our arms and pressing the wounds together so that we're bonded forever."

Lou Anne looked like she was going to cry. Bob truly hoped she wouldn't do that. More than just about anything, he hated tears and scenes.

"Come on down with me, Lou," Bob said. "You're part of this deal, too, and there are still some very important details we have to go over."

"I have to get dinner ready," Lou Anne said.

"Dinner can wait," Bob said, turning so that she could get by, but only in the direction of the basement steps.

She hesitated, so Bob edged behind her and pushed her a little.

"Come on, sweetie," he said. "We finish this deal and then we can all go out to Little Italy and celebrate."

"I don't really like Italian food," Lou Anne said. "Besides, I'm on a diet."

Bob smiled in a pained way and picked up the grappling hook, which he'd placed on the table next to the dried black-eyed Susans.

They were halfway down the basement stairs when Lou Anne smelled the blood.

"What's that horrible odor?" she said.

"I don't know, Lou Anne," Bob said, walking behind her. "It's not my house. But my guess would be dead vermin. Do you have rat traps down here?"

"I don't think so," she said, her voice trembling.

She was far enough downstairs now that she could see Dave, who was propped up in his old rocker, with his back to her, just a few feet across the basement room.

"Dave," she said, and Bob could hear a mixture of hope and panic in her voice.

"He's busy looking over our agreement," Bob said.

She turned to look at him.

"You've written it all down?"

"Yes, we have, Lou," Bob said. She really was too stupid to live.

He sliced through the air with the grappling hook and caught her in her mouth. When he pulled the blade out, half of Lou Anne's tongue came out with it and landed on his shirt.

What to do with them both? Where could he hide their bodies? The best thing, Bob began to think, was to get them down to Bogert's Cove. But Christ, that meant boxing them up, carrying the box from the house to the car. What if the neighbors saw him?

Oh Christ, why had he been so damn impulsive?

A smart murderer would have lured Dave down to the cove, killed him there, and dumped him in. But not him . . . oh no, he had to kill them right here in their own house.

And what of tomorrow? When they didn't show up for the wedding? What about that? Wouldn't people come looking for them? Of course, they would.

Why had he picked up the damn grappling hook?

He looked out at the street. On the corner a bunch of alcoholics banded together, after their AA meeting. There was always something going on at that bloody corner, if not there, then at Brandau's bar up the street. There was no way he could sneak them out.

He had to wait . . . think . . .

Wait a minute. There might be a way.

Maybe he should simply leave them here, go to his wedding tomorrow as scheduled. Dave and Lou Anne don't show. So what? Dave got drunk or Lou Anne was protesting because she didn't get to be maid of honor.

But what if somebody stopped by to check on them and found their bodies? Wouldn't it be obvious that Bob had killed them?

No, Bob reminded himself. You only feel that way because you did it. No one else will have any idea.

No, Dave was his best friend, the guy who made him famous. Why on earth would he kill Dave? And even more so, if he *were* going to kill him, would he do it the day before his wedding, when anybody knew the bodies would be found? Of course not.

Bob began to laugh. The very impulsiveness of it all had worked for him. Who kills the best man at his wedding the day before his very marriage ceremony?

Only a lunatic.

And over what?

No one else knew what Dave and Lou Anne knew about Bob. To the rest of the world Bob was a selfless hero. In an age of reevaluation of the spiritual life . . . post 9/11, Bob stood as an emblem of purity, of courage and commitment.

His kind of goodness transcended petty nationalism, transcended even religious differences.

People needed him to be heroic. They wouldn't want to believe he had anything to do with it.

Yes, he was bulletproof.

It would be a terrible shock to Jesse, of course. Almost unbearable. Bob would have to take care of her. Nurse her back to mental health. Which he'd do, with all his gentle care and skill. With all his heart. And money.

But now the question was what to do with them? If only there were an old trunk sitting around like at Emile's? But there wasn't. . . .

The thing was he had to make sure they kept until tomorrow. They couldn't start smelling up the block. That was a real problem. Of course, he could turn the air-conditioning up. Yeah, he could do that. They'd keep until tomorrow afternoon.

He looked down at their bodies, Dave propped up in his chair and Lou Anne on the couch.

Lou Anne's eyes were still open, like she was staring at him.

He wanted to walk over and shut them, but he was afraid to touch her again. He wiped off the grappling hook with his bloody shirt.

He was going to have to borrow one of Dave's old jackets to get home. And he had to leave soon, before Jesse got back from her trip to the Etta gown shop.

Her parents and sister were coming. Later that night. God, he had to play host to them after he had just killed his best friend and his wife.

Jesus, looking down at them gave him the creeps.

It was like Dave and Lou Anne were goofy teenagers on Halloween. Like they were playing a gag on him. Yeah, that was exactly how it felt. They'd covered themselves with some pig blood they'd gotten at the butcher's and they'd had fun painting each other's faces. Then they'd situated themselves in the cellar like a couple of mutilated corpses and they called Bob and they waited for him to come over. And as soon as he reacted—"What the hell's going on, you guys?"—they'd jump up and say, "Happy Halloween!"

Except it wasn't Halloween and they wouldn't be hopping up again in this life. Not now. Not ever.

He'd killed them both.

Oh God, don't think about it. Don't let it get to you.

But what to do with them?

Nothing. Just clean up, turn the AC up real high, so they didn't start to smell right away, then get the hell out of there.

Go home. Get rid of the bloody clothes.

Act like it never happened.

And tomorrow, marry your girl, get through this, and have a tremendous third act in your life.

Fame, wealth, and glory.

If you can just get through this.

Bob took a last look at them, checked to see if the drunks were dispersed on the AA corner, and headed out the front door.

Please God, he thought, as he closed the door behind him and wiped the doorknob clean, just let me get through this and I'll share my money with the poor for the rest of my life.

# CHAPTER TWENTY-FOUR

Bob found himself walking briskly, with perfect posture, down the dark street. It was funny, he thought, when he was a kid his mother had always told him not to "slouch." She had warned him that "slouching" might lead to other bad habits, like "smoking" or "drinking" or "gambling" or "worse." Bob had always wanted to ask her what "worse" might be. "Fucking," maybe, or "sucking" or trying to become a saint?

How about "double homicide"?

That was funny, so very funny. A block away from his house. Walking on this perfect spring night, with all the little tendrils budding on the lonely street trees, Bob began to laugh hysterically.

It was positively hilarious. "Slouching" was the crack in the dike, right?

He would have been all right if he just hadn't "slouched."

Well, he wasn't slouching now. No, he was walking tall and proud, taking long, quick (but not panicky) steps toward home. Over his blood-splattered shirt, he wore Dave's old Baltimore Colts jacket. Funny, he'd always wanted one of those, but had never gotten around to getting one.

Walking along, with his Colts jacket on. Just like a good old Baltimorean. One of the guys. "Hey, ain't it a shame that Johnny U died." "Hell yes. Never was a better man, no sir."

And not slouching. Uh-uh. No slouching for Bob Wells, the hero of Baltimore.

Bob Wells, ready at the fore, sir. Bob Wells, grappling hook in hand, ready to serve, sir. Fire the cannons, get ready to board ship, Cap'n Dave!

He came to American Joe's and crossed the street. Better not to run into anyone else. Then he had a truly disconcerting thought. What if he looked inside American's and Dave came out to talk to him?

"Hey, Bobby, wassup?" Dave talking like a black gang member so he could still pretend that he was young.

"Hey, Bobby, get any new patients? I know it's tough, kid, but hang in there."

"Hey, Bobby, I'm really making progress on my novel. I really am. The great American working-class epic lives! Of course, I'm through for today, so why not come in and join me for a little drink, buddy?"

He could really see Dave walking out of there, a grappling hook in his head, just as cheerful and optimistic as ever, followed by Lou Anne, babbling away, behind him. Though it was impossible to understand precisely what she was saying, since she didn't have a tongue.

Bob felt faint. His head seemed to be swirling in big loopy circles, so he hitched up his posture another notch. No "slouching," a dead giveaway for bad character. Garrett sees him coming down the street like this, a sloucher, why he'll know ... know at once ...

Only a hundred feet or so until he got home, Bob felt like he was going to puke.

Inside his house. Jesse not home yet. Time to take the blood-stained shirt off. But what to do with it?

Burn it in the fireplace? But what's he doing building a fire in April?

Wash it? But can't some invisible bloodstains be detected by the police nowadays? Christ, with the computers and laser technology they have now they can see anything.

Bury it out back? But what if a stray dog wanders in from the alley and digs it up?

Why hadn't he thought of all this before he lost his temper and sliced his friends in half? Had he done that? Wasn't it all just a joke? A bad dream?

Why . . . why hadn't he just agreed to pay Dave off?

Because . . . because Dave would have come back over and over again, like all blackmailers.

Because Lou Anne wouldn't be able to help herself. She'd talk and talk and talk some more. He could just see her at the hairdressers:

"You think your cousin's a lunatic, hon? Well, let me tell you 'bout a *real* lunatic. Bob Wells, the so-called hero. I can tell you a thing or two about him, you best believe it, sweetie."

She could never keep her mouth shut. No way.

But that wasn't really it, either.

No, he had killed them because they knew. He would have done it even if he'd been one hundred percent sure that they wouldn't say a word. They knew and they would always look at him differently. They would always hold it over him. Dave and Lou Anne, inferior people to him in every way, knew that Saint Bob was a liar and a thief and he couldn't bear the thought of it.

They knew he was a fake, that all the years of serving others and saying how "giving is its own reward" and how "true happiness is helping a troubled kid" was just so much bullshit.

That in the end, Dr. Bob Wells, the kindest and the best and the most true, was really the greediest and most egomaniacal of them all. They knew that he had waited and waited for some sign, from the world at large or from God himself, some sign that his good works had been recognized . . . that the Rudy Runyons of the world wouldn't take it all, and when that sign failed to manifest itself, he'd collapsed and become the very thing he hated most. A user, a predator, a liar, and a thief.

Bob ripped off the shirt and got a pair of scissors out of his medicine chest in the bathroom. He began to snip apart the shirt, dropping the pieces in the toilet, like bloody confetti. When that was done, he'd have to do the same thing with the Colts jacket. Jesus, that was a shame. He could probably get an easy two hundred bucks for it on eBay.

What was he thinking? He had five million downstairs.

He had to get used to that idea. That he was rich. That he didn't need to scrimp and save.

God, Dave. Old Dave. His pal. His bud.

Christ, the guy could really get on your nerves, but still . . . the truth was he was going to miss old Dave. Dave McClane had been his one real fan. It was true. Through thick and thin, Dave worshiped Bob for his purity of purpose and though Bob had laughed at him and his sentimental "workers of the world, unite!" bullshit, he now realized how much he was going to miss Dave's sweet and hopeful rants. Why, there was a period of Bob's life, in the not-so-distant past, that all he'd had to look forward to were afternoons in American Joe's, where old Dave propped him up.

Bob snipped away at the shirt and felt as though he was cutting up Dave's body. Yes, Dave had loved him. It wasn't just hubris for him to say that he'd really been Dave's hero. Which made the way things turned out a little more understandable. You could even say that it was *better* . . . really, it *was* better for Dave to be dead than to have to give up worshiping Bob. Because once he knew that Bob wasn't for real, Dave had lost his own sense of self, too, and had become a mere cynic. And idealistic, sentimental Dave made a lousy cynic. No, that wasn't him, the true and kind Dave, at all. He had only become that way because . . . because . . . (Bob suddenly couldn't bear the thought) because Bob had caved in, gone for the money. Because he didn't want to be alone when Bob and Jesse split the scene for good. Which made Bob kind of responsible for Dave's lame attempt at blackmail. Didn't it?

No, no, no . . . that was absurd. We're all individuals. We're all grown-ups, aren't we? He couldn't be responsible for Dave's actions any more than Dave was responsible for his, could he? That was the way it was now, right? Everybody was out there in the jungle fending for themselves, and an adult, a grown-up male in his fifties for chrissakes, doesn't have any right to blame some-body else for his moral failures, does he?

It comes down to weakness really. It comes down to moral weakness. The thing is, Dave wasn't strong enough to do what had to be done.

Doesn't it come down to that? In the end, Bob thought, tears flowing down his face, doesn't it come down to something like, "Dave was in over his head. Way over his head"? Doesn't it come down to something like, "If you play with the big cats you're gonna get scratched"? Doesn't it all come down to that?

Isn't all that "I am my brother's keeper" stuff bullshit? Doesn't everybody know that's only a pipe dream, something you tell kids . . . but nobody really believes?

Yeah, of course it is. The brother's keeper, the Good Samari-tan, those are all just fairy tales, right? No different than, say . . . Santa Claus.

Of course . . . of course . . . so why was he crying so hard. Thinking of Lou Anne staring at him, her tongue all torn out of her head.

Bob snipped away at his bloody shirt, dropping it piece by piece into the toilet.

The way to think of it, the way to position it in his head was that Dave McClane's death, and Lou Anne's, as well, had been necessary.

He looked down at the bowl and flushed it, watching the bits of bloodied shirt going round and round and he said out loud, so as to confirm the reality of his new stance:

"Thanks, Dave. You did it, man, you played your part. I'll miss you. Both of you. 'Bye, buddy. I'm sorry, man. But, as a wise man once said: It be that way sometimes."

# CHAPTER TWENTY-FIVE

Jesse's parents, Chuck and Diane, and sister, Darlene, arrived late that night from West Virginia. Bob was delighted to see them. Hard-working, good people. The old man liked to drink, which was fine with Bob. He stayed up late with him, listening to his stories about Jesse when she was a kid. That was fine, getting a little head on, just what he needed to stop thinking about Dave and Lou Anne.

That and the kind looks and loving glances from Jesse.

In spite of the horror of the afternoon, Bob began to feel a warm glow, partially from the whiskey, of course, but partially, too, from being part of a real working-class American family.

They liked him. They were impressed by him.

After Chuck had half a snort on, he told Bob that he'd seen him on TV. Bob smiled and said, "Oh that?"—like it was nothing—but old Chuck put his arm around his shoulder and said:

"You ain't nothing like I thought you'd be."

Bob winced a little. Here it comes, he thought, the jealousy and bitterness. He half expected Chuck to call him a phony, a creep.

But old Chuck smiled and squeezed his shoulder.

"Onna TV," he said, "I thought you were gonna be a damn saint and all, but you're just a good old boy, like me. And I'm right proud to have you inna family."

Bob suddenly felt a flush of emotion and had to wipe the tears away from his eyes.

"Damn," he said to Chuck. "That's how I feel, too. I love you guys and I love your daughter more than anybody in the world."

The two men, overcome with raw emotion, hugged as Jesse and her sister watched from the dining room. And Jesse wiped away a tear or two of her own.

The church, Saint Stanislaus Cathedral, a huge concrete mausoleum of a place built in the early 1900s, looked especially imposing and impressive that early spring day. Or at least it seemed so to Bob, as he drove up to the curb with his new family. He had never paid much attention to the place as a house of worship. Mostly the church had been used back in the social activist days for community action meetings. Now, two thirds of the congregation had moved away and there was constant talk of the church closing its doors forever.

But today, Bob thought, as he walked inside, slapping hands with well-wishers, the old place seemed austere and somehow a little frightening. It was almost as if God was sending him a message through the marble pillars and that message wasn't "Gentle Jesus meek and mild," but "Fear me. Fear the wrath of God."

Bob remembered feeling that way when he went to church as a kid. That the whole thing was scary, fearful, and now as he saw all the artists and people he'd worked with over the years, he began to shake a little inside.

He recalled, out of nowhere, an old preacher he'd heard once, who kept staring at him and saying, "Remember this, boy. By your acts ye shall be judged." And he remembered taking an inventory of his acts that very Sunday afternoon, and already feeling even then, at the age of twelve, that his acts didn't in any way assure him of a berth on the Heavenly Express.

And now . . . today . . .

No . . . he supposed not.

Not with two blood-splattered corpses sitting in a freezing basement just about a mile away.

But no need to think of that. Not now. No need to think of that at all.

Instead, think of all the people who had attended the church today. Bob peered down the aisle and felt a little better.

There were Ida Washington and Fannie Mae Edwards, the two old black women whom he visited every week for years and years. Why, they had loved him so much that they made him cakes and played spirituals for him on their piano. And there was old Wyatt Ratley, a man who suffered from a terrible burn he'd gotten working at Larmel Steel. He'd been so depressed he'd considering taking his own life, but Bob had worked with him for years, not only in the office but had actually made house calls to see him when he was too depressed to come out. Bob smiled seeing Wyatt there, and the old gentleman with the terrible scar smiled and waved to him from the fourth pew. And there was Ethel Roop, looking like a chubby Easter egg, all dressed up in a purple crepe dress that did nothing to hide her girth, but she was smiling at him, too . . . and just a few seats behind her was Perry Swann, looking neat and under control, and maybe, Bob thought, maybe I have helped them. And the wild Finnegan Brothers had come, too, Jack and Tommy, dressed in black leathers, their fierce beards and mutton-chops making them look like Visigoths . . . and they'd brought half of their biker gang . . . and now they were waving to Bob from the back pews . . . and he thought to himself, yeah, well, that should count, too, shouldn't it? Giving pleasure to people through music? You can't judge a man for his one bad act, can you? Okay, three bad acts. One robbery and a double homicide. (And could maybe God think somehow of the Dave and Lou Anne thing as,

like, one murder? Like a package deal of some kind? Twofers?)
Standing there waiting for Jesse and Father Herb Weaver, the
activist priest, Bob tried to imagine how God might tote that up.
Like how many good acts does it take to discount one murder?

And how many dollars would one have to donate to the Church
to wipe off the blood on one's hands?

And as he looked around he suddenly got it, why Mafia dons
made big donations to the Church. Not only to seem like big
shots and pillars of the community. No, to buy their way into
heaven. Of course, and who knew . . . maybe they could.

Which was a very odd way to think, because before he'd killed
Dave and Lou Anne he'd never really thought about heaven
much, nor worried one way or the other about it.

Now, though, killing his friends had seemingly awakened a
dormant sense of sin and a religious impulse he'd never experienced since childhood.

Wasn't that strange?

Wasn't it strange that he felt connected to these people, many
of whom he'd helped. There was Barb Silenski, whose mother
had died of cancer and needed grief therapy and Bob had seen
her through. And there was Eileen DeLuca, who had had such a
terrible time when her husband had walked out on her, but Bob
had been there for her. And sitting next to them, on the aisle,
were Ronnie and Leslie, the kids whose lives he had saved. They
beamed up at him with such admiration, such gratitude, that Bob
could barely stand it. He tried to tell himself that the fact that he
had stopped to save them did mean something . . . that the bomb
wasn't really his responsibility . . . that, after all, he couldn't possibly know they'd be there . . .

Fuck it, he silently said to himself. Put it behind you. This is
the first day of the rest of your life. Funny, how moronic clichés
like that could be useful sometimes. The thing he had to concen-

trate on was that he loved them . . . he loved them all . . . he really did. It was like a fire burning inside his chest.

They were all there to see him married and for the first time since this strange obsession had begun, Bob suddenly felt relieved by it all. . . .

He loved them all, and they loved him. It was that simple.

It occurred to him that it didn't matter if he was acknowledged or not by the media. It didn't matter if he was rich or not, if he could buy fancy cars or not . . . or if he could fly around the world or not, that none of that was him. Not at all.

And, as he talked to Curtis Frayne and told him that he didn't know what had happened to Dave, and he'd be honored if Curtis would be his best man . . . just then Bob felt that the strange question was why . . . why had he thought money and fame and glory mattered so much?

Why, it was as though he'd been infected by a virus, a virus that ravaged him as surely as any bug would, and the virus had been greed and jealousy and bitterness . . . and now, here at the church, on the day of his wedding, the virus had burned out of him, and he was able to be the sweet, kind, good guy that he'd always been before the infection had set in. His eyes began to tear up. He had been a good man before, and maybe now that he had regained his sanity he could be a good man again.

Yes, why not.

He was Bob Wells, goofy but nice leftist shrink, who loved people and was only too happy to help them, and his people, his flock, as it were, were all there, bikers, steelworkers, teachers, old welfare recipients, and even, in the back pews, a couple of his old shrink friends . . . and they were there because they loved him, respected him for what he used to be—a good man.

And all the rest, the fame and money and worries about being celebrated by the media, all of that was sheer madness.

Yes, he thought, this is my real reward, and how could I have not seen it? How could I have forgotten what goodness and kindness meant?

And then he heard the organ playing and saw Jesse, walking down the aisle dressed in white, the white lace veil obscuring her face, and he realized that she loved him more than any of them. Because she knew him at his worst and loved him anyway.

Well, not quite his worst.

No, not quite. Not yet.

As he looked at her hips, her slender legs, and her small but full breasts and lips, Bob felt such overwhelming love for her that his knees buckled.

He would marry his lovely bride and they would live as before, helping people, both of them leaders, models of compassion and goodness. Maybe, Bob thought, as Jesse walked toward him . . . maybe the greatest turn-on of all time was being good. Wasn't that why they all loved him, after all? Yes, it must be that . . . his former kindness, goodness (or were they all only here because he'd been on television? God, don't let that be so).

Father Herb Weaver regarded him with a compassionate and respectful smile on his face and began:

"We are here today to join together two people, Bob Wells and Jesse Reardon, in holy matrimony."

Bob looked at Jesse, and his heart swelled with such a tenderness and happiness that he actually thought that it would burst. His love for her, he felt, was magnified a thousandfold by the love he felt emanating, in waves, from the crowd of well-wishers, people whose lives Bob (and now Jesse, too) had enriched.

Bob smiled at Jesse with tears in his eyes and heard Father Herb say the words:

"If any man has reason why these two people should not be joined in matrimony, let he or she speak now or forever hold their peace."

It was just then that from the back of the room Bob heard what sounded, at first, like a cough. A loud, choking cough.

But the sound wasn't merely a cough. No, not at all.

Someone was trying to say something. You couldn't make out the words through the cough. But then, then finally the words were understandable:

"They're dead. They're dead, Dr. Bobby."

Bob turned and looked at the back of the church. He watched in shocked disbelief as Barry Lansing, aka 911, staggered up the aisle, his hands and cheeks soaked in blood.

"Dr. Bobby, I had to tell you. Your friends. They're both dead."

Jesse clutched Bob's hand, as the crowd stood up and began buzzing excitedly. Bob watched 911 steady himself on a pew back and then slowly move forward.

"I seen it," he said. "Dave and his wife, Lou Anne. They're both dead."

"Throw him out," Old Finnegan screamed, his face contorted by rage. "The man's wasted!"

"Let's kick his ass!" Young Finnegan said.

"No, let him talk," Ronnie Holocheck said.

Jesse turned and pulled up her veil.

"What happened to you, Barry?"

"I went over there to Dave and Lou Anne's house," Barry said, his voice trembling.

"You went to their house?" Bob said. He couldn't quite grasp this.

"Yeah," Barry said. "It was 'cause of what you done for me. I mean, getting me into AA. See, the thing is you get in there and they tell you you gotta try and make amends to people you hurt while you were drinking. And I made a list . . . a really long list . . . and I decided I'd go see Dave 'cause I kicked him in the . . . the crotch that night at the Lodge. So I thought I'd go over and, you know, apologize . . . and I rung the front doorbell and they didn't answer, so I started to leave. But then I thought maybe I'd try the back door. And I went around there and looked in, and I seen them sitting onna couch downa cellar, and I rapped on the door over and over, but they didn't get up. That's when I knew something was really wrong. So I broke the pane of glass and went inside, and, oh God, it was awful . . . they was all hacked up, ripped to shreds."

There was a collective gasp from the audience. Bob looked out at them all, people who only minutes ago were happy and calm, awaiting a great and glorious day, were now sitting with their mouths agape, their eyes bugged out in horror.

"I came over here 'cause I thought you'd want to know, Bob, you being my sponsor and everything," 911 said. "I'm real sorry I maybe messed up your wedding day."

"He's real fucking sorry," Old Finnegan yelled, moving down his pew toward 911. "Well, maybe you can explain to me how you got that blood all over your shirt, pal."

"I don't know," the homeless man said. "I might have tried to, you know, help them. Pick them up . . . I don't remember."

"Oh, he don't remember," Young Finnegan said, his face curling in a violent sneer.

He looked as though he might start crying.

"But they were already dead when you got there, right?" Perry Swann yelled. "So why'd you go and pick them up?"

"I don't know. The way they were sitting there on the couch was so awful. I wanted to lie them down, so they would look right."

"What bullshit," Old Finnegan screamed, now only a few feet from 911's face. "You did it. You killed them . . . then you came here to confess, ain't that right?"

"Yeah," Young Finnegan said, joining his brother. "You went over there to rob them. And when they resisted you, you killed 'em both dead. Right, you homeless fuckhead?"

"Yeah, that's it. You scumfuck murdering bastard," Old Finnegan said.

The church, only moments ago, a haven of kindness and love, had undergone an instant and violent revolution of consciousness.

One after another, the wedding guests moved toward the bloodstained messenger with hatred on their faces.

"I didn't go there to hurt them," 911 said, staring wide-eyed at Old Finnegan. "I went to apologize."

Bob watched in horror as the crowd moved from the pews to the aisles. He saw Wyatt Ratley, the burn victim, moving toward 911, his grotesque face twisted with fury. He saw Ethel Roop blunder forth, pushing people out of the way. All her life people had laughed at her for being fat, and now . . . now, by God, she had a chance to exorcise her pain. He saw Perry Swann, the public masturbator, jumping over pews to get to the aisle, where he could ejaculate his wrath onto 911. All of them were moving around like a great, many-headed beast . . . ready to kill.

911 looked up at Bob with a piteous gaze.

"You believe me, don't you, Bob?"

Bob watched as the crowd stopped for a second, their eyes turned toward him.

"Yes," Bob said. "I believe you."

The crowd stopped and looked at him in mass disbelief.

"Awww, that's just Bob," Old Finnegan screamed. "The softy son of a bitch thinks everybody's good, even me! But we know you, you asshole. We know you for the murdering scum you are! Let's hang him!"

He reached out and grabbed 911 by the collar, jerking him off his feet. Young Finnegan leaped into the aisle and kicked the fallen man in the head. Ethel Roop joined him, lashing out with her portly leg, and got in a powerful kick to the kidneys.

Bob froze in horror as he watched the crowd go mad, smashing and kicking bloodied Barry.

All he had to do was let it happen, he thought.

His incredible run of good luck was still holding.

The crazed, blood-smelling mob were capturing, indicting, trying, and punishing the man they thought responsible for Dave and Lou Anne's murder. He was off the hook.

It was almost, he thought, as if it were written.

He looked at Jesse, whose face was frozen with horror.

"Bob," she said. "Stop them!"

He felt something happening to him, something terrifying and strange. Goodness and kindness and compassion attacked his soul like blood-sucking vampires.

All he had to do was let it happen . . . and yet looking out at the man curled in the fetal position, covering himself up from the angry, bitter fists and feet, it was almost as he himself were lying there in the aisle. He could feel the bikers' boot heels pounding on *his* ribs, the fists cutting *his* eyes.

He watched Father Herb scream at the crazed crowd and try to pull them off, but he was thrown back into Jesse.

"Good God," he said, "somebody stop it. They'll tear him apart."

All he had to do was let it happen . . .

And he would have Jesse, and the money and fame and glory.

The stolen money, the phony glory.

All he had to do was . . .

And yet, Bob found himself moving forward, with a kind of strength and determination he hadn't felt since . . . since he had led the neighborhood people against the cops and city hall all those years ago.

He had, God help him, the strength of his convictions.

"Stop it," he screamed. "Stop it at once! Now!"

The crowd heard his strong voice and, though confused (why was Bob trying to ruin their fun?), did as he said.

Old Finnegan, his beard covered with Barry's blood, squinted up at Bob.

"The man killed your best friend. Dave and his wife. And you want us to stop?"

"Yeah," Bob said. "I do."

"Why should we, Bob?" Ethel Roop said. "He deserves it."

"No," Bob said. "He doesn't. Not like this. He deserves a fair trial, like anyone else."

The crowd looked back at Bob like kids who were being pulled away from a birthday party. They let out a collective "awwww."

911 looked up, trembling in fear.

"I'm telling you, Bob. I dint do it!"

Bob moved toward the seething mob and picked Barry off the floor. He put his arm around the whimpering, blood-soaked homeless man and carried him up to the altar.

"Jesse, call the police," he said, handing her his cell phone.

"Okay, Bob," she said.

Bob watched the crowd as she dialed. There they were, he thought, the ones he'd helped and worked with all these years. True, most of what he'd done was useless. That he'd ever believed, as he had when he was young, that these people could be welded into a revolutionary force that would strike down capitalism and start a more humane world now struck him as the most absurd thought he'd ever had. Even more absurd than his attempt to become a colorful bad guy. And yet they were his people, even the lowliest of them. That was how he'd felt before he'd lost his own mind, and it was how he felt once again.

They were his people, *especially* the lowliest of them.

Bob saw things clearly again. It was as though someone had come along and given him a new pair of glasses.

The truth was he had murdered his friends. "Slain" them, as the old defeated Bible might have said.

He had slain them and somehow he had to find a way to make things right. But what that thing might be he had no idea. Perhaps, he thought, as he sheltered Barry from the crowd of bloodthirsty wedding guests . . . perhaps he should simply confess. Right here and now, in front of everyone, but then they'd tear him apart and what would be the point of that? No, there had to be a better way. And he promised himself that he would think on it, make it happen. After careful study, serious soul-searching, he would find the right way to make amends. He would, he told himself. This wasn't just rationalizing bullshit. He meant it. He did.

"No one here will touch this man again," Bob said.

"Why the hell not?" Wyatt Ratley said. "He's a goddamn killer."

"No," Bob said. "We can't judge that. And besides, it's my wedding day and I will not allow mob violence to mar the most important day in my bride's life."

The crowd mumbled again. There was a great disappointment. It was rare that a person could feel justified in ripping another human being apart, but if ever there was a moment that cried out for vigilante justice, this surely was it. But nooo . . . Bob Wells, Mr. Humane, had to go and ruin the whole deal for them. They grumbled and glared at Bob and one another, but once Old Finnegan said, "Well, damn Bob . . ." and sat down, the rest of the wedding guests capitulated. They sat back down in their pews and tried to concentrate on the original reason they'd dressed in their finery and come to the church.

"Well, if we cain't kill the son of a bitch," Old Finnegan yelled, "at least let's have us the damn wedding!"

"Yeah," the mob yelled.

"Get the fuck married, why doncha?"

"Come on, for chrissakes. Marry up."

"Do it, Bob. Get hitched, asshole."

"We want the wedding!"

"We want the wedding!"

"We want the wedding!"

They stomped their feet and looked up at Bob and Jesse with more than a hint of belligerence in their eyes. This was it. They'd come for a spectacle, goddamn it, and a spectacle they expected to get. In a way, Bob thought, they didn't really care if he got married or they killed 911. Because the important thing was that something big should happen, something ritualistic that would take them out of their sad, defeated selves, and give them the happy feeling of belonging to a community, and beyond that, a larger spiritual truth.

They wanted significance, Bob thought. And it didn't matter what kind it was.

"Well," Bob said, looking at Jesse. "You want to go through with this, hon? I can let your folks there hold onto Barry here until the cops come."

Jesse looked at him with a cocked eye.

"Sorry, Bob," she said. "I kinda lost my taste for a wedding today. I'm going home."

Bob was only semiflabbergasted.

It had, after all, become a most difficult day. Indeed, he felt confused, and as though he lived in a world ruled by hideous whimsy. His friends were dead (had he really done it? It didn't seem possible), another man was being arrested for the murder, and his marriage was, at least for today, ruined.

He looked out at the crowd who were staring at him hard, their faces tense with anticipation.

"I'm sorry, you all," Bob said. "The wedding is temporarily postponed. But I want you to go over to the Lodge and drink some beer on me. I mean, we got the kegs, so let's use them."

There was a brief moment of silence and then the wedding guests gave a great cheer and headed out of the church like stampeding cattle.

Maybe, Bob thought, as he took 911 by one arm and his bride by the other, maybe they didn't want significance after all. Maybe they just wanted to get totally fucking drunk.

And in that, he really wanted to join them.

# CHAPTER TWENTY-SIX

The wedding guests, who had almost stomped a man to death, quickly dispersed and headed over to the Lodge to get drunk, and to discuss the murder of Dave and Lou Anne. Bob and Jesse and Jesse's relatives stood by the church doorway, watching them go.

"They look kind of happy," Bob said.

"Yeah, well, they think they caught the criminal," Jesse said.

"You don't think he did it?" Chuck asked.

"No, I do not," Jesse said.

Bob looked away, as if he were suddenly interested in the fascinating roofing shingles on Saint Stanislaus Cathedral.

"Well, we going with 'em, honey?" Chuck said.

"No," Jesse said. "I don't feel like partying any more than I do getting married. You all take the car. I think Bob and I will walk home. We'll meet you there."

"You sure, honey?" Diane said.

"Yeah, we'll be there presently," Jesse said.

She smiled and kissed her dad and mom and then looked up at Bob.

"Let's walk through the park, hon," she said. Her voice made an attempt to be cheery, but Bob could hear the heartbreak in it.

He smiled at her, but inside he felt as if his head was filled with frizzed-out electric wires. He didn't want to take this walk . . .

though it was through the gloriously budding park, it seemed more like a walk down a long concrete hallway toward a room waiting with a gurney replete with leather straps and an IV drip full of poison.

"Sure, Jess," he said, offering her his ice-cold hand. "Let's go."

They walked through Patterson Park in utter silence. Bob was waiting for Jesse to strike the first blow. In fact, he wished she would stop walking and just stand there in her gorgeous wedding gown and start screaming at him. But she just walked beside him . . . walked in a stiff and unnatural way, her body filled to the breaking point with tension.

Finally, as they neared the old Chinese pagoda, she tore away from him and threw herself down on a green bench. Her legs were splayed open and her lacy dress rustled in the wind.

Bob approached her carefully, waiting until she was settled before sitting down next to her.

She looked at him and shook her head.

"This could have been the happiest day of my life," she said.

"I know," Bob said. "It's just so terrible. I mean, I knew 911 was violent, but I never thought he would do a thing like—"

Jesse turned and slapped him in the face. Bob's head snapped back and an old man hobbling past gave them a shocked look and managed to limp quickly away.

"Don't . . ." she said. "Don't even say it."

Bob felt like a fool. He hated lying to her, and yet now that he had headed down the path he had chosen, it seemed all that he could do.

"What?' he said. "You don't think 911 killed them?"

She managed a bitter laugh.

"No, Bob," she said in a voice ripe with contempt and mockery. "I don't."

"Well, who then?' Bob said. "People who worked with Emile Bardan? I thought of that one, too. I mean, he must have had people lined up to buy the mask. And maybe they thought that Dave knew something, and came around to talk to him. Maybe there was a fight and things got out of—"

"Shut the fuck up, Bob," Jesse said. "I know who did it. We both know, don't we, Bob? Just tell me why. Why did you kill our two best friends?"

Bob looked down at his feet. He wanted to tell her. He wanted badly to confess. Never in his life had he wanted anything more, not even the money. The thought that he had gashed his friend's eye and sliced Lou Anne's tongue out of her head was . . . so unlike him, he thought. He was a kind man, a radical humanist, an old revolutionary, wasn't he? This other guy . . . this monster who had done these things . . . well, that was just an aberration. Really . . . it was like someone had come along, some criminal, some devil . . . maybe even *the devil*, and shoved themselves inside his body, totally *taking him over*, committed those terrible crimes, and then left him, headed somewhere else to infiltrate some other poor unsuspecting *good person*.

He wanted to explain all that to her. His darling, his life . . .

But he doubted . . . no, he was positive she wouldn't be able to understand. No, he thought, ignorance of the devil is no excuse, ha ha ha.

"You're not answering me, Bob," she said.

"What can I say?" Bob mumbled. "That you would think that I . . . I had anything at all to do with these murders . . . makes me sick. I can't believe you'd think . . ."

She said nothing more, but continued staring at him, and he met her gaze in a steadfast way.

"I didn't do it," he said. "You know I could never hurt Dave or Lou Anne."

A tear ran down her cheek.

"You swear it?" she said. "On your life?"

"I swear it," Bob said. "On my life."

"On Jesus Christ our Lord?" Jesse said.

"On Jesus Christ our Lord," Bob said.

"And on your unborn son's life?" Jesse said.

"On my . . . *what*?" Bob said.

She nodded her head slowly and Bob felt a bolt of fear and anxiety shoot through his arms.

"I was going to wait until tonight to tell you," Jesse said. "Until after we were married."

More tears rolled down her lovely face.

"My God," Bob said. He was filled with equal parts ecstasy and horror. What kind of father would he make? Christ, he was too old, too burned-out (not to mention a double murderer). The thought of changing diapers, staying up with a sick child . . . going to school plays. Why, having given himself to the poor—his surrogate children—all those years, he would now have to give the rest of his life to a child. Why, he'd be a slave . . . all over again. And forever.

He'd have to forget all his dreams, everything he'd struggled and killed for . . . his pleasures, his life of ease, travel, beauty, art, great dinners, expensive wines, fine cars, the good life he was so close to living. The good life he had sacrificed everything for. No . . . no . . . it was all wrong. He couldn't make this trip, no way.

"A boy?" he heard himself say. And for a second he could see the shining child smiling up at him from a soft blue blanket. Bob Junior would look at him adoringly and say, "Dada." But no, no, no . . . he had to resist that shit at once. Pure sentimentality. It was way too late in the day for fatherhood.

"Your own little boy," Jesse said. "How does that make you feel, Bob?"

"I don't know," Bob said carefully, as his emotions ran riot. "It's just so . . . unexpected. Are you sure you want this now, Jess? What of our plans? You and me traveling . . . being together . . . just the two of us."

She smiled at him in a shrewd way.

"Going from place to place, Bob? Spending all our time to-gether . . . living the high life?"

"Well, don't say it like it's nothing," Bob said. "That's what we dreamed of."

"No, Bobby," she said. "That's what *you* dreamed of. When I met you I thought I'd finally hooked up with a serious person, an intellectual. A man with ideals. The kind of man who, if he just had a few breaks, would make a great husband and father."

Bob began to rock back and forth a little like a catatonic. He felt sick to his stomach. Dizzy. There were voices in his head . . . voices of babies crying, screaming . . . babies, like vampires, sucking the life out of him.

"You never said anything about it before now," Bob said. "You told me you were on the pill."

"I was," Jesse said. "But I began to think about it. I talked to Lou Anne. She and Dave were going to do it, and I just thought how wonderful it would be, how it would be the thing that would finally get you to put it all together. Be the man I knew you could be, instead of this . . . you know, dreamer."

Bob felt a wave of nausea pass through him. Well, of course, he thought . . . of course . . . in the end it was what they all wanted. A child. It was never about him . . . never. He began to laugh then, in a crazy way, as he sat there shaking and rocking.

"What's so funny, Bob?" Jesse said.

Bob could barely speak he was laughing so hard.

"I used to worry," he said. "I used to worry . . . this is really funny . . . that you were only after me for my money . . . and all along . . . all along it was the baby you wanted. Oh God . . . God . . . I'm such a child."

"No," Jesse said. "You're a man. At least I thought you were. Until today. Bob, you're getting old . . . who knows how long you'll be around? Don't you want to leave something fresh and pure in this world?"

Bob shook his head.

"Leave something?" he said. "Yeah, I used to want to. See, I wanted to transform the whole world. I wanted peace and love and to tear down the walls, pull down the rich and make all men and women really equal. A humane, loving socialism, a revolution of consciousness. That's what I wanted."

Now Jesse began to laugh in a harsh, mocking way.

"Yes, and that was fine, when you were a kid, Bobby. But that was all a thousand years ago. In case you haven't noticed the world moved on. Vietnam is over. Two of the Beatles are already dead and the other two are billionaires with grandchildren. And you said it yourself, all of your other heroes grew up."

"No," Bob shouted. "Not grew up. Sold out! They all sold out!"

"Whatever," Jesse said. "The point is no one cares anymore. The world you hoped for is long gone. There's a new war, terrorists have blown up the World Trade Center, and might blow up our city tomorrow. And you? You're headed into old age. Are you just going to waste the rest of your life like you wasted the first two thirds, living in a fucking dream world?"

Bob felt a bolt of anger shoot through his chest and zap his brain. It was as though someone had stuck a live electric wire inside him.

"Waste my life?" he said. "I'm a hero in this town! I'm the last radical, the only one who never sold out."

"Ah, Bob," Jesse said. "Aren't you forgetting something? The fact that you, Mr. Purity, robbed his own patient? You ought to get over this innocent thing you're into, honeybun, 'cause when you caved in, you caved big time."

Bob felt the same terrible rage he'd experienced at Dave and Lou Anne's just the other day. He suddenly wanted to rip Jesse's head off. . . .

"Don't bring that up," Bob said. "Don't ever bring that up again."

She shrank back from him, panic in her eyes.

"What are you going to do, Bob?" she said. "Kill me and your son? Is that next on your agenda?"

Bob suddenly realized that his hands were extended in front of his body in clawlike grasp. Jesus, he thought, I might have done it, just then. I might have strangled her . . . and the thought frightened him so badly that he stood up and willfully made himself put a few feet between himself and Jesse.

"Of course not," he said, dropping his hands at his side. "Of course not. It's just that all this is a shock, coming on the death of Dave and Lou Anne. Give me a little time to get used to the idea . . . of becoming a dad. Yeah . . . maybe you're right after all. Maybe being a dad would be the best thing possible."

Jesse smiled weakly and nodded her head.

"Okay," she said. "We better get back to the house. Mom and Dad will be wondering where the heck we are."

"Yeah," Bob said. "We don't want to upset Mom and Dad."

They headed back across the park and Bob looked up at the old, half-collapsing pagoda and thought he heard a baby's cries.

# CHAPTER TWENTY-SEVEN

Jesse's parents left two days later, and Bob was sorry to see them go. Not because he had any great fondness for them, but because once they were gone there was no way he could avoid having a real showdown with Jesse regarding her new dream—having a family. The thought of which made Bob ill. No . . . there was no way he could deal with it. And he already knew that there was no way she was going to have an abortion. Oh no, she wanted that baby more than Bob wanted to be one of the rich and famous.

Now it was clear to him . . . that this was always her dream and that she had expected him to "come around," like any other guy. You give the guy a little sex, you make him a few homemade meals, you kill somebody for him, and let yourself believe he didn't murder your two best friends, and boom, he'll come around. Sure, why not?

He'll see that this idea of sailing around the world drinking and eating and looking at art and being feted as a saint is just a bunch of adolescent crap, and that if your life is going to mean anything at all you have to have children and a wife.

All that other stuff . . . was just empty boy's fantasies. The kind of thing a man might think when he's spent too much time alone. Why, once he's hooked up with the right woman he'll forget all that silly shit . . . and realize what's truly important.

The next generation. The new kids on the block.

The horror of it was too much for him. To think that he'd lived almost his whole life for the Great Revolution that had never come and now the woman he loved, the great mythical comes-out-of-the-rain blues singer who was not like any woman he'd ever met before—this vision of earthiness and sex—had turned out to be strictly from squaresville.

She didn't want the cool life Bob had killed for . . . no, she wanted a fucking kid, and that was only for starters. Now Bob saw the future unfolding before him. Oh yeah . . . he saw it all. Why, of course, it wouldn't be just one kid. No, no, no . . . Jesse would soon want more kids because, after all, everybody knew only children were spoiled brats. So you had to have another kid to make sure that the first one came out okay. And then, hey, wouldn't three be a nice number? After all, they are all so adorable. Sweet, loving, great . . . oh God, he could see it all . . . this was his life . . . and all the money would go, not into his pleasure, not into their own great adventure, but into . . . God help him, schools. 'Cause everybody knew that the public schools were shot to hell so he'd better have plenty of dough to send them to Gilman or St. Paul's or Boys' Latin . . . oh my God . . . and after that, well, colleges were a tad steep and of course they couldn't just go to a state school, but to Hopkins like good old Dad had, or even worse (because more expensive) Yale or Harvard or Princeton. Oh my God, he saw it all before him. Not a life of fun as rich celebs flying around the globe from capital to capital, but his ultimate horror, worse even than falling apart at American Joe's with Dave every day.

Life as a bourgeois!

The very thing he, the last hipster, had rebelled against all his life. This was the life she wanted, Bob now knew. How long before she said, "Let's move out of this shitty downtown 'hood and get out there to the burbs with the rest of the bright people"?

But, of course, of course . . . he couldn't have a child because he *was* a child. A child who had never seen it coming. The ultimate trap . . . not the death penalty, not the fallen beatnik activist, but the man in the gray flannel suit.

This was his fate.

The minivan, the ballet lessons, the fund-raising school car wash, the school picnics . . . oh God, the horror of it.

And he was trapped. Trapped . . . there was nothing at all he could do.

Unless . . . unless he made a run for it. Took the money out of the wall. And headed out. Book out of here at once.

Yes, he thought, what could she really do to him? She had killed Emile Bardan, not him. If they ever found the little shit's body they would probably find her DNA on him, as well. So she couldn't really turn him in. No, not with her child on the way.

That was it, Bob thought. Make nice, hang around for a few days, and then disappear. Yes, during the next few weeks he'd scour the Internet to find the perfect place to go. He'd heard that Quito, Ecuador, was great. Yes, maybe he'd chill in Quito for a while. Get himself a nice native girl . . . live in a hut . . . do the whole Heming-way thing. (Funny, he'd always thought Hemingway was an ass-hole, but now . . . now . . . he could dig it, he really could.)

This was his plan. He hadn't gone through all this crap to end up a bourgeois jerkoff living in Baltimore County, watching his kids turn into little yuppies that blew his fortune on drugs and cars and trips that he should have taken.

No, no, no, fuck that. He'd given all he ever would.

Now he would escape . . . escape social-climbing, family-loving women, as well as society.

He was living for himself now. Like a real outlaw, like a real man!

In just a few months he would make his move. Good-bye, Jesse . . . good-bye, dead Dave . . . good-bye, Lodge . . . good-bye, poor folk . . . good-bye, patients . . . good-bye, 911, it's a shame you have to take the fall for me, but that's the way it goes . . . good-bye, good-bye to old Baltimore once and for all.

He, Bob Wells, was finally and forever on his way.

# CHAPTER TWENTY-EIGHT

They came two days later at 6:30
A.M. The two hated, dogged detectives. Garrett and Geiger. They
leaned on the front door bell, and kept leaning on it, until a weary
Bob and an exhausted Jesse staggered down the steps and let
them in.

"What's this all about?" Bob said.

"Sorry," Geiger said. "We didn't want to bother you."

"Yeah," Garrett said. "We know how a star like you needs his
beauty sleep."

"Just thought you'd be interested to know that we're letting
Barry Lansing go."

Bob tried not to flinch at this news. But Jesse took a step away
from him, as if he'd just been diagnosed with leprosy. Christ, he
thought, what if the two detectives noticed that?

"Really?" he said. "How come?"

"Because," Geiger said, "he didn't kill Dave and Lou Anne."

"You know that?"

"Yeah, we sure do," Garrett said. "Just got the lab report.
Clearly shows that the deceased were already dead for twenty-
four hours before Barry boy arrived on the scene."

"So maybe he killed them the day before," Bob said, suddenly
feeling ill. Why hadn't he considered this?

"Yeah, we thought of that, too," Geiger said. "But it seems the day before Barry has an alibi. He was with an AA group the whole day down Ocean City, Maryland, playing in the waves."

"Yeah," Garrett said. "Twenty people saw him. So he's ruled out. You know what I think?"

"No," Bob said. "But I bet you're gonna tell me."

"That's right," Geiger said. "We think you did it. We think Dave knew what you were really doing that night in the brewery and maybe tried to blackmail you. You lost your temper and killed him. Then you had to kill his wife, too . . . which meant you must have waited in the house until she got home."

Bob felt himself swallow and noticed that his right hand twitched.

"You look a little nervous, Bob," Geiger said. "You got a bad conscience?"

"No," Bob said. "I'm just shocked that you guys are so anxious to get me that you would invent a scenario in which I killed my two best friends."

"Yeah," Garrett said. "We're very clever that way. But be that as it may, we'd like to ask you what you were doing that day."

"I was here," Bob said. "I was getting ready for my wedding."

"And you, Miss Reardon? Were you here, too?"

"No," Jesse said. "I was out shopping most of the day."

"I see. So you can't verify Bob's story."

"Not really," Jesse said. "But it's ridiculous. Dave was a great journalist. If he said Bob was a hero in the brewery, then he was. He wouldn't have made any of that up."

"No?" Geiger said. "Well, maybe you didn't know this, but the fearless journalist was sued three times over the years for writing fanciful versions of people's lives."

"I know all about that," Bob said. "Those were exposés about the rich and powerful and Dave was sued by people who feared him because he told the truth."

"Maybe," Geiger said. "But he was lying about you, Bob. I want you to know we're talking to all kinds of people about you, and your friendship with Bad Ray Wade. You shouldn't plan to go anywhere for a while, pal."

"I'll go wherever I want," Bob said.

"Okay, Bob," Geiger said. "But even if you run, you aren't going to get very far."

"That's right," Garrett said. "It's kind of funny, Bob. A few months ago if you'd taken off, we'd have had a hard time finding you. But now that you're famous, everybody knows your face. There's nowhere a guy like you can go where they won't know you. But just in case you want to run off to, say . . . South America or some other foreign country . . . we've had your photos sent there, ahead of time."

"You can't do that," Bob said. "That's a breach of my civil liberties."

"Yeah, well, take it up with your lawyer, Bobby. You can sue us if you want. But you ain't getting away, pal. You're a murder suspect, and you're his accomplice, Miss Reardon."

"Me?" Jesse said. "What are you talking about?"

"Well, it's only reasonable to assume that if Bob here committed a double murder you'd know all about it. And if you keep what you know to yourself that makes you his accomplice."

"That's how it works," Geiger said. "Well, we gotta get going, Dr. Bobby. So many people to interview and so little time."

"Yeah," Garrett said. "Sorry to wake you two up. But we just thought you'd want to know where the investigation stood."

"Yeah," Bob said, through clenched teeth. "Thanks for coming by, detectives. It's always a treat."

The two detectives smiled at him as they walked out the door.

* * *

Bob peered through the curtains as they pulled away. He dreaded the scene that he was sure would follow. Recriminations, fury, panic . . . God, there was no end to it. He turned back to the living room, steeling himself for Jesse's torrent of abuse, but was surprised to find she wasn't there.

"Jesse?" he called. "Where are you?"

No answer.

Then he heard her moving around upstairs. The toilet flushed and a minute later he heard the shower.

Christ, he thought, what did that mean? Waiting for her to blow her stack was almost worse than the actual thing.

Suddenly he felt tired, so very tired. He couldn't handle fighting them much longer. He had to clear out of here, the sooner the better.

But not just now.

Bob sat down on the couch, and as soon as he put his head back he was fast asleep.

When he awoke he felt a chill pass through him. And suddenly he wanted to see his money. But where was Jesse?

He called her name. No answer. Maybe she'd gone out to think things over. Jesus, he had to deal with this once and for all. That was the hardest part of the criminal life. It was merciless. As an intellectual he had always railed against security, but now . . . now just a little wouldn't be so bad. Like knowing you were going to live the whole day without a bullet in your back or a knife in your neck. That would be kind of . . . well, refreshing.

Bob pried himself off the couch and headed through the kitchen, then quickly descended the old rickety stairs to the basement.

What bullshitters the cops were. Pictures sent in advance to South American countries. That was an obvious lie. They were just trying to scare him into confessing, but he would never do that. The pigs wouldn't get to him. No way. He'd been a street-fighting man, after all . . . he'd stood up to the cops before. He'd always been on the side of the little guy, the people, and now the people were him.

He went to the back of the cellar and heard the shower still running.

Good. Good. Just wanted to check. Think over his options.

He walked over to the loose board and pulled it out with his fingernails. His left forefinger nail ripped from the skin and began to bleed, and Bob cursed the police again. Look what the sons of bitches had done to him. He'd fought them all his life. But there was no escape from their relentless persecution, none.

He reached deep inside the wall hole to get the briefcase with the money and the mask. Felt down into the blackness . . . his hand grasping around . . . grasping once, then again.

There was nothing there. Nothing at all . . .

The money and the mask were gone.

"Son of a bitch," Bob said.

Then he heard someone breathing behind him. He turned and looked at Jesse. She stood there in front of him. In one hand was the briefcase, and in the other a gun.

"Sorry, Bob," she said. "I took the money and that other thing while you were sleeping. I'm still planning to give the mask to some museum."

"What are you doing, Jess? You're crazy."

"Could be," she said, laughing. "But you killed Dave and Lou Anne. You have . . . what is it you shrinks call it . . . bad impulse control. I think a lot of people in your generation had that problem. It's funny, Bob, if you have a problem controlling your impulses when you're young—you know, like driving too fast, drinking, doing dope, and screwing around—people think you're way cool. But have the exact same problems when you get a little older and they call you a psychopath. Seems hypocritical to me."

Bob blinked. He had never heard Jesse talk this way.

"I didn't realize you were so up on psychological theory, Jess," Bob said.

"Well, if you spend time in mental hospitals you get quite an education," Jesse said. "And I've been to two of them. Did I forget to mention that?"

"Two?" Bob said.

She smiled from the corner of her mouth and made a funny little sound, more a bark than a laugh.

"Yes," she said. "I keep getting my heart broken, you know, Bobby? I keep falling in love with assholes. Singers and bikers and the lot. But this time, I really thought I'd hit the jackpot. A sensitive guy, a smart guy. When we talked in the park the other day I was still ready to give it another shot. What's that called, Bobby, denial? Yeah, that was it. I was in denial regarding you and Dave. But come on, Bobby . . . even a stone romantic like me can't swing with this one. How did it happen, Bob? Did the cops have it right?"

Bob bit his lower lip and nodded his head.

"Yeah," he said. "They had it right. Dave and Lou Anne found out what I'd done. He wanted money, a lot of it. He was a black-mailer, Jess. Maybe I should feel bad about it, but I don't. I couldn't let him bleed us like that. And you know Lou Anne would never shut up."

"I see," Jesse said. "And how long would it be before you decided I was in your way, too, Bobby? Me and the baby."

"Never," Bob said. "Who do you think I am?"

"Well," Jesse said, "that's a good question. I'd say looking at it in one way you're a good man who got spooked by being old and poor and went on the wrong path. But looking at it from another way you were this guy all along . . . this thief and hustler, and now murderer, Bob. This guy was the real you just waiting to get out."

"That's wrong," Bob said, edging toward her a little. "You know I'm not like that."

"I don't know," Jesse said. "Maybe there's a third way to look at you, Bobby. Like a broken-down car, sort of."

"Huh?"

"Well, my uncle Clyde had himself an old Chevy back in Beckley. It was a good ride for a long time, then one day it got stuck in one gear. Reverse. Couldn't get that clutch to kick in any other gear. Only went backward. That's you, Bob. You got stuck in your youth, baby. In visions of purity and innocence and some kind of ultimate justice. Other people grew up and went on, but you stayed in the past. Everything you see and do is in reverse, Bob. You judge everything from the viewpoint of about 1968. From there you can justify anything you want to do."

Bob shuffled a little closer to her. The bitch, talking to him like this, to *him, Bob Wells, who had given up everything for the poor, the needy, the tired, the hungry, a man who had sacrificed because he loved humanity, had a vision, a real vision of equality and racial harmony and love and peace and compassion . . . he, Bob Wells, how dare she . . .*

"You know," Jesse said, "my mama used to act the same way you did. Only she wasn't no liberal. She was a churchgoing woman, and she believed God was on her side, and she could justify jest about anything with Him hanging on to her. She and my uncle Clyde once killed a black man in the neighborhood and I overheard 'em talking all about it, how that nigger threatened them, how they was good, kind people but that nigger's mere presence was enough of a threat to justify him disappearing into the Gauley River. That's you, Bob. You talk better and have read more books, but you're a fanatic. Ain't no difference between you and my mama or for that matter some Muslim terrorist. All of you are sure you are pure. Well, I say if there ever was a revolution in this country, the first thing we oughta do is shoot the pure, 'cause they are the worst of the worst, and we'd all be better off without 'em."

Bob felt a great pressure building in his temple. What was she saying? Him, a fanatic? No, no, no, he'd spent his whole life defending the poor against the fanatics, the rich, the evil, the powerful . . . he was the only one, the last one of his generation with real morals.

"You don't understand anything about me at all," Bob said, raising his voice. "You ignorant redneck. You don't understand. I didn't play the situational ethics game. I stood up for my beliefs all my life. I was practically a saint. But that wasn't enough. They wanted me to die, see? They needed me to die, to justify their own selling out. And I wouldn't let 'em do that to me. That was why I had to take matters in my own hands. That was why I had to steal and kill. They wanted me to die in the gutter, so they could shake their heads and say, 'He never grew up. He never learned how to be an adult,' as if there was only one way. Being like Rudy Runyon, a phony phone voice on the radio dispensing bullshit advice about feelings, conning people into thinking they felt better for ten minutes while emptying their pockets into your back account. I wouldn't settle. Never."

He took another step toward her and Jesse moved back.

"You can't have it both ways, Bobby," Jesse said. "Saints don't look for a big payoff. Not to mention they don't kill their friends and let another man swing for it. You're no saint, Bob. You're an egomaniac, and if you take one more step toward me you're gonna be a dead one."

"You cunt. Talking to me that way?" Bob said. "Threatening my life?"

He took another step toward her. Now he was nearly within reaching distance.

"I'm leaving now," Jesse said, backpedaling. "There's a hundred thousand dollars on the dining room table, Bob. That should see you through for a year or maybe even two of drinking yourself to death. Forget about looking for me. Because if you find me, it'll be the last thing you ever do."

"Bullshit," Bob said. "You don't have it in you."

He took another step toward her, his hands reaching so close that he could nearly touch the gun barrel.

"I knew it," he said. "Now let's get serious."

"No problem," Jesse said, then shot him once in the stomach. As the blood seeped out of him, Bob looked at the bullet hole in disbelief. Then he sank to his knees.

"You did it," he said. "You shot me."

" 'Bye, Bobby," she said. "Thanks for the education." She quickly turned and ran from the room.

Bob waited for some indescribable pain, but instead felt as though air was whistling through his innards. He pulled himself up by leaning on his chaise longue and, after retrieving his gun, he limped to the front porch just in time to see Jesse's car driving two blocks down Aliceanna Street.

He staggered to the curb and opened his own car door. Fell heavily into his seat, his mind a whirl of pain and Jesse's voice delivering her catastrophic insults. At that second he wanted to choke the life out of her, more for what she had said than for the fact that she had stolen his money and shot him.

The indignity of it. He had been on the *Today* show and in *The New York Times.*

And she was a mere hillbilly girl who he had allowed into his life.

Why, hadn't he done the whole thing for her? Stolen and murdered to keep her around? It was almost, almost as though she had ordered him to do it.

Anyone could see that.

He twisted the key in his car and roared off down the street.

# CHAPTER TWENTY-NINE

Bob figured that she'd be heading for the beltway. Once she made it there she'd go to the airport. Of course. She must already have a plane reservation. And probably under another name.

Christ, the airport was huge. Once there he might never find her.

And which country would she go to? He had no idea. And he was pretty sure she had no idea, either.

Or had she already arranged some kind of offshore banking deal?

Christ, that made perfect sense. She'd been planning it ever since they got back from their happy little visit with Emile.

Yeah, the whole Dave and Lou Anne thing was just an excuse.

She had always planned on taking the money. Of course, and good old, softhearted Bob hadn't seen it.

He made it to the stoplight at Broadway. There was a giant National Bohemian beer truck in front of him. He leaned on the horn, but the truck didn't move.

Then he saw her. She'd been stuck in traffic, as well, and was just on the other side of the truck turning right at Broadway.

If he waited he might lose her forever. There was nothing left for Bob to do but drive up on the sidewalk. He heard the muffler dragging as he bumped over the curb. A woman screamed in front of him and narrowly dove out of his way. Though his stomach was throbbing now he started to laugh wildly. Was this a new kind of fun? He drove across the wide sidewalk and smashed into a parked car, smashing his own front bumper, which now hung from the grille.

People screamed at him, waved their arms, and a man threw something at him. It bounced off the window and Bob caught a glimpse of it through the window. It was a Cal Ripken puppet. Well, yes, he thought, of course.

He turned the wheel frantically to straighten himself out and then floored the car, shooting a block and a half in barely thirty seconds.

There she was, in her shitty Honda, turning at Lombard. Trying to get to the freeway, but he could cut her off if he could just get by a taxi that was blocking him.

He wanted to honk his horn, scream at the guy, but didn't dare. If she heard it and looked behind her, she'd see him. So he tailgated the taxi driver and waved his arms. The guy shot him the finger back and Bob rammed into his rear.

The taxi driver, an Indian man, relented and moved over. As Bob passed him the man waved his arms and cursed him.

But Bob paid no attention to him. Now she was just on the left of him. He pulled up next to her and gave her a couple of quick blasts on his horn.

She looked over and Bob saw the shock on her lovely face.

He hit the window button and stuck his head out.

"Pull over and give me the money," he said. "Now!"

"Fuck you, Bob," Jesse said.

That left him no choice. He rammed into her side, sending her into the far left lane. She managed a turn on the other side of Broadway, but slid off the road, overcompensated to her right, and smashed into a light pole.

Steam blew from the engine like a geyser.

Barely able to stay on the road himself, Bob pulled up on the street in front of her, parked, and jumped from his car.

He walked toward her, but was surprised to see her leap from the car and run into the Aero Theatre.

Bob tried to run after her, but felt something shift inside his stomach. He looked down at himself and saw the blood making a thick, red stream down his shirt and pants.

And suddenly he was aware of the pain. In the car, he had been so focused on driving that he was numb, but now Bob couldn't believe the radiant throbbing he felt from deep inside. It was as if someone had placed a hot coal in his intestines.

He had to get to the hospital. But the thought of giving up the money was too ugly. It was his and his alone.

He staggered up to the Aero's door, opened the doors, which said COOL in big wet-looking letters, and went inside.

A fat, little black man looked at him and shook his head.

"You a mess," the man said. "You need to get yo'sef to a doctor."

"I'm with the Baltimore Police Department," Bob said. "Detective Geiger. I'm following a woman who is suspected of being a terrorist. I saw her enter here."

"Yeah," the man said. "I was, like, working over at the snack bar and she run right in there. I was jes getting ready to call a cop when you came in. She shoot you?"

"Yes, she did," Bob said, staring down at the blood stream, which ran steadily down his pants.

"You want me to call the cops?"

"No," Bob said. "This whole deal is undercover. Top secret."

"Whoa," the ticket man said. "Ain't that something?"

"Keep the crowds back," Bob said.

"Right," the man said, looking at two junkies who were

eagerly staring at Jesse's wrecked car in front of the theater. "Hey, like, be careful in there, Officer. Bitch still has her piece wif her." Bob opened the two gold doors that led into the dark theater.

Inside, the blackness blinded him as he stood by the door. It occurred to him that she could be standing right in front of him, her gun aimed at his head. He quickly dodged into the back row and took a seat while his eyes got used to the darkness.

While he waited he looked up at the screen and saw two women making love to a man dressed in some kind of superhero costume. The man Bob recognized as the repulsive porn star Ron Renzle, a man Rudy Runyon had recently interviewed on his radio show. The two of them had discussed the liberating aspects of porn, and Bob had to suppress a desire to call in and scream at Rudy for selling porn as freedom. The nerve of him. What had happened to the left? Now they sold anything as freedom, anything that could make money.

Bob got so mad at Rudy Runyon (the phony, the cad, the wife stealer) and the porn star that for a second he forgot why he was in the Aero Theatre at all. He fell back in the seat and wanted badly to go to sleep.

But the pain in his stomach kept him awake and a second later he remembered why it was that he was here.

Yes, of course, he had to keep focused.

He was here to kill his fiancée and take back his money. The money he had stolen and killed for. (But it didn't seem that way. Somebody had killed for it, yeah, but was it him? Really? No, it couldn't be, could it? Not he who so loved the world . . . )

He could see in front of him now.

Twenty or thirty men in the old theater, where Bob had once seen *Rocket Man* serials, old Roger Corman movies, like *The*

*Invisible Eye*, and was it watching him now? Oh yes, it could be, and wasn't it always watching a person? Yeah, you know it was. It was always there, and it was sometimes Jesus' eye and sometimes it was Karl Marx, and sometimes Bakunin and sometimes R. D. Laing and they were all watching him all the time . . . they were. It was kind of a no-escape deal and he felt the blood leaking out of him and he forced himself up and saw a man bobbing up and down in his seat to his left, a newspaper over his lap. And Bob realized he was here in jackoff city in the hot afternoon, and yet when he looked at the man again, a long-haired guy with a round face, he was sure he knew the guy.

Wasn't that Billy Stetzle, the old activist? Hadn't they taken part in some of the greatest street battles of the early seventies? Yeah, that was him. Bill Stetzle sitting in a porn theater with a copy of the *Sporting News* over his pants. How weird was that?

The man looked up and when he saw Bob's face, he blushed and kind of pulled his hand out of his lap and waved.

"Hey Bob," he said.

"Bill," Bob said.

Bill looked deeply embarrassed.

"I don't usually do this so much," Bill said.

"Of course not," Bob said. "You see a blonde come in here?"

"She have a briefcase with her?" Bill said.

"Yeah, that's right," Bob said.

"I saw her go somewhere down front," Bill said. "Not too many girls come in here."

"Right," Bob said. "Well, keep working it, Bill."

"Yeah," Bill said, looking away.

Bob looked at the screen and saw the two men and the woman starting to have sex with a huge, hairy thing with one eye. Behind them was a paper moon.

Bob felt ashamed for being in such a place.

He slipped out into the main aisle, light-headed, and walked down toward the screen. He looked in each aisle, many of which held two or three single men, all of them with newspapers on their laps.

On the screen a character was saying, "We are the gods of Venus," and Bob had a thought that soon we could send porn to other planets. Porn and sex toys, and wouldn't that be fine.

Yeah, eventually a scientist could look through the Hubble telescope and see a used condom on the moon. Hey, hey, hey!

He felt faint again and for a second forgot why he was here in the . . . theater, which he could no longer name. And in fact, was it even the theater, or was it the Lodge? He peered down the dark rows, his gun in his hand, and saw someone else he thought he knew . . . who was that?

The guy looked like Young Finnegan, and he was really working it there, up and down with his hand, and making "ahhhha ahhhh" noises. What was he doing here, Bob thought. Why was Young Finnegan here at the Lodge jerking off to a porn movie? Bob staggered on, his throat dry, the pain now radiating all over his body like a radio signal, and he had forgotten just why it was . . . and how . . . and he wished the couple on the other planet would stop humping the moon man.

He was in row three when he saw Meredith and Rudy and they were screwing right there in their seats and they were very young and had long hair and they saw him and gave him the black power sign, the old clenched fist . . . and he heard this dripping and felt hot stuff leaking down his legs and into his groin.

Oh yeah, this was the dawning of the Age of fucking Aquarius, didn't they all know? Why don't we do it in the road?

And on the screen there was a dog in the story now and he had on silver underpants and Bob didn't want to look at that for too long.

He walked farther down the rows and saw more people he knew, or felt like he knew . . . people wearing berkas, and in the second row there was something lying there that might have been a body, but it had no head, and Bob felt as though he would throw up, and there were all his old patients in row one, smiling and waving at him, Ethel and Perry and whoa . . . Emile, too . . . but with a bashed-in head . . . Bob felt a wave of compassion for him . . . tenderness even, and gratitude, too, because he'd obviously forgiven Bob and come here to the Lodge today or tonight, whatever, to hear the Rockaholics play.

And then there was something else, something he hadn't counted on. There was a hot, red rain leaking down from the roof, and at first he couldn't understand what it was . . . but then he remembered the three other kinds of rain from the hospital and he knew that this was it, the fourth, the last.

A red rain, dripping down and covering them all . . . all his friends and all his enemies sitting in the COOL theater in the middle of the afternoon.

And he knew what it was, of course. He knew exactly what it was. It was a rain of blood.

And wasn't that something? They said no man could make rain—why, only God could do that—but Bob had proved them wrong.

He had made this rain without any divine assistance. Yes he had, a rain of blood dripping down over all of them, and he knew Utu would like it, too. . . .

Yes, he would. Wasn't that what he was about? Wasn't that what all gods were about. Four kinds of rain, but only one was fit for mankind.

Then he saw somebody coming from out of the left side of the theater and he looked up and saw Jesse running for the left exit and he felt so happy to see her. What a great combination they were onstage. He wanted to get over to her, tell her what the playlist was going to be tonight, today . . . but she was already at the exit door. And she was working it, really working it, pushing the exit bar on the door, but the bar was stuck . . . ha ha, in reverse gear, Bob thought.

She couldn't get out, either. No one could escape the past, why even try? You try and try and try to transform yourself, but you won't make it, dude . . . all you can do is change your hair. Ha ha.

He was standing next to her now and he touched her back.

She turned around and looked at him.

"Get away," she said, pointing the gun at him. "I'll kill you. I will."

Bob smacked her in the face and her head snapped back. He reached for her neck, but she smacked him in the head with the briefcase and he fell back.

She ran by him, up the battered little steps to the stage in front of the screen, and Bob looked at her up there, caught in the spotlight, the movie playing over her face, and when he looked back at the crowd he saw old friends waving to him, old movement pals who had long ago moved to the burbs and left their politics behind. He saw his mother and father out there, as well, and they were looking out at him and shaking their heads in disapproval, oh, but what did they know?

And there was the *Today* show crew with their cameras, and there was Dave and Lou Anne with their faces bleeding and their eyes and tongues gouged out, but hey, they'd made it. And there was the old gang at the Lodge screaming for him and Jesse to get up on the stage and do their thing one more time. Old and Young Finnegan and Abbie and Nixon, too . . . all of them out there like the old *Sgt. Pepper's* album . . . and Lenny and Terry and all the wise guys.

And then from behind him Bob heard a moaning sound, and

he turned toward the screen and saw the fat little actor wearing the mask of Utu as he severed off one of the actress's pale arms with his electric saw. That was perfect, Utu had shown up, too, and maybe, maybe he was running it all. . . . Yes, wasn't it funny if the old Sumerian god had been playing with them all this time strictly for his own entertainment.

Bob had always laughed at such ideas as Fate, but now it seemed entirely possible. Anything seemed entirely possible. . . .

They were all there except two guys and now remarkably Bob saw them coming in at the back of the theater. The gendarmes. Yes, Geiger and Garrett were there, too. All of them convening for a very special episode of *The Life of Bob*.

The two detectives were standing there in the back of the theater talking to the little black ticket man and he was pointing down the rows, and the cops were holding their hands over their eyes and squinting and trying to see through the pouring red rain, and now Jesse was up on the stage, frozen there in the spotlight, and Bob was somehow up on the stage with her, not ten feet away, but she was blinded by the film and he aimed his pistol at her head.

"You deserve this, you bitch," he yelled.

Jesse turned and tried to lift her own gun, but she was several seconds too late. Bob had her dead in his sights. Dead on, and wouldn't this be a treat for the bloody crowd who might just be too jaded for a simple rock concert. No, they had all been through way too many oldies concerts to get any kick out of them anymore. They needed something raw. Something rawer and realer than reality TV, something that could match the blood dripping from the ceiling. And Bob knew just what it was they needed.

She was his.

He held the gun on her, staring her down, wanting to pull the trigger, wanting so badly to do the one right thing, the definitive thing . . . *blow the bitch away* and with her all the years of hap-lessness and failure. . . . He needed to do this, he should just go ahead and pull the trigger, but instead he found himself thinking of the baby, the goddamn baby he never wanted. The kid, his kid with blue eyes and a round, smooth, pink-cheeked face.

The child who looked up at him and smiled. And said, "Daddy."

It was no use, no good.

Bob turned the gun away from her. And saw Garrett and Geiger racing down the aisles, their own guns drawn.

Bob aimed the gun at the first one. Saw him clearly. Saw him so clearly, and held his hand lightly on the trigger.

Good old Geiger, Bob thought, as the first bullet tore through him.

He felt it rip through his arm (whoa, that hurt), and behind it, a second one hit his chest, and finally, the third came for him from the left side.

It did what he had never been able to do, take his head out of gear.

And as he fell he saw them all out there waving and screaming his name. They loved him, they all loved and understood his sac-rifice, Bob thought, all of the people he had known and would like to have known . . . cheering and calling his name.

"Bob . . . Bob . . . Bob . . . Bob . . ."

The third bullet blew out his brain, and as he faded Bob saw an assemblage of stars, and in the distance a lovely woman, running, running over a starry staircase and disappearing into a whirlpool of red rain.

"Where'd that Reardon woman get to?" Geiger said, as they watched the ambulance pull away.

"I don't know," Garrett said. "But she's a waitress without much dough. How far can she go?"

"Heard she's from West Virginia," Geiger said, as they watched the wrecker tow Jesse's car away.

"So we'll get out an all points there," Garrett said.

"Only one problem, though," Geiger said.

"What's that?" Garrett said.

"She does have some money and runs to a foreign country, I'm not sure we can bring her back for questioning. I mean, we got nothing else on her."

"Yeah," Garrett said. "That's right."

"Anyway, that's the sad end of Dr. Bobby. Know what?"

"What's that?" Garrett said.

"Between you and me? I'm gonna miss that guy."

"Miss messing with him, you mean," Garrett said.

"Well, yeah, what else?" Geiger said, as he got into their Crown Vic. "But there was something about the guy. You gotta admit. He was a special kind of asshole."

"Right," said Garrett. "I'll give you that."

"Yeah," Geiger said. "Funny thing."

"What's that?" Garrett said.

"Thing is," Geiger said, "I had a real jones about shooting that son of a bitch. But when I finally did it, it didn't feel right. 'Cause just before I fired I saw his face."

"Yeah?" Garrett said.

"Yeah," Geiger said. "And the bastard was smiling at me."

"Weird," Garrett said. "You think it was death by cop?"

"Yeah, I do," Geiger said. "And I ask you, partner, where is the great satisfaction in that?"

"Know what you mean," Garrett said. "The pleasures in this job are few and far between."

Geiger nodded in agreement, then stomped on the gas, and the two detectives shot down Broadway toward a crab cake, a bottle of beer, and a shot back. At Bertha's, their favorite hang.

# CHAPTER THIRTY

The beach at Maya, Mexico, is white and the surf is perfect. In the morning Jesse walked down it to a little palm frond bar called the Frog and had coffee and eggs with *chili verde*. Then after reading the *International Tribune* and talking to a couple of Canadian expats, she went into the small town where she'd found a woman, Sylvia Hernandez, who had agreed to teach her Spanish. Jesse had worried that she might not be able to pick it up, the same worry she'd always had since she was a kid. That she wasn't too bright, that she couldn't learn things that other people took for granted. But as usual, she was wrong. In fact, Sylvia said as they studied on the back porch, she had a real aptitude for languages. Of her five new students, Jesse was by far the best.

That was good, Jesse thought, because she wanted her boy to be multilingual. The world was changing so quickly. What was important was to keep up with it, to understand that the changes didn't come every ten or fifteen years now but within weeks, or months.

Everything was connected now, she thought, through computers, satellites, and what you knew one day was outdated the very next.

Of course, there were some things that changed more slowly, and here in the village by the sea she could enjoy them for a while. The sea, the beach, the trees, the birds . . . the Mexican music. In town there was even a bar where a blues band played. She heard them as she rode by on her bicycle just the other day.

She could feel the tug of the place. The idea of going in there and singing, playing blues again . . . it was pretty appealing. Maybe after she had the kid she'd stop down, see if they needed a singer.

That was what she missed most when she thought of Bob. He was a great guitar player, unselfish, not the kind that went on endless jams but spare, playing only enough notes to make the tune work.

That's what had attracted her most about him. Not his endless talk, his anger, his obsession with money. Just the way he played the guitar and hung out with the band after the gig. She'd only asked him about the money so they wouldn't end up broke. What she really liked was everyday life, not having to struggle just to make ends meet. And that was what she wanted to give Bob Junior.

Yes, she thought, as she walked down the beach. She'd call the baby Bob, after his dad. She owed him that much. He was a madman who lived in a dream world and she saw now that he had always wanted to die. That was the point of the whole thing, she thought, as she felt the warm water rush over her ankles.

If he couldn't make the past come to life then he would hurry the present to its end. He hadn't thought that was the point of it all, but really it was. Bob would have never made it as a roving citizen of the world . . . he had invested everything in the past. That was where he was comfortable, living in a dream. A dream of purity and goodness, and anything less sent him into some kind of rage.

Well, when the baby came, Jesse thought, there would be no more of that. The sixties would never be mentioned in her house, nor would any of its heroes or ideals. The past was an oc-topus, and its tentacles would pull you right down to the bottom of the sea.

She looked up at the moon and felt the wind on her face. It felt so good, so clean, and Bob Junior was growing daily inside her.

She wondered what he would look like, of course, but even more so, she wondered what he would be like. Strong and practi-cal, she prayed, with maybe a musical bent.

And helpful, she thought as she felt the waves splash on her legs. Yes, she had no doubt that Bob Junior would be a very bright and helpful child.

Like his dad used to be, she thought. She wished she'd known him then.